El Diablo

Kathryn Dodson

Renegade Reads

Contents

Chapter 1

Mediation could be hell, and this case looked headed for the courtroom. Grateful her boss dismissed her to begin drafting a sure-to-be-denied settlement offer, Jessica escaped the tension in the boardroom and hid in her cubicle just around the corner. Over the past eighteen months, she'd seen a lifetime's worth of divorce cases. She'd put a bullet through her brain before she'd go through that.

Not that she'd ever divorce Angus. Her life had changed two years ago when she decided to clean up her act, marry her best friend, and become a lawyer. Angus kept her sane, even though her supposed dream job began and ended with arguments between people who used to love each other. She'd expected a legal career helping women out of tough situations, something she'd experienced. Instead, the boring business contracts and mind-numbing divorce cases made her head hurt. She shoved away the thread of doubt about her current life choices.

This case, not her new life, was the problem. The couple she'd just left in the conference room took spite to a whole new level. She opened the fat file folder. Wealthy and with three kids, they had a humongous house overlooking El Paso and a seething hate for each other. Perhaps not unwarranted, since the husband evidently couldn't keep it in his pants and had impregnated one of the wife's tennis partners.

The wife had cowered in the boardroom, makeup-less and with red-rimmed eyes. She was easy to feel sorry for, although the lack of foundation exposed flawless skin and a perfection that seemed surgically enhanced. As did the breasts on a frame that looked far too light to support them.

"You!" Suddenly, the wife hovered over Jessica as if she'd jumped out of her thoughts.

"Holy shit, you scared me." One hand protectively flew to Jessica's chest, while the other quickly closed the folder. The meeting had ended faster than she'd expected.

"You need to make sure Jeff doesn't screw me over again." The mousiness from the boardroom had vanished, replaced by narrowed eyes and a fierce voice.

"Ma'am, I'm just the paralegal," Jessica said.

"Everyone in this office needs to understand what happened in our marriage. He's probably hiding funds from our family, and I will protect my children. I want to cut his fucking balls off." The last sentence came out in a growl.

How should she respond to that? Bodily injury wouldn't help the woman in her divorce proceedings. "Your attorney, Alma Rey, she's the best. You should talk to her about this."

"I'm going to talk to everyone about this. Especially you. You do the grunt work, right? Writing up documents and such? Low-level people like you have more power than you think. I'll be watching you."

Half right. Jessica was definitely low-level but had zero power. "Okay . . . I'll do my best, and I'll let Ms. Rey know about your concerns."

The woman stalked away. Jessica admired the pro bono immigration work Alma did, but it took handling divorces and a hundred other boring cases to pay for those good deeds. Something treacherous in her wanted to go screaming through the halls, begging her colleagues to work on more important, exciting cases. She shoved that unruly thought back into its box and snapped the lid closed.

Her second year of law school had just ended. One more year of yawning textbooks packed with dull legal theory, then she would look for a different job. She'd love to work as a public defender, focused on the community and helping people with few resources. But given her father's conviction for destroying evidence while the district attorney in this very city, she'd never apply. One Watts had done enough damage to El Paso.

Jessica headed for Alma's office, but another couple already sat at the corner table. She sighed and slipped to the edge of the glass window, peering into the office. Until then, it looked like yet another divorce.

A pretty blond who couldn't have been more than twenty-five stared at her hands, not engaging with Alma or her husband. Her pastel floral dress had long sleeves and a high neck. She could have stepped out of a print ad from 1952—demure housewife. It might be another act, but this woman didn't seem as victimized as the last one had during her performance. Instead, she looked like she wanted to fade into her chair.

The man had the opposite vibe. He'd turned a sportscaster smile on Alma, with double dimples and intense blue eyes. Charm came easy for guys like this. He'd probably slept around too and would likely take that poor girl for everything she had.

Jessica tiptoed backwards, praying Alma wouldn't see her and call her into the room. She couldn't handle another divorce right now.

Instead, she yearned for the excitement of the past. Interesting real estate deals in Mexico, the search for a missing woman, the satisfaction of not knowing what tomorrow would bring. Back then, Jessica had pursued justice in a bumbling and dangerous way.

But she'd left that life behind, had gotten her act together. Now, she'd do things right. By the book.

Except that part of her would rather live on the edge than die from boredom in an office cubicle. Divorces and business deals resembled two-sided demons with each side battling to screw the other. Nothing heroic about that kind of work.

She wished she could split her skin in two, have the real Jessica crawl out and flee into the desert to search for victims and get started on good deeds. She would leave some automaton husk of herself to handle the divorces.

She shook her head. *Stop being ungrateful.* Alma took a chance hiring her. Angus took a chance marrying her. She needed to behave, live a normal life. The path lay before her, straight and narrow.

Alma walked by with the couple in tow. Soon she returned, handing her notes to Jessica.

"Another divorce?" Jessica asked.

"Not this time. A real estate deal. They're purchasing a hundred and fifty acre ranch on the border of Hudspeth County."

"That's pretty far out in the boonies."

Alma met Jessica's comment with a dull stare. "I thought, with your commercial real estate background, you'd appreciate this deal."

"I'm happy to work on this." Jessica reached for the folder. "And I appreciate this job and everything you let me do here."

Alma visibly relaxed, even smiled. "I think you'll really like this one. It's unusual. A religious man known as Brother Bill Hardaway ran what might be considered an informal rehab program out there. He passed away a few months ago and left the entire ranch to a woman who stayed on to help him after she went through the program. Evidently, she's selling the land to the Wrights over time and at a discount. I'll need you to research the title and draw up a contract."

"This does sound interesting. Who represents the seller?"

"According to the Wrights, the woman doesn't have an attorney. We'll need to look into that. Her name is Nora Riggs."

"I'm on it," Jessica said with real enthusiasm, something that had been missing from her work life for quite a while.

***

Flooded with sun, San Jacinto Plaza in downtown El Paso usually brightened Jessica's day. Buildings from an earlier century surrounded the square. Some were white with wedding cake scrollwork. Her favorite had fantastical gargoyles as decoration. Shiny, sculptured alligators frolicked in a fountain in the middle of the square. She'd heard they commemorated the real alligators that once lived in the fountain. In El Paso, anything was possible.

She turned her face to the sun, letting it warm her air-condition-cooled skin. She'd stopped for hot coffee on the way to the plaza. It would pair perfectly with the burrito Angus had made for her the night before. Somehow, she'd found a man who packed lunch for her before he went to bed. She made coffee each morning, delivering a mug to his nightstand and kissing him awake before she left for work.

When they'd first moved in together, these small acts seemed as fragile as glass. How could she have a successful marriage, one grounded in details her badass single self would have made fun of? But day after day, their traditions strengthened into something more permanent. They came home from work and had a drink on the porch before worrying about dinner or more mundane tasks. Terrified of losing this best thing, she viewed their rituals like an addict, afraid a single misstep would bust the happiness apart.

Angus made the boring parts of her life worth it. She bit into the burrito, machaca, her favorite. It also meant Angus had been to his parents' house. She'd recognize his mom's particular mix of eggs, shredded beef, and vegetables anywhere. The warmth of this simple meal made the desert sun and scalding coffee seem frigid in comparison.

Her phone buzzed, and she expected a text from Angus. Oddly telepathic, he often reached out when she thought about him.

Instead, the text was from Lucía Rey. Why would Alma's sister's kid text her?

Jessica's close ties to all three Rey sisters reached back to when her parents abandoned her after her dad's conviction and her parents' flight from El Paso. Alma, her boss, had lived with her until she moved into the college dorms. Luz, one of Jessica's best friends, let her live on a tiny house on her property until Jessica and Angus bought their own home. The oldest sister, Paz, raised Lucía on her own, and Jessica had babysat for her often. But that hadn't happened in years. Now, Jessica rarely saw the highschooler except at family gatherings.

"Meet me for coffee today?" Lucía texted.

"Sure. After work. Lmk where"

"Starbucks@UTEP. Don't tell mom."

Not good news. She didn't want to hide things from any of the Rey sisters, especially Paz, who worked as a paralegal beside Jessica at Alma's firm. But high school sucked. She'd hear the girl out.

"CU there"

Chapter 2

That afternoon, Jessica ordered a coffee at the same Starbucks she'd worked at in college, then took a table by the window. She hoped Lucía, a junior in high school, would go further afield than UTEP. The bookish girl had a bright future, but she needed to explore the world a little. Jessica worried about women who stuck too close to home. A little street smarts went a long way.

Lucía came in wearing jeans and a cute cotton top. Unlike half the young women in the coffee shop, Lucía's jeans allowed her room to breathe, and her top didn't reveal half her stomach and all of her cleavage. Jessica hadn't been so conservative in high school, but then, she'd done a lot wrong.

Lucía ordered a drink, then dropped into the chair next to Jessica with an apprehensive glance. She was usually perky and full of smiles, and Jessica wondered about this unsettled version of the young woman.

"You have to promise me you won't tell my mom." Lucía barely raised her voice above a whisper.

That only meant bad news. The Rey sisters should be the first ones called when trouble arose. More than entrenched in the family, Jessica and Lucía practically grew up together, although the fourteen years between them meant Jessica had been caretaker more than friend.

Jessica agreed to Lucía's demand, caveating, "for now."

"I'm here to talk about a friend." Lucía's eyes shone a little too brightly at the words. "We both attend the Christian Kids Fellowship program after school and on weekends. We have bible sessions, study halls, plus we raise money for charities and volunteer for service projects. That's how Grace and I met freshman year. She's a really good kid and one of my best friends." Desperate pleading filled Lucía's eyes and voice.

Jessica wondered what drove the expression. Perhaps this would spin into the tale of a good girl gone bad. Jessica could relate, not that she'd ever been the church group type. "So, what happened? Why did you want to meet?"

Lucía's eyes dropped to the tabletop. "A few months ago, a new pastor arrived at Grace's church. The old one, Mr. Soto, he just disappeared. We never heard what happened to him. The new pastor preached at some of the services and now he leads our youth group too."

"Lucía, look at me. What's going on?"

Lucía briefly glanced up before returning her eyes to the table. Her cheeks turned pink. "The pastor, he's kind of handsome. Blond hair, blue eyes. He looks like a movie star. Some of the girls got a crush on him."

Aah. Jessica braced herself against the coming revelation. She hoped the conversation veered toward inappropriate feelings rather than improper actions. "That's okay. I've been known to have a crush on a teacher or two."

"It's not like that. We're not like you were."

"Ouch." Jessica's once Olympic man-izing, or whatever the opposite of womanizing was, had disappeared the night she asked Angus to marry her, but a reputation is a difficult thing to overcome. She hadn't realized it had seeped down to Lucía's generation.

"I'm sorry." The red in Lucía's cheeks deepened.

"Don't be. I deserved that. And if you ever need to talk about guys, I'm your girl. So, what happened with this friend?"

"Well, she started hanging out with him, like not just at regular group times. She started visiting his classroom for lunch and she'd stop by after school. She was all proud when he took her down to the river."

"Um," Jessica broke in. "There aren't a lot of reasons to go to the river. You're either there to exercise during the day or make out at night." The Rio Grande didn't have a lot of water anymore, but it had wide grassy banks and plenty of hiding places along its winding route. Parties, drug deals, and hidden trysts had happened along the banks of that fabled stretch of water for centuries.

"Yeah. That's what I thought. I think she believed he was interested in her, but he's married. I've seen his wife. She came to one of our functions, and she's beautiful."

"Marriage vows aren't always sacred, even among religious types." Especially among them, although Jessica wouldn't burst Lucía's bubble.

"I think you may be right."

"So, you're worried your straightlaced friend might be getting too cozy with this guy?"

"I'm worried because she hasn't been at school in a week." A shallow groove between Lucía's brows marked her concern. "I called and asked her parents where she was, and they said she'd been invited to our group's college camp. That camp's not for a month and a half."

The hairs on Jessica's arms prickled with alarm. "Do you think she lied to her parents?"

"I don't know, but they didn't seem worried."

"Could she still be at home?"

"Maybe. I don't know. I asked if I could talk to her, but her mom said no. It's just not like Grace not to stay in touch. I asked the pastor if he knew where she was. He said she was fine, and I needed to focus on my own relationship with God."

What a rude thing to say to a teenager, although Jesica didn't have much tolerance for religious figureheads. "I admit her disappearance sounds a little weird, but why wouldn't you want to tell your mom about this? She probably knows Grace's parents and can talk to them."

The girl dropped her head into her hands and took a few labored breaths. "I had a crush on him too." The words came out in a whisper.

Jessica's gut belted in fear. "Did anything happen with him?"

Jessica heard a sob, and Lucía's shoulders shook. She pulled her chair close to Lucía's and reached an arm around her, as a comfort and a shield. She wished they'd met at a quieter locale. The chances of someone they knew walking into the busy coffee shop near campus were high.

Eventually, Lucía's sobs quieted, and she turned a tear-stained face toward Jessica. Jessica handed her the napkin from under her cup and ran a finger under her own eye to signal mascara stains.

"Did you sleep with him?" Jessica asked.

"No, Jessica! Never! I'm not that type of girl." Lucía began crying again.

What was she going to do with this girl? She grabbed a few napkins from a nearby dispenser and handed them to Lucía. "You need to tell me exactly what happened between you and this pastor."

Lucía wiped her eyes and her nose. Jessica watched her try to pull herself together, but something in the young woman had torn. Probably her image of herself. Jessica was familiar with that particular wound.

"He's so nice. When you talk with him, he really listens. Adults don't do that much. I met with him a few times after school. I've been really stressed out lately. There's so much homework and Mom and my aunts are always pressuring me about where I'm going to college. They want to know what I'm going to study, and I just don't know yet. I feel like I don't even have a life. I'm sixteen and I've never been on a date. I've only kissed one boy. Most of the guys at my school don't even like me. Sometimes I just hate my life. When I talked to him, he made me feel better."

Jessica shook her head, stunned at the wordy confession and wondering what to address first. "How did you kiss a boy if you've never been on a date? And you are beautiful and wonderful, and someday the right guy will see that in you. But there's no hurry. You have the rest of your life to be an adult. Enjoy being a kid for another year or two."

Lucía sniffled and looked up at her. "David Valdez kissed me in a movie theater once. He's part of our group, and we all saw the same movie together. He tasted like Flamin' Hot Cheetos popcorn. It was disgusting."

Jessica laughed. "Yeah. That sounds pretty terrible. I guess I had the wrong idea about those Christian high school groups. Who knew kissing was allowed? Now, tell me more about this pastor and how he made you feel better." Jessica worked to portray calm and caring. She already wanted to kick this guy's ass.

"He asked me to stop by after school once, on a Tuesday, the day Grace has violin practice. I started going most Tuesdays. I'd visit him in an empty classroom, and he'd always pull his chair close to mine. Like I said, he really listened. Sometimes he put his hand on my leg."

"That's creepy."

Lucía crossed her arms and narrowed her eyes at Jessica. "Maybe I liked it. I felt like he cared about me."

Jessica closed her eyes, sheepish. She knew how touch staved off loneliness, especially for girls without fathers. "Is that all that happened?"

"He told me I was beautiful once. We were standing by the classroom door, about to leave. He told me he could see the light of Christ in me. That I was unbearably beautiful. He touched my cheek." Lucía ran her hand along her jaw, a faraway look in her eyes.

What a fucking creep. "Anything else?"

Lucía dropped her eyes. "Once, his hand accidentally brushed my breast. I know he felt my nipple get hard."

"Oh, sweetie." These poor girls who grew up so innocent.

"He said I had a little of the devil in me too. He's right."

"He is not fucking right. And I doubt his touching you was an accident. He manipulated you." Jessica struggled to hold back her fury. This asshole had mentally toyed with a vulnerable girl. Jessica wanted to rip him into pieces. But Lucía needed something different right now.

"You are beautiful and good and have done nothing wrong. Don't ever let a man make you feel bad about yourself."

"It was an accident. And he's right. I liked it. I wanted him to touch me again. I am bad." The words came out in wracked sobs, and people turned toward them.

Jessica wrapped the girl in a hug and glared at the other customers until they turned away. She'd protect this girl with everything she had. "Honey, it is not bad to feel things. It's biology. Your body reacted exactly how nature intended it to. You are young and just learning these things. I guarantee you this man already knew how your body would react and used this natural response to make you feel bad about yourself. How old is this guy anyway?"

Lucía's sobs slowed, and Jessica hoped she'd listened. "He's not as old as my mom. Maybe he's your age?"

"And he works at the school, but isn't a teacher?"

"Our group is a club, but the school sets aside a couple of rooms for club activities. He spends a lot of time at school." Lucía's eyes remained fixed on her lap.

Jessica wished she could take her shame away. She hadn't done anything wrong. "Lucía, look at me. We have to tell the school about this guy. He shouldn't have touched you like that."

"I don't want you to get him in trouble. I shouldn't have been there. I shouldn't have let that happen. I knew Grace liked him. This is all my fault." Lucía had an endless supply of tears.

"You should have been there. It's your school. And I'm worried that if he's done this to you, he'll do it to other girls. Or something worse."

"That's what I'm worried about too."

"With your friend?"

"Yes."

"Let's talk to your mother about this. I promise she'll understand."

"No!" The word rang out across the coffee shop. "You promised."

"I said maybe."

Lucía raised her head and glared at Jessica. "I always hear about how you helped a young woman who needed to get away from her family. I'm all my mom has, and she worries so much about me I can barely leave the house. Now, I need help. I think my friend might need help. But if my mom gets involved, it will all blow up. Please don't do this. I thought I could trust you."

"You can trust me." Frustration boiled in Jessica. "You can trust me to do the right thing." She crossed her arms and sat back. It hurt to be a teen, and she hadn't had parents to turn to. Would she have if they'd been there? Probably not.

Lucía looked at her with puppy dog eyes and a face ruddy and swollen from crying. Shit.

"What's this guy's name? I'll do a little sleuthing, and I won't say anything to your mom today. But we're not done with this conversation."

Lucía huffed and crossed her arms. "His name is Pastor Wright, but please don't talk to my mom without talking to me first."

The familiar-sounding name made the hairs on her arms rise, as did her promise to go behind Paz's back. Hopefully, a visit to the school would take care of the crisis.

Chapter 3

J essica's phone rang before she made it back to the office. She pulled to the side of the road to answer in case Lucía had something else to discuss. Someday, maybe once she had her law degree, she'd make enough money for a new truck, one that would connect with her phone.

She pulled her phone from her pocket. Not Lucía.

"Hey, Mom. How's it going?"

"I'm so glad you answered. I need to talk to you about something." Her mother paused, leaving dead air between them.

"And?" Jessica finally asked.

"I'm thinking about moving to El Paso."

Jessica had expected this hammer to drop. Her mother had no one in Fort Davis, the small town in the middle of nowhere, Texas. Her father had moved there shortly after being sentenced to house arrest because he believed staying in El Paso endangered his family. Of course, his wife followed him instead of staying with her only daughter. Jessica refused to speak with them after that.

Not long after moving, her father had a stroke. Since Jessica's mother was his only caretaker, it left little time for her to make friends. His death six months ago had left her mom isolated and lonely.

Jessica had reached out to her parents two years ago when she needed to get her life together. She had rebuilt a tenuous relationship with them.

"You'll have to sell your house in Fort Davis." Jessica refused to ask her mother where she thought she'd live in El Paso, in case she mentioned Jessica's home. They had way more work to do on their relationship before that could be a possibility.

"Yes, I've called a realtor. There's not a lot of demand here in Fort Davis, and she warned me it might take a while to sell."

Relief flooded Jessica at the bought time of a soft real estate market. "I can come down and help you get the house ready to sell."

"I'd really appreciate that. Bring Angus down too, I could use his brawn. I think I'm ready to move. The house will sell whether it's vacant or not."

Shit. Jessica forced the next words out. "Where are you planning to stay?"

"Well, since you've moved into a new home, I thought I could take over the little cottage you rented from Luz and Sarah."

"Mom, have you seen that place? It doesn't live up to the word cottage. It's not exactly roomy. Or pleasant." The tiny home had served as a refuge for Jessica for years after she'd moved out of the dorms at UTEP, but she couldn't imagine anyone else tolerating the ancient building. At least not a person with standards.

"That's what Sarah and Luz said. They offered me a room in their house, but I don't want to intrude. Besides, I think I'd like my own space. Anyway, I'd at least like to visit and take a look at it."

"When? You're welcome to stay with Angus and me when you visit." There. That hadn't been so hard, even though she felt like puking. She wanted to spend more time with her mom, she really did. But the two of them always turned the drama up to eleven, and it exhausted her.

"Thanks, Honey. Maybe next time. I'm going to stay with Luz and Sarah. I'll be there on Friday for happy hour. Are you coming?"

The offer reminded Jessica of a police entrapment case that had recently gone through the law firm. Jessica had attended Friday night happy hour, a long-standing tradition at Luz and Sarah's, from the beginning. Once a week, her friends surrounded her with strong margaritas and delicious Mexican food. Happy hour had become her respite when her job and her personal life grew dangerous.

Of course, since she'd married Angus, since she'd changed careers, danger had crept far away. She no longer needed happy hour the way she once had, but it remained constant, her safe space. Until now. "I'll be there. Are you arriving this Friday?"

"Yes, Honey. I'll see you then."

Jessica ended the call but didn't pull back into the road. She'd have to talk to Angus. Her mom would hate the rental at Luz and Sarah's. He might insist she move in with them. He'd always been the nicer one.

Jessica popped the top off her beer, then joined Angus on the generous front porch. He sat in an armless leather chair, strumming an acoustic guitar. She lounged on the wide swing they'd built together, with his dad's help, when they moved into the small house.

She rocked gently, appreciating the cold, bitter brew. Her eyes scanned the lawn, the Bermuda grass turning beige and crunchy after the first freeze of the year. The mountains that sliced through El Paso glowed amethyst in the evening light of the setting sun.

Purchasing the house had stretched them financially, but that and marrying Angus had been the two best decisions Jessica had ever made. Sometimes she still couldn't believe they owned their own home. If she had to sit through boring legal cases to come home to this little slice of paradise, then it was worth it.

She swore Angus hadn't changed since high school, all shaggy-headed and smiling with a guitar in his hands. With a mischievous sparkle in his eye, he crooned, "Did you have a good day at work?"

"I don't know. It was odd."

Angus set his guitar aside. "Odd sounds better than the boring and painful divorce days you've been complaining about lately."

"Oh, I had one of those too. Wild divorce lady stopped by my office and threatened to cut her husband's balls off."

"Ouch."

"Then my mom called. She's serious about moving here. Soon."

"Do you want her to live with us?"

"That would cut my balls off."

Angus laughed. "She's not so bad. Except for the leaving you on your own at sixteen part."

Jessica had tried to bury the pain of her parents' departure for years, but it had fed one bad decision after another until she finally confronted them. Now she got along with her mother, or at least tolerated her. They still tiptoed around the bruises they'd caused, but the crying and screaming had mostly passed. "Being on speaking terms with someone and living with them are two entirely different things."

"I'd like to think if something happened with my parents, and they needed to move in, we'd find a way to accommodate them." The end of his sentence lilted up in a question.

"Of course we would. They can move in tomorrow. Hell, your mom's the best cook in El Paso, and I adore your dad. I'd kick you out if I got those two instead."

Angus chuckled. "You'd sell me out for my mom's tamales?"

"And her enchiladas and gorditas and picadillo."

"You're making me hungry, good thing you got steaks." Angus took her hand and turned serious. "If our parents need us, we should try to find a way to help them. But staying here should only be a temporary solution. You never know when we might need that extra bedroom."

Good time to change the subject. "Hey, Lucía wanted to talk to me today. She's worried about the guy leading the school's Christian group. Seems he's getting a little handsy with some of the students."

"Did you tell Paz? Do you guys need me to go kick his ass?"

Jessica rolled her eyes. "Lucía didn't want me to tell her mom. I figured I'd do a little snooping around first."

Angus scowled and picked up his guitar again. "I think you should tell her mom. She needs to let the school know about this."

"Did you tell your parents everything in high school?"

"No, but you know how you get."

"What does that mean?"

"You get overinvolved. Things go south from there."

He wasn't entirely wrong. Jessica had loved the excitement of taking on a drug dealer in college. He now rotted in a Mexican jail. More recently, she'd searched the hemisphere for a missing woman and ended up having to escape the woman's angry father and jilted lover who both wanted to kill her.

She missed the heady excitement her darker self craved, but she'd made the decision to leave that Jessica behind and become the kind of woman who deserved Angus and a real job. Condensation ran down the bottle she held. She took a long sip to ground herself. The new Jessica could handle this.

Chapter 4

The next morning, Jessica parked outside El Paso High. She hadn't returned to her high school since, well, high school. She'd hoped to never walk through those glass doors again, much less go through security, then tread the hallways toward the principal's office.

She wavered between the teenage girl of the past and the self-possessed woman she'd become. Back then, she carried the embarrassment of her dad's conviction and the gutting of their subsequent abandonment. Only sixteen when the high-profile case hit the media, it not only took down her dad, it left a teenager with a serious chip on her shoulder navigating high school and life.

As she walked down the hallway, she wanted to hide behind the thick dark hair and heavy black clothes from that earlier era. This morning, she'd pulled her hair off her face and worn black slacks and a thin sweater that offered no protection.

She pulled open the door to the principal's office. The ancient, hard-faced secretary of her high school years must have been put out to pasture. A woman Jessica didn't recognize sat at the desk. She looked like a middle-aged mom, perhaps Jessica could get somewhere with her.

She still hadn't decided which story to use to dig up information about the youth group Lucía had mentioned. She could pretend to be a mom, but if anything got back to Paz, she'd be in trouble. The law student angle seemed the most honest. She could claim an assignment to investigate the group. She could come clean and admit to being Lucía's aunt, but that would also likely get back to Paz. So, she went with attorney, where she could hide behind privilege to keep from spilling information.

"Hi, I'm Jessica Watts with Cohen Garcia Law Group. How can I find out more information about one of your extra-curricular groups, the Christian Kids Fellowship?"

"Vice Principal Jackson handles that. Would you like me to see if he's available?"

Jessica nodded. While the woman picked up the phone, Jessica took a minute to look around the office. Still all sports trophies, mostly football. You'd think the building housed an athletic club, not an academic institution. Some things never changed.

"Mr. Jackson will see you momentarily. You're welcome to have a seat."

Before Jessica could slide into one of the vinyl-coated chairs, a large Black man came out a door. "Ms. Watts, I'm Charles Jackson. You wanted to meet?" He offered his hand.

"Yes, thank you. I'd like to talk to you about one of the groups that meets on campus." She reached out and shook his hand, then followed him into his office.

Given his size, she expected him to be a football star, perhaps a linebacker. Devoid of sports memorabilia, his office instead displayed a green helmet, an American flag, and a wall full of awards. That made sense. The Fort Bliss Army Base cut a swath through east El Paso, then stretched north for over a million acres. Many soldiers who served there retired into civilian life in El Paso.

The big man sat in a chair behind his desk and gestured for Jessica to take a seat across from him. "How exactly can I help you today?"

"I'd like more information on the Christian Kids Fellowship group that meets at the school." She decided to stay away from cover stories as long as possible.

"What kind of information, and why are you interested in this group?" He seemed genuinely curious.

"Someone I'm working with, a client, had some questions about them and asked me to learn what I could about the organization."

"And you're an attorney?"

Her lies were already tripping her. "No, I'm a paralegal. I'm just doing preliminary research."

"I see." He studied her for a moment as if trying to determine the truth. "I think you'll need to go to the school district for information. That group is approved by the district to operate at area high schools."

"Is that normal?" From what Lucía had said, Jessica had assumed the group only met here.

"It's not terribly abnormal. Most new student groups arise from student demand and need a teacher sponsor. However, this group has operated at the local high schools for many years. At some point, long before I got here, the district took over some of the administration."

"I heard they recently got a new minister."

"That's true. Alfredo Soto ran the group for many years, but he recently resigned. They did appoint someone new a couple of months ago. Again, you can probably find out more at the district."

"Is there a teacher liaison for the group at this school?"

"I'm sure there is, although I can't remember who it is off the top of my head. Give me a minute." He started typing on his keyboard.

His size must intimidate the hell out of the high school bullies. Jessica smiled. That could be a good thing. She wished she'd had someone big and strong to look after her back in the day, although, frankly, she'd have likely visited his office because she'd done something wrong, not because she needed protection. Mostly, she'd just tried to survive high school by hiding beneath a tough exterior.

"The club liaison is Mr. Douglas."

"Doug Douglas?" she asked. He nodded.

"I can't believe he's still here." Coach Douglas had been old in Jessica's day. He taught American government but was best known as the football team's defensive coordinator. Jessica still remembered how he'd started their first class by explaining how the government was set up like a football team. Only in Texas.

"You were a student here?" Jackson asked, a hint of suspicion creeping into his voice.

"Yes. Do you have an issue with my talking with Coach Douglas about this group?"

"Be my guest."

Jessica thanked him, then left the office. The secretary told her Coach Douglas would be teaching in twenty minutes and gave her a school pass. Jessica trudged down the hallway. Almost every locker and water fountain unlocked a memory, most of them bad. She arrived at Coach Douglas's room and found it empty.

Jessica entered the classroom and stepped back in time. The windows along one wall still showed the treetops where birds scuttled about. She'd watched them, bored out of her mind by the inside of the classroom. The clock at the front of the room still ticked loudly, reminding her of each second of her life passing while she sat behind a desk. Thank god, she didn't have a clock like that at work.

Five minutes before the class's start time, several students had already filtered to their seats. Coach finally came in. She approached his desk and saw a confused look on his face.

"Didn't you used to be a student here?"

"Yes. Can I ask you some questions about the Christian youth group that meets at the high school?"

Confusion returned to the man's face.

"You're the teacher sponsor of the group." She prompted him, hoping for some kind of response.

"Really? I didn't know they still had me on that list. It's a great group, by the way. Is there anything else? I need to get class started."

"Yes. Do you know who replaced Mr. Soto as the group leader?"

"Alfredo is gone? I didn't know that."

Just then, the bell rang. Jessica left the class, defeated. Coach Douglas had never been the smartest teacher at the school, but now he seemed almost willfully ignorant.

***

Back at work, Jessica placed a call to the school district. The woman who answered the phone abruptly told her someone would call her back. Jessica wanted to keep working on this case. She'd prefer finding a perpetrator who preyed on young girls to whatever boring legal issues Alma would throw her way. But unfortunately, she needed to pay the bills.

She pulled out the real estate deal. Jeremy and Emmy Wright. Surely no relation to the evil pastor. Her luck couldn't be that bad. Besides, the guy she'd glimpsed in Alma's office looked like a salesman, not someone who'd hang around a high school. And the name was common enough. She still needed to contact Nora Riggs and find out if she had legal representation. The file didn't have the woman's phone number, and Jessica couldn't find her online, a rarity these days.

She looked up the original owner, Brother Bill Hardaway, and found a website for the Gospel of God Renew Ranch. Evidently, Brother Bill liked alliteration. She called the number. It rang six times before a tinny sounding voice recorder asked her to leave a message.

"This is Jessica Watts calling for Nora Riggs. I'm with Cohen Garcia Law, and we've been asked to work on the transfer of your property. Would you call me back and let me know if you have an attorney I should work with?" She left her phone number and began writing up the contract.

The deal surprised Jessica in its generosity. The Wrights, the couple she'd seen in Alma's office, could take possession of the property immediately with almost no money down. They could pay off the property over fifteen years with no interest, and they could also buy out the entire contract any time they wanted.

No wonder Alma had wanted her to find Nora Riggs. The contract severely favored the purchasers. One provision did help Nora. She could continue to live on the ranch rent free until the buyers paid fifty-one percent of the purchase price, although she'd have to vacate the main house. After that, she'd have to leave.

What Jessica wouldn't have given for a deal like that. Not that she wanted to live in the middle of nowhere. Although, it might work for her mother. She shook her head. She had to quit thinking about her mother as a burden.

The phone rang. "Law firm, Jessica Watts speaking."

"Hello, this is Rosa Muñoz from the school district returning your call."

Finally, a chance to make progress on this case. "Yes, I'm looking for information on the Christian Kids Fellowship at El Paso High."

"What kind of information? You're calling from a law firm. Is there a legal issue?"

"No. I'm not calling on behalf of the firm. I've got some concerns about how the liaison is interacting with students." She wanted to jump in with the inappropriate behavior claim but worried the person would hang up.

"Um, that's a pretty serious accusation."

"Honestly, I don't know enough to make an accusation. I just promised a student I'd look into it. Can you tell me anything about the new man who's leading the program?"

"New? I don't know about that. The program is led by Alfredo Soto."

"That's odd." Jessica couldn't keep the suspicion out of her voice. "Both my niece and Vice Principal Jackson said he'd been replaced." The other end of the line when silent. "Are you still there?"

"Yes, I'm sorry. That program is overseen by school board member Dick Saunders. I need to reach out to him." The woman sounded flustered.

"The ex-mayor?" Surely not. Goosebumps pricked the flesh of Jessica's arm. The old feeling of being on the trail of something exciting gripped her.

Jessica quickly typed the district into her computer. Dick Saunders, current school board member and ex-mayor, stared back at her from the board of directors' page. "Why would he be involved in a program like that?"

"I'm sorry, Ms. Watts, but I'm going to have to get back to you. Thank you for calling." The line went dead.

Chapter 5

Alma dropped the updated divorce folder on Jessica's desk. It landed with a thud. Jessica stared at the thick folder, set a hand atop it, her curiosity about the earlier phone call ebbing away. Back to the jilted wife playing roles to get her way and her philandering husband. There must be more important work out there. Something that wouldn't suck her soul through the muck of other people's lives.

She turned to the real estate folder instead. At least this one would be clear cut, unemotional. Nora hadn't returned her call. Jessica might have to go out there. She could prepare the contract and leave a copy with Nora.

She'd used the firm's standard real estate form, modifying it to reflect the unusual deal. She filled in their client's information. Jeremy and Emmaline Wright. Again, the name stopped her. Could it be the same guy who led the youth group? The man who'd touched Lucía? A cold chill crawled up her spine. She had to find out.

As soon as she'd finished the contract, she took it into Alma's office. "Would you take a look at this? I've left a message for Nora Riggs but haven't heard back yet. Maybe they're in the process of changing the phones, and I just couldn't find the right number for her. I thought I'd drive out there and see if I could meet her in person."

"That's a long drive. But, I guess if it's the only way to reach her." Alma set the contract on top of a hefty stack of papers in her inbox.

"I could go out there this afternoon if you wanted to take a look at that now." Jessica tried to keep the pleading from her voice.

"It's four o'clock, and it would take you an hour to get there. This case isn't that urgent. I'll review it tonight, and you can go in the morning." Alma turned back to her computer.

Jessica hid her emotions even though she wanted to growl in frustration. If this was the same guy Lucía had mentioned, she wanted to get to work. Only she couldn't tell Alma this because she'd promised to keep it quiet. She turned to leave.

"Hey, have you updated the Jordan file yet? I need to call Tina tomorrow." Alma's voice reached her before she made it to the door.

A sigh escaped, loud enough for Alma to hear. Jessica tried to make herself sound chipper. "No. I'll get right on that." She needed to appreciate her job, and everything Alma had done to help her get it.

***

The next morning, Jessica arrived at work early. She'd stayed late yesterday to finish the updates to the latest divorce. This morning, she reviewed them before sending them to Alma. A peace offering for all the eye rolling and snide comments about divorce cases.

Alma had always believed in her. As her guardian and the main adult in Jessica's life after her parents left, Alma had remained her friend and guided her career. When Jessica finally decided to become an attorney, Alma gave her a job so she could gain experience and afford school. Jessica could never repay her for all she'd done, but she could become Alma's best employee.

Alma strode toward Jessica's desk, carrying the real estate deal folder. "Good job on this. And good luck finding Nora. The Wrights are getting a sweetheart deal, so if she doesn't have an attorney, please recommend she find one. I'm not sure what her relationship with Bill Hardaway was, but she might be grieving. We wouldn't want to litigate this because she felt undue pressure from the Wrights or anyone else."

"Great, I'm on it."

The drive into the morning sun burned her eyes, even behind sunglasses. She took Montana Avenue, a street that started in downtown El Paso and headed due east. The avenue quickly changed from tall commercial buildings to the once-stately homes of rich El Pasoans from over a century earlier. The two-story colonnaded buildings now mostly housed restaurants, galleries, and an assortment of other businesses. After that, the street changed to an endless stream of strip shopping centers and stoplights, the suburban hellscape seeming to last forever. Finally, she reached the outskirts of town, where only tire stores and junkyards braved the encroaching desert.

The avenue turned into a highway, and the El Paso mountains glowed bright from the morning sun in her rearview mirror. She could see distant mountains on the front horizon as well, perhaps the Guadalupe Mountains National Park. The land she drove through between the mountain ranges was the flat bed of a sea that had vanished millions of years earlier. Sage and creosote dotted the stark country. It would be terrible to have a flat tire out here, or to get lost somewhere in all this sand.

Eventually, she turned off the road and headed north toward the New Mexico border. Jessica had driven this road a few times. It led to Hueco Tanks State Park, a land where hills of boulders erupted from the desert. Climbers loved the place. Jessica couldn't imagine much worse than climbing up hot boulders under a scalding desert sun, but she'd explored the park with her mom and dad several times as a child. The boulders had been home to the ancient Mogollon Native Americans, and they'd left hollows in the rocks for collecting water and beautiful paintings on hidden rock faces.

Today, she turned off the road to the park several miles before the entrance. The narrow two-lane road quickly shed its pavement for gravel. She'd hoped to follow GPS, but after she passed a low hill, her signal dropped. She followed the directions she'd jotted down far into the desert, making one turn and then another, hoping she'd gotten it right.

Just over an hour after she'd left the office, she came to an iron archway over yet another dirt sideroad. It had a horse centered on top. She turned under it and crossed a cattle grate. Hopefully, this was the place. If not, she'd have to be careful. People out here didn't like visitors, that's why they chose isolation. They also tended to be armed to protect their property, and they wouldn't hesitate to use their guns on trespassers.

At least the road had improved from the earlier washboard gravel that shook her truck to its bolts. This place had been cared for. She clocked more miles on her truck, weaving through a few barren hillocks before finally seeing buildings.

A brick ranch house surrounded by the area's only trees sat to her right. Ahead, a small wooden barn looked recently constructed. Two freshly painted buildings sat to the left. They looked a little like bunk houses at a horse camp she'd attended once. Made of wood, like the barn, she didn't know how they, or the barn, would withstand spring's desert winds. A couple of motor homes dotted the nearby desert, along with a decrepit old school bus that had clearly driven its last mile. The entire place seemed creepy.

Jessica parked close to the ranch house. She hadn't seen anyone and figured it was the best place to start. She trudged down the cement path, then up two concrete stairs. The place seemed deserted, and she hoped she hadn't made the long drive for nothing.

She rang the doorbell, or buzzed it, given the horrible noise it made. Nothing about this place welcomed her. Silence. After a few moments, she buzzed it again.

"Just a minute." A woman's voice.

More than a minute passed before the door opened. The woman she'd spied in Alma's office stood before Jessica. Church-girl. The term flitted through Jessica's mind before she could quash it. But still, the young woman wore yet another demure flowered dress. Her blond hair shone as if just brushed one hundred times, and she had a heavily powdered face and freshly applied lipstick.

"Good morning. I'm Jessica Watts from the law firm you and your husband are using to purchase the ranch. I'm looking for Nora Riggs."

A look of confusion passed over the woman's face. "Nora? Why do you need to talk to Nora? Don't you work for us?"

"Well, yes. But in order to protect you, we need to understand if Nora has legal representation. I would have called her but couldn't find a phone number."

"I think you should talk to my husband. Unfortunately, he's gone to El Paso to meet with some people." The woman blocked the doorway with her body and seemed to want to end the conversation.

Jessica tried another tack. "It's just part of our due diligence. I'm happy to call your husband about it if that would make you feel better. Is Nora here?"

The woman sighed, then stepped back from the door. "Please, come in."

Jessica entered a living room that probably hadn't been updated since 1973. The woman gestured her toward a rough twill sofa in a hideous orange. It and a dark wooden coffee table with several worn patches and glass ring marks sat atop an orange and green rag rug. A lounge chair with ripped leather arms flanked one side of the coffee table, while a light wooden spindle chair flanked the other. Jessica wouldn't have been surprised to see the furnishings pulled to the curb on trash day. They seemed completely opposite to the woman in the flowered dress.

Jessica sat on the edge of the sofa, afraid to sink too far back into its lumpy cushions. Who knows what had happened on that couch over the years?

"May I get you something to drink? A glass of water?" The woman moved her hands to her neck, where she'd certainly have clutched pearls had she worn any.

"No, thanks. I'm fine. You're Emmeline, right? How long have you lived here at the ranch?" It surprised Jessica that they'd already moved in, given the unsigned contract in her bag.

"Please, call me Emmy." The woman seemed to relax slightly and perched on the edge of the spindle chair. "We've just moved out here. We had an apartment in El Paso for a few months."

"How do you like it so far?" It embarrassed Jessica to ask the question. This woman did not fit into the kitsch ranch house or dry desert air. Her discomfort showed in her tight smile and the way she sat on her chair with the disdain of a cat.

The woman dropped her eyes. "It's different than Big Spring. I've never been so isolated before." A deep sadness trickled through her voice. Then she transformed, sitting impossibly straighter, and focusing on Jessica. "My husband has a job to do here. He has a calling." Any bit of warmth vanished.

Just when Jessica started to feel sorry for her, the woman turned into an ice queen. Jessica thought about asking after Nora again, but figured she'd probe a little deeper. "So, what does he do that brought you all the way out here?"

"He's opening a home for wayward girls."

Jessica almost choked at the odd response. Whatever it was, it sounded horrifying. "What does that mean?"

"You know, girls who get in trouble. Ones who aren't on the right track." The woman stared at Jessica as if challenging her to ask further.

More than a few times in her past, people would have thought that about Jessica. Although, her path had been harder than most. "You mean like most teenage girls at one point or another?"

A stain of red crawled up the woman's throat, even though she continued to stare at Jessica. Emmy's oddly sinister glare unsettled her. Was she some kind of Stepford wife? Her modest dress, perfect posture, and steely blue eyes suggested it, but the perfect neighborhood she should have inhabited had turned to sand and sage.

"You'll have to talk to my husband about the program. I am not involved." Just like that, a door shut in the woman.

"Does Nora still live here?" Jessica asked. "Since she officially still owns the ranch."

"Yes. She moved into one of the trailers."

"If you tell me which one, I'll be on my way."

Emmy's gaze pinned Jessica to the sofa. "You probably shouldn't come out here."

What was with this woman? "I'd rather not have, but I couldn't find any other way to contact her. Do you have a phone number for Nora?"

"No. I'm not sure where she is right now. Check the silver motor home."

"Thanks." Jessica stood. "Hey, is your husband the same guy who's involved with the youth high school Christian programs in El Paso?"

Emmy laughed, brittle like dry straw and broken glass. "I met him in one of those programs."

"Really? But those programs are for everyone, right? Not just wayward girls?"

Emmy's eyes looked straight through Jessica, focusing on some point on the far side of where she stood. "Aren't all young women wayward in some respect?"

"No, they're not." Lucía flashed before Jessica's eyes.

"I think you're wrong." Emmy stood. "You should be able to find Nora outside. Get what you need, and I recommend you not come back."

"Why?"

"You're not the kind of woman anyone out here is looking for." With that, any emotion in the back of Emmy's eyes shut. She opened the door for Jessica and waited for her to leave.

Part of Jessica wondered if the Wrights had come to this place so far out in the desert because Emmy had some sort of mental illness. It was like she played a game Jessica couldn't see, with her changing attitudes and confusing words.

Back outside with the sun on her face and the door to the house firmly closed behind her, the ground felt firmer. Jessica walked to the ancient Airstream motor home. A small silver land blimp shining in the desert sun, it had to be intolerably hot during the summer. She knocked on the door but got no response.

She wandered over to the barn and stuck her head in a partially ajar door. "Hello?"

"Yes? Just a minute." The muffled voice came from inside. Jessica stepped into the aisle and let her eyes adjust from harsh sun to dark interior. A slim woman with wavy brown hair stepped into the corridor.

"Oh, I'm sorry. I thought it was Emmy." The woman wiped her red-rimmed and puffy eyes.

"Are you all right?"

"Yes. I'm sorry. I shouldn't be crying. It's just that Jeremy insisted on getting rid of all the animals. They've been such a big part of my life since I've been out here, and it's just hard."

"Animals?"

"Yes. We had cows and pigs and dogs, among others. Now we're down to the last two. The alpaca leaves today, and then it will be just me and the barn cat."

Just then, a white animal with a long neck and delightfully fuzzy face stuck its head out of a stall door.

"Oh, how cute."

"This is Marshmallow Max." When the woman approached the animal, he stretched his head toward her for a scratch behind the ears.

"May I?" Jessica reached her hand toward the animal.

"Yes. But be careful. He's a little nippy."

Jessica avoided the lips that extended toward her fingers and patted the animal on the forehead. "He's incredibly soft."

"He sure is. I'm going to miss him with my whole heart." Tears leaked from the woman's eyes. She wiped them away with the back of her sleeve. "I'm sorry. I'm Nora. You caught me on a bit of a hard day."

"I'm Jessica Watts. It's nice to meet you. You're the reason I'm out here."

"Me? Why is that?"

"I'm sure you know that Jeremy and Emmy Wright hired a law firm to draw up the contract for the sale of the ranch. I work for that firm, and I wanted to find out who represents you in the transaction."

"I don't have an attorney." Nora sighed heavily and stroked the alpaca as he nibbled on the hem of her shirt.

"Why? Brother Bill left the ranch to you, and he owned it free and clear." Even a ranch in the middle of nowhere had value in Texas. Jessica's suspicions went on alert.

"Well, Bill's realtor came to talk to me about six weeks ago. He told me the taxes on the ranch would be astronomical, way more than I could afford. If the county foreclosed, they'd take the ranch away. Fortunately, the realtor had a buyer. I didn't want to lose Bill's ranch because I couldn't pay the taxes. That would be a terrible thing to do to his legacy." Tears dripped down the woman's eyes again.

"But if it operated as a working ranch, you would have gotten a Texas property tax exemption."

"I just don't know." Nora sobbed, then wiped her eyes again. "Cade said it would be too difficult to do on my own. He's the realtor. I'm sure he's right. Everything's just been so awful since Bill died. Bill was my rock in the world."

Jessica laid her hand awkwardly on the woman's back. She never quite knew how to comfort people, especially ones she didn't really know. She'd wanted people to leave her alone when she was down. It gave her the chance to pack away her anger, tears, whatever, so no one could see it. At least that's what the old Jessica had done. The new Jessica had vowed to be better. In fact, she'd vowed to help women in trouble, and Nora seemed to have trouble in spades.

"Nora. If you're having second thoughts about selling the ranch, we need to know this now and get you someone to represent you. My firm can't work both sides of the deal, but I promise, it's better for everyone if you're sure about your intentions going in." This is exactly why she'd driven out here. If they'd done the deal and Nora felt coerced, she could sue to get her property back. People hired law firms because of due diligence like this.

"It's fine. I have to buck up, just like everyone says. I need to figure out what's next in my life. I just never thought I'd have to do it without Bill. Or without—using."

Jessica re-evaluated Nora. She originally placed her in her late forties, but she might be quite a bit younger than that. Her eyes seemed older, like she'd been through a lot.

Nora broke her gaze and looked down at the packed earth of the barn aisle. Then she straightened her spine and her eyes met Jessica's. "Did you know that Brother Bill used the ranch as a kind of halfway house for people with drug problems?"

"I'd heard that." Jessica kept her eyes locked with Nora's.

"That's how we met. I was one of his first customers. That was seven years ago. We became—well, we lived together. After I got better."

"I understand. And really, none of that is relevant to what our firm is doing. If you have any doubts at all about selling this property, you need to get an attorney."

Nora looked up at Jessica with beautiful eyes the color of cinnamon. They held so much pain Jessica almost looked away. She thought of Angus and the chasm that would open in her life without him.

"I can't imagine staying on the ranch without him," Nora said. "I also have no idea where I might go. The deal with the Wrights works for me, at least for now. I'll stay on and manage the ranch for them, at least for a while."

"But the contract is written so that when they've paid half, they'll be able to kick you out. Here, I've brought it for you to review." Jessica pulled the document from her bag and handed it to Nora.

"An attorney might be able to provide you with some protection, at least give you a certain number of months' notice." Jessica tried to channel Alma. The line between representing the firm's clients and giving advice could be thin. In this case, having both sides know their rights would likely make for a stronger agreement.

"I think I'm doing what Bill would want. He truly believed that Jesus saves lives. He would want the ranch to help people. That's why he first came out here. He had his own problems back in the day. Before he learned how to lean on God instead of his vices."

"What do the Wrights want to do out here? Emmy said something about a place for wayward girls." The old-fashioned term irked Jessica. Kind of like Emmy, the word would have fit better in the 1950s than today.

"They haven't told me much about it yet, but they want me to get the bunk rooms ready. I think it's a great thing. If I'd had someone to help me when I was a teen, my life might have turned out differently."

"Do you think they plan on bringing girls here against their will?" Lucía's fear for her friend caused Jessica to probe deeper.

"Why would you say that? I don't think that's what's going to happen at all. You know, your life might have been all roses growing up, but there are a lot of girls out there who suffer."

Jessica stared at Nora, unsure of what to reveal. Her life had definitely been worse than many girls, but she'd made it through without falling into an addiction to drugs, something Nora hadn't avoided. "Believe me, I understand better than you can imagine. I just don't know whether being out here would have helped."

The alpaca tossed his head, perhaps in agreement, more likely from boredom. Nora pushed his head back into the stall and closed the upper door before hooking the Dutch doors together. "Well, it certainly would have helped me. It would have gotten me away from the people who hurt me. It would have taught me about our savior and about personal responsibility. If you'll excuse me, I've got to get Max ready. The trailer should be here to take him away any minute."

Nora's moment of anger had faded back to sadness. Jessica wished she'd convinced her to get legal help. "Hey, can I get your number in case we need to call you about the contract?"

"I guess." Nora slipped a phone out of her pocket.

Jessica input her information, texted herself, then handed Nora a business card. "Call me if you need anything. I understand how hard transitions can be."

Nora slipped the card into her jeans, then opened the alpaca's door. "I'll be fine," she said. Then she stepped into the stall and left Jessica alone in the aisle.

Jessica left the barn and took one more look around the property before leaving. It raised the hair on her arms that this was the same guy involved in the school. She couldn't imagine anyone worse running anything for girls, but she'd gotten what she came for and had no reason to stay. She wanted to explore the bunk rooms and learn more about what would go on here, but she had a real job back in El Paso, and those divorces weren't going to resolve themselves.

Chapter 6

Back at the office, Jessica buried herself in busywork. When Alma swung by, she explained that Nora didn't want representation.

"Well, you tried. Thanks for that, and put it in the case file." Alma seemed ready to move to the next subject.

"But I'm not sure she really feels that way. She was pretty broken up. Evidently, the Wrights decided to sell the animals on the ranch, and she seemed devastated. It's like she didn't realize she still owned the place and got to decide what happened." Surely this was exactly the type of person they were supposed to help.

"You asked her if she was represented by someone and if she wanted to be, correct?"

"Yes, but I think she's being manipulated." Jessica wanted to protect Nora, but the Wrights had contacted them first.

"The Wrights are our clients. You know that. I'm sure you did your best to talk Ms. Riggs into getting an attorney, but you can't help people who don't want to be helped."

Jessica hung her head. Alma was right, but she'd gotten into this to help people like Nora Riggs. That woman had walked a tough road. Plus, Jessica had some severe concerns with Jeremy, and frankly, with his wife after her weird performance at the ranch.

As if her words had incited action, Jessica's cell phone rang. Lucía's name and photo flashed on the screen. Jessica grabbed for the phone, but not before Alma saw it.

"Why is Lucía calling you?"

"Oh, you know, teenage stuff. Do you mind if I take this?"

"Nope. Tell her hi for me." Alma sauntered away.

"Hey, what's up?" Jessica whispered into the phone.

"I just heard from Grace. Her parents are convinced she's done something wrong. They've kept her locked in her room and are threatening to send her away." Lucía semi-shouted into the phone. She sounded on the verge of tears.

"Shhh. I'm at work. Alma was just at my desk."

"No, you can't tell Tía Alma or my mom!"

"I won't. I promised you that. But if you keep yelling, they're going to find out. If you heard from her, that's a good sign. Maybe we can talk some sense into her parents."

"Maybe. But she won't tell me what's going on. She sounds scared."

"Did she say anything about Pastor Wright?"

"No." Sniffles crackled through the line. "I asked her about him, and all she would say was that none of this was his fault."

"But you don't believe that."

"I don't know. Maybe I had it wrong."

"Did he put his hand on your breast?" Jessica kept her voice calm but firm. She remembered how easy it was to be influenced by others. Especially older men. She'd run into that kind of trouble in college and barely escaped from a horrible man who had drugged her and probably had despicable things planned. She hated that memory. Two years ago, someone who'd hired her to find his daughter had tried to kill her. She couldn't imagine trying to best an older man in high school. One who was probably a master manipulator.

"Yes. But I told you it was an accident." Lucía sighed heavily on the other end of the line.

"He shouldn't have been close enough to you to touch it. Did you give him permission to touch you?"

"No. But—"

"There are no buts. I know they teach you about consent these days. If you don't learn this now, you'll never be in control of your relationships."

"Okay. But this is about Grace, not me."

"If this weren't about you, I wouldn't be involved." Jessica rolled her eyes. This girl was going to drive her to drink, or to drink more anyway. "Let's make a plan."

"You should go talk to Grace's parents, adult to adult."

"Doesn't your mother know them? Honestly, I think it might be better to involve her."

"Please, Jessica. Please just do this one thing for me. Let's put Grace first right now. I need more time to think about what I might say to Mom. She's liable to freak out."

Jessica considered it. It might be a great way to get more info on Jeremy, and the parents needed to know about this guy. Although, she hated not telling Paz.

Jessica's phone beeped. "Hey, Angus is on the other line. I'll do this one thing, but if anything is off, we're letting your mom know. Text me their address."

Jessica clicked over to the other line. "Hey, Ang. What's up?"

"Your mom just stopped by the house."

"What? What did you do?"

"I talked to her. It's no big deal."

"But she wasn't supposed to be here yet. Does she want to stay with us?" A fine tremor of panic thrummed in Jessica's chest. So many times in the past two years, she and her mom had found ways to disappoint each other. Living under the same roof likely wouldn't improve their relationship.

"She said she's staying with Luz and Sarah. Just like you told me she would. Why are you so wrapped around the axle about this?"

Jessica inhaled and let the breath out slowly. "I don't know. I just don't trust her yet. You remember the first weekend I visited them? She begged us to go to her gallery opening and then stood us up. It felt like she'd abandoned me all over again. And then after the funeral . . ." The shame of her mother's accusatory words slid over her skin.

"Yeah. She said some terrible things." Angus's voice filled with compassion.

"And then she locked us out of the house. I was furious." Memories became oxygen, and the flames of anger burst into life.

"But you took her call. You accepted her apology."

"I took, like, her seventeenth call. And I did forgive that, but I feel like I'm responsible for her now that Dad died. Having her around is complicated."

"We'll get through it. You and I can get through anything. Besides, I think the last thing she wants to be is a burden."

"Then why did she stop by when she knew I'd be gone? She can't deal honestly and openly with me yet. She's using you as a go between."

"It kind of worked. I invited her over for dinner tonight."

"Oh, shoot. There's something I have to do after work." Jessica didn't look forward to confronting Grace's parents and had no idea how long that might take.

"I'll push it back to seven-thirty, and I'll take care of dinner."

"Why don't we postpone it to another date?" One far in the future when Jessica had her life and relationships figured out.

"I'm here to help you with this. Let's go ahead and do it. The sooner you deal with her living in El Paso, the easier it will be. I promise."

"Fine. Thanks for handling this. I'll see you at home." Perhaps everything would be fine, although nothing had been fine with her mom for a very long time.

***

Jessica rang the bell of the white brick home with a bright blue door and shutters. The paint matched the yard, which had a lawn of acorn-sized, sparkling, crushed white rocks instead of grass. A few blue rocks had been scattered in with the white. The color-coordinated gravel defended the home rather than welcomed visitors.

Jessica had never understood the penchant for some El Pasoans to rock their lawns. Sure, grass died in the desert heat and used too much expensive water. But there were plenty of gorgeous desert plants that made for interesting and environmentally friendly yards.

In El Paso, rocks graced every surface. She'd sold commercial buildings with aggregate walls, basically gravel stuck into concrete. Some homes had gravel-topped roofs, and rock walls divided one home from another. Scarce trees meant scarce timber, but unlike most, these rocks didn't reflect the surrounding desert. Who knows where they'd come from?

Jessica rang the bell again. Lucía had said Grace's parents locked her in her room. Surely, someone was home with her. Jessica would have figured out how to escape within five minutes of being left alone.

"Who is it?" a woman asked from the other side of the door.

"This is Jessica Watts." She wondered what else to say. If she brought up Grace, the door might not open. "I'm a friend of Lucía Rey's."

The door opened to a tiny Hispanic woman with huge brown eyes and hair pulled into a severe bun.

"What do you want?" the woman asked, barring the door with her body.

At five-ten, Jessica had no trouble seeing over her into the home's living room. She did not see a teenage girl.

"Lucía is super worried about her friend. Is Grace okay?"

"You should go. I think Lucía has been a bad influence on my daughter."

"That's impossible." Jessica sputtered the words. Lucía was the most straightlaced teen Jessica had ever met.

The woman started to close the door.

"Please," Jessica said. "You remember what it was like to be a teen. Grace is Lucía's best friend. When she disappeared from school, Lucía got worried. I'm just trying to help."

"Who's at the door?" A man's voice. Aggressive and angry.

A look of fear crossed the woman's face, then the door opened wider. A heavy-set blond man as tall as Jessica stood beside the woman.

"This person is asking about Grace. She says Lucía is worried about her."

"Who are you? You're not Lucía's mother."

"I'm a friend of the family. Lucía was just worried about Grace missing school and wanted to know how she was. She's happy to pick up homework for her if you'd like."

"How my daughter is isn't your business. She needs a new school and a new set of friends. You can tell Lucía that."

"Is Grace, okay? Physically? I'm worried about those girls." Jessica was desperate to get beyond the walls these people had put up and figure out what they knew.

"Is Lucía in trouble too?" the woman asked. The man grabbed the back of her arm and Jessica saw a brief flash of pain cross her face.

"Lucía's not in trouble, but there's this Christian group leader that I'm concerned about. Do you know a Jeremy Wright?"

"You think there's an issue with Pastor Wright?" Mr. Randolph asked. "He's an upstanding man. In fact, he met with us about our daughter. We are a Christian family, and unfortunately, Grace started to stray from that path, and that's a problem for us. Without Pastor Wright's help, we never would have known."

"Are you sure? I mean, Lucía says Grace is a wonderful girl." Jessica heard the pleading in her voice. Her opinion of Jeremy Wright differed from this guy's immensely. "And I have some issues with Pastor Wright's behavior."

"Pastor Wright is like a father to these girls, or at least an older brother. Grace admitted what she'd done wrong, but not until Pastor Wright let us know. You should check with Lucía also. Girls these days can't be trusted." The man practically sneered.

"I think you are completely wrong. If there's someone I don't trust around here, Jeremy Wright is at the top of the list." Jessica wanted to shake this guy. Anyone who took a creepy adult male's side over a teenage girl's needed his head examined.

"You need to get the hell out of here." The man practically growled. His face flushed with anger.

"Can you please just let me know if your daughter is okay? Are you planning on sending her back to school?"

"Grace is fine." Finally, the woman spoke. "She will not be back at school for at least the rest of the year. They are not teaching her the things we'd like her to learn."

"You better go check the splinter in your own eye." The man yelled as he slammed the door. Jessica stood on the stoop, stunned by the overreaction.

She'd hardly driven a mile before her phone rang. Paz. Of course, they'd called Lucía's mom. She let the call go to voice mail. It immediately started ringing again. Jessica pulled to the side of the road. If the Randolphs had called Paz, Jessica needed to deal with her anger before she called Lucía.

"Hey, Paz. How are you?"

"Did you just go to the Randolphs' house?"

"Um. Yeah. I wanted to check on Grace."

"They are furious. Why would you do that?"

Jessica wasn't sure how to get out of this one. If she told the truth, Paz would be angry that Jessica hadn't involved her earlier. Of course she should have. "I'm sorry. Lucía and I were talking, and she was worried about her friend. I didn't think it would do any harm to stop by Grace's house. But that was before I met her father."

"You can't just go check up on Lucía's friends. That's not your role. When did you talk to Lucía? Why didn't you mention it at work today?"

"Listen Paz, I'm sorry. Lucía and I were just talking about stuff. I remember how it was to be a teenager, and I was trying to make her life a little easier. Please don't get mad at her. This is all my fault."

It took a long time for Paz to respond. "Listen. I think it's great that you and Lucía spend time together. But we've got to set some boundaries. If she's in trouble, I need to know about it. If she needs someone to talk to a teacher or a friend's parents, it needs to be me."

"Got it." Jessica wondered about the hand on breast thing, but Lucía seemed to have learned her lesson there. As long as she stayed away from that preacher guy, any danger had passed.

"Listen, I'm not trying to be a hardass. You'd know if you had kids, especially if you had a teenager, that it's hard to stay close to them. They want to push you away and step into adulthood, but they're just not ready yet."

"I've got it. Really," Jessica said.

"Thanks. And by the way, Grace's dad's a complete dick. Definitely stay away from that guy."

"Yep. I already learned that one the hard way. I feel bad for his wife."

"I pretty much feel bad for all wives, given my experience."

Jessica laughed. Paz's husband had cheated on her and then abandoned them years earlier. As far as Jessica knew, he'd never paid a dime of child support, and he certainly never attended any of Lucía's sports or performances. "Thanks, and I'm sorry. I'll tell Lucía she needs to talk to you."

"Don't worry about it. I'm glad she has other adults to talk to besides me. Just remember the boundaries."

***

Boundaries. Jessica pulled into the driveway behind her mother's van. The big picture window showed Angus and her mother chatting in the living room. She'd never noticed how easy it was to see into the house at night. Although she and Angus spent far more time on the front porch than on the living room sofa.

Some clawing need to protect the bubble of space she and Angus had created scratched at her. Especially today, after dealing with Emmy, Nora, and Grace's parents, she didn't need more drama. But she'd vowed to be a responsible adult, so she climbed the steps, opened the door, and met their gazes.

"Hey, why don't we go to Rosa's Cantina instead of staying here?" Jessica asked.

"That would actually be great," Angus said. "I haven't been home long because Robbie was late showing up for his shift."

"No surprise there," Jessica said. Angus's former bandmate and current employee had never been punctual.

"You don't want to stay here?" A worried look crossed her mom's brow. "I can whip something up."

"Have you ever eaten at Rosa's? It's some of the best food in town, and that's saying a lot. Come on, it's my treat," Jessica said. Rosa's also had some of the cheapest food in town. And ice cold beer.

They piled into the front seat of Jessica's truck, with Angus sitting in the middle. The van might have been more comfortable, but that meant giving up control. If the night needed to end, Jessica wanted to decide when they'd drive away.

They found a table underneath one of the TVs permanently set to the rodeo channel, except when the Cowboys played. Nothing but cowboy TV in this place. Plenty of cowboys here too—lots of dusty boots at the bar.

Jessica immediately ordered a beer and considered a tequila to go along with it. Her mom ordered a strawberry margarita, and Jessica fought to control an eye roll at the sugary choice. She ought to tone down the judgement, but every little thing annoyed her tonight.

She glanced at Angus, but he'd buried his face in the menu. They'd eaten here so many times he probably could have recited it to her, so he must not want to meet her gaze. At least someone in the family tried to keep the peace.

Her mom anguished over the menu, despite Jessica telling her to get the Mexican plate. One taco, one enchilada, one chile rel-leno—the perfect meal.

When the server returned with their drinks, her mom interrogated the woman over the menu, finally choosing a guacamole tostada. Angus, as usual, got the green chile cheeseburger. Jessica ordered another beer.

This time, Angus did meet her eyes. He mouthed "I'll drive."

Bless him. Tequila would help the conversation with her mom go down easier, but she figured she'd save that one for later in the meal if needed.

Thirty seconds later, when her mom started crying, she wished she'd ordered the tequila. "What's wrong?" she asked.

Her mom patted under her eyes with a napkin, not that it kept the new tears from falling. "I miss your dad, and I just don't know what to do with myself."

Angus reached over and rubbed her back in comfort. "It's going to be okay. I'm sure you miss him."

Jessica didn't know what to say. Mostly, she just wanted her mom to stop crying in the restaurant. She understood the loss. Heck, she'd just started getting to know her dad again when he died. But she didn't know how to make it better, and wasn't her mom the adult in this relationship? Jessica almost kicked herself at the thought. She was thirty, an adult in anyone's book.

"Are you still painting?" she asked her mom, hoping to get the conversation on better footing.

At that, her mother's head lifted, and she patted under her eyes one last time. "Yes. That's the only thing keeping me sane. And I'm hoping it can provide my livelihood at some point. I'm meeting with a few galleries while I'm here."

"That's great, Mrs. Watts. Your paintings are beautiful."

"Angus, I've told you a hundred times, please call me Clarice." She squeezed his arm.

The reprieve didn't last. Halfway through her tostada, Jessica's mom started crying again. Jessica took a long pull from her beer, then sighed. "What is it now?"

"I just feel like my life was on a certain path and now everything has changed, and I have to start all over again. Nothing is turning out like I thought it would. I had my life planned, and that fell apart when your dad died. Now, I don't know what to do. Do you ever feel that way?"

"Yeah. Damn near every day."

Angus shot her a wide-eyed look.

He was right, she'd chosen to reopen this relationship. She could be more compassionate. "Hey, Mom. It's going to be okay. We're here to help."

"Oh, thank you, Jessica. And Angus." The tears turned to sobs.

What would get her mom to stop? Just then, her phone rang. She slipped it out of her pocket. Nora. Jessica took the call.

Her mom looked at Jessica and her sobs inched up a notch in volume. Angus cast Jessica an angry glare. Someone turned up the sound of the country music streaming through the joint. Jessica's head felt like an atom bomb ticking down. She could only handle one crisis at a time.

"Nora, it's Jessica. Can I call you back in twenty minutes?"

"Sure. Jeremy's going back on his word. I want to talk to you about what you said about cancelling the deal." It was hard to tell with all the noise, but Nora sounded sad, maybe even crying. Welcome to the club.

Jessica ended the call.

Chapter 7

Jessica woke up before the alarm the next morning, her brain foggy from too much tequila. For some reason, she'd stretched herself along the very edge of the bed. Not even a sheet covered her, and the cold air of the desert morning had chilled her to the marrow.

She rolled over and crawled into the cocoon Angus had made with the down comforter.

"Oh my god, you're freezing." Sleepy voiced, he pulled her into his heat, throwing an arm and a leg around her.

Jessica burrowed into him, her body slowly warming. She remembered the tequilas they'd had after her mother had left. Between what she'd drunk at dinner and the nightcaps, it's no wonder she hadn't slept well.

They made it through the rest of dinner, but back at the house, the conversation with her mom deteriorated. She'd taken a look at the house on the outskirts of Luz and Sarah's property. While she didn't exactly say the place appalled her, she did ask Jessica how she had lived there so long with it in that condition. The judgment burned Jessica. She wasn't the one who'd run out on her daughter. They antagonized each other so easily. They'd gone from heated yelling to icy cold as her mother stomped to the van and drove away.

Thus, the late night tequila and an even later night drunken discussion with Angus. He wanted Jessica to lighten up on her mother. Something about the respect and duty his parents had instilled in him. But it only worked if it ran both ways.

He'd mentioned the possibility of letting Clarice live with them. Jessica would have preferred to take in a stray.

Dogs. On top of everything else, it turned out that Tela, Jessica's Catahoula Leopard Dog, absolutely loved her mother.

She'd have to talk to Angus again. There had to be a solution they hadn't considered yet. How would they have mornings like this, when her mother would probably already be up and making coffee and breakfast?

Already, she wanted to defy this woman who threatened the peace Jessica had so carefully stitched together. Her house. Her man. Her realm.

With passion, she kissed Angus's chest, wrapped an arm around his waist, and stroked his back. Her kisses moved up from his chest to the sensitive spot where collarbone met neck. He moaned and dipped his head to catch her lips with his own. She stretched herself along his body, determined to feel every inch of him.

Later, when they lay next to each other, satisfied, she pulled herself up on one elbow just before he fell back asleep. "You know, it's going to be much harder to do that if my mom's in the house."

He opened one eye and gazed at her. "I'm sure we could find a way to work around it. Although, point made."

With that, she smiled and kissed him one more time. "I'll go make the coffee."

***

Jessica called Nora again once the caffeine kicked in. It rang then went to voicemail, just like it had when Jessica tried calling her back last night. Jessica apologized again for not taking the earlier call and asked Nora to return the call. Damn it. She should have walked out on her mom and taken Nora's call first.

What had Nora meant about wanting to cancel the deal? Jessica had found the signed contract on her desk that morning. The receptionist said it was delivered late yesterday. At this point, Nora would have to go to court to cancel it. Either way, Jessica needed to warn Alma.

She tried Nora one more time before she reached Alma's office. Still no answer. She found Alma half-buried under the stack of files on her desk.

"Hey, I got a weird call from Nora last night. She said something about wanting to cancel the deal because Jeremy Wright had gone back on his word."

"But it's too late. Both parties have signed."

"Yeah, I know. I wish I knew more. I told her I'd call her back because I was at a noisy restaurant with my mom. I've tried her multiple times, but she hasn't picked up." Jessica shook her head in frustration.

"How did that go? I heard your mom was in town."

"Fine, I guess." The last thing she wanted to discuss was her mother and her lack of housing options in El Paso. "The Wrights did have some obligations to meet in the contract."

"True, but they're mostly financial." Alma sighed and shook her head. "This is why people need to have their own attorney review a contract before they sign it. I don't think either party has the money to litigate this. I guess I'll call the Wrights and see if Nora mentioned the issue. Aren't they all living on the ranch together?"

"As far as I know. They were when I went out there."

"Have a seat. We might as well get this out of the way." Alma gestured to one of the chairs in front of her desk.

Jeremy picked up on the first ring.

Alma introduced herself, said he was on speakerphone, and let him know Jessica was on the call as well. "Nora called Jessica yesterday and seemed concerned about the deal. Did she express any issues to you?"

"No, not at all. In fact, yesterday afternoon, she told us she was so thrilled with how things were going that she would leave the ranch in our hands and go stay with some friends for a few days."

Jessica shook her head. Nora had told her something completely different and had sounded extremely agitated. The roiling in her gut told her something was wrong. Of course, it might have been the tequila.

"Will you let me know if you hear from her?" Alma asked. "If either of you have any issues, it will be far better to try to work them out quickly. It could be costly if she decides to sue."

"Of course. But I doubt you'll hear from us. Everything seems great at this end. I'm not sure what Jessica heard, but Nora is happy. We don't want anyone stirring up trouble. Especially from the firm we paid to get this deal done. Is that clear?"

"Of course. We're just trying to look out for your best interests. If you do hear anything, let me know. Thank you." Alma pushed the button to end the speaker call.

"I swear, that's not what she told me. And she sounded really upset." If only she'd stepped outside the restaurant instead of telling Nora she'd call her back. Nora had needed her, and Jessica hadn't even taken the call.

"Perhaps it was a bit of seller's remorse," Alma said. "Leaving a place where you've lived for a while can be emotional. But she also may have told the Wrights everything was fine. She's been through a lot lately. You told me that. She lost her lover, sold the animals she'd taken care of, and decided to sell the ranch. That's a lot to go through. It wouldn't surprise me if she swung back and forth about whether she'd made the right decision."

Jessica bit her lower lip. Should she press Alma to let her look for Nora or just accept this as over?

"It's okay. You haven't done anything wrong." Alma's brow furrowed.

Jessica wondered what in her expression had caused that response. "Thanks. I am worried about her."

"I understand. Give it some time. If Nora contacts you again, let me know."

"I will." Jessica paused a moment. "There's something else. Jeremy Wright runs the Christian group at El Paso High. Lucía is a member."

"Huh. Well, I knew he was a pastor."

"I don't think he's a good guy."

"Jessica. He is our client." Alma shook her head, frustration evident on her face. "We have concluded the deal, so I suggest you keep your personal feelings out of this. And I expect you to do the same with our other clients, like Tina Jordan. The other day in the boardroom you looked at her like you wanted to strangle her. She is paying us a lot of money to handle her divorce. If you can't keep your personal feelings to yourself, you won't make a good lawyer."

"Got it." Jessica turned away. Maybe Alma was right. Someday, she would choose her clients carefully instead of taking anyone who came along.

When she'd sold real estate, she hadn't cared who hired her. She'd found the best building for her client's company and dealt with plenty of unsavory characters over the years. What had changed? She'd thought being an attorney would make her a better person, and she could leave the old, broken Jessica behind. Instead, she felt trapped between two versions of herself, and she wasn't happy with either one.

The second she returned to her desk, she tried Nora again. Still no answer. Perhaps Alma was right. Jessica just wished the feeling in her gut agreed with that logic. Something was off with Nora, and she didn't trust Jeremy Wright.

Chapter 8

The next morning, Jessica woke to a ringing phone. "Lucía's gone. She took my car and left her cell phone on the kitchen table." Paz's voice held an unfamiliar strain.

"What do you mean gone? Where would she go?"

"I think she went to find Grace. She left a note saying Grace had texted her and said she'd never see Lucía again. She said she had to go find her." A heavy sigh, or perhaps a sob came through the line.

"How can I help?" A knot formed in the pit of Jessica's stomach. She should never have encouraged Lucía without talking to Paz first. Waves of anger and desperation made their way through the phone. They morphed into guilt as they hit Jessica's ears.

"I've already called Alma. We've got the day off. We have to go find her."

"I'm on my way. I'll be there in fifteen minutes. Maybe less."

Jessica sped out the door, her thoughts spinning. If Lucía had gone to the Wright's ranch, she might be in the clutches of that filthy Jeremy Wright already. Or those of his strange wife. She asked her phone to call Nora. It amazed her that an ex-drug addict seemed like the most trustworthy person on the ranch. Still no answer. What had happened to Nora?

When she arrived, Paz waited for her on the front stoop. She trotted down the stairs and jumped into the passenger seat almost before Jessica had stopped.

"You know where she went, right?" Paz shoved the panicky words at her.

Jessica shook her head. "Let's focus on where they might be. Grace's dad seems to think Jeremy Wright walks on water. Jeremy's weird wife said he's setting up a home for wayward girls. They even have what look like bunk houses at the ranch."

"Oh, no." Paz's voice had softened, as if she hadn't intended to say the words out loud. "So, this guy is a pastor, and he's keeping young girls at his place. Is he a perv?"

"Maybe. Should we go check it out?"

"Where is this place? And how much does Lucía know about it?"

"It's way the hell out near Hueco Tanks. Lucía knows about it because I told her." Jessica wished she could go back in time and insist Lucía tell her mother everything.

Paz sighed, probably in disappointment, then shook her head. "Let's go find my daughter. You can tell me the story while you drive." She crossed her arms over her chest like she was trying to hold in all the worry.

"There's a Christian group at school and they got a new leader."

"I know. The gorgeous Mr. Wright."

Confused, Jessica glanced at Paz. "I don't think he's gorgeous."

"No, but Lucía did. I heard all about him. And about how he seemed to prefer Grace."

"Yeah, about that. Evidently, he hit on both girls."

"What?" Paz's voice boomed through the truck cab.

"He's a real creep. Lucía told me he touched her boob, although she swears it was an accident. Over her shirt." Like the last phrase made the rest of it any better.

"You are kidding me. And you didn't think you needed to tell me this?" Paz's anger flew toward Jessica. And she'd earned it.

"It sounded like a one-time thing. I talked to Lucía about how to deal with it. Seriously, sometimes it's better to have a sounding board outside the family."

"How would you know? You didn't have any family when you were her age."

"Touché." Jessica wouldn't protest. Not when Paz's barbs flew from a place of fear.

"I'm sorry. I'm just really worried about her."

"Me too. Do you have any idea when she left?"

"The text from Grace came just after five o'clock this morning. She probably left about five thirty. I'd have heard her after that." Paz pulled Lucía's phone from her bag.

"Parents sending me away. Don't want to go. Won't see you again. Scared." Paz read from the screen.

"Why do you think Lucía left her phone?"

"She didn't want me to know where she was. She probably knew I'd follow her."

"What? Do you track her phone?"

"Yes, of course."

Jessica glanced at Paz. "And that's okay with you?"

"Yes. She tracks me too. Welcome to the modern world of relationships."

The drive to the ranch took forever. Jessica hated that she had to stop and get gas, but her truck only had a quarter of a tank. They couldn't risk getting stuck in the desert.

"Where the hell is this place? It's desolate out here." Paz shuddered in the seat beside her.

"It's only a few more miles. Unfortunately, all of it is on this crappy dirt road."

They finally reached the turn to the ranch. Jessica stopped the truck. The wrought iron horse above the entrance had been replaced. Capital letters now spelled out DOMINION.

"Well, that's fucking ominous." Jessica turned the truck into the drive.

When they pulled up to the house, Jeremy Wright waited for them outside the front door. Jessica realized he must have seen the truck's dust trail from at least a mile away. She scanned the parking area but didn't see Paz's white Camry.

The women exited the truck simultaneously. Jessica spoke first. "We're looking for Lucía Rey. Has she been here this morning?"

"She's gone."

"What does that mean?" Paz sounded on the verge of hysteria.

Jeremy sighed heavily and shook his head, as if he couldn't be bothered with two emotional women showing up on his doorstep. "She was here earlier. She said she was looking for Grace Randolph. I sent her away."

"Is Grace here?" Jessica asked.

"That is certainly none of your business. Why do you keep showing up at my property?" He pointed at Jessica. "My wife told me about you coming here the other day to harass her."

"I didn't harass your wife. I was looking for Nora Riggs, on your behalf. We needed to talk to her about the real estate contract. By the way, is Nora here?"

Jeremy visibly stiffened. "Nora is gone. I told you that."

"Where did she go?"

"I don't know. She said she left to visit friends. In fact, she left after you talked to her. What did you say to her?" He stepped toward Jessica, accusation in his voice.

"I just asked her if she had legal representation. That was my job."

"You work for my attorney, so you better do what I say. Right now, I want you two to get off my property."

"I need to find my daughter." Paz's voice trembled. "Where did you send her?"

"Ma'am, you clearly have no control over your daughter. It's a terrible thing when a woman is asked to raise a child alone. And from what I've heard, you are not a good role model. Lucía told me that she never sees her father."

Jessica looked over at Paz. This would not go well.

"That bastard left us before she was born. And who are you to judge me, anyway? Or my daughter? She told me what you did to her." Paz nodded toward Jessica.

Jeremy's eyes turned to steel. "I have no idea what you're talking about."

"I think you do." Paz's voice went rough and dirty. "Preying on young women like that. You're an adult. How dare you touch my daughter in that way? It's time the school learns who you really are."

"I'd be very careful if I were you." A sneer accompanied Jeremy's remark.

"You're the one who needs to be careful. I've already talked to Vice Principal Jackson, and I think it's time for another meeting," Jessica said.

"How dare you? You work for me." Something wild glinted in his eyes, and his skin turned ruddy.

"The contract is done. As far as I know, that was your only business with us."

"Well, I can promise you, my first call after you leave will be to the head of the law firm. I don't think you're the type of person they want representing clients."

"Fine with me. I want to look in the bunk rooms to make sure Lucía isn't here."

"You'll do no such thing. Leave my property now, or I'm calling the sheriff."

"Screw you." Jessica headed toward one of the white buildings. Jeremy's footsteps tracked behind her.

"You are trespassing. Get off my property!" he yelled. A few feet from the stairs, he caught up with her, grabbing her arm and pulling her around.

"Get your hands off me!" Jessica twisted out of his reach.

"You better leave now." Jeremy grabbed his phone from his back pocket, punched a few numbers, then held the phone to his ear. "Sheriff Burns, this is Jeremy Wright. I've got a problem here at the ranch."

Shit. Surely, he was faking it. This guy had only been in town a few months. How did he know the sheriff already?

"Well, actually, it's not going so well," Jeremy continued. "I've got a Jessica Watts here at the ranch. She's trespassing and demanding to enter the buildings. This doesn't seem right since I'm a customer of the law firm she works for. Do you know anyone over at Cohen Garcia?"

"Yes. I would appreciate it if you'd put in a call for me. See if you can have them make their employee leave my property."

Thank god he didn't know Paz worked there, also. Jessica climbed the stairs to the building. If she was going to get fired, she might as well make it worth it. "Hey, why is there a padlock on the door?" She jumped off the porch and walked around the building.

"Where is my daughter?" Paz asked Jeremy in a voice loud enough to carry around the building.

"What kind of mother are you that you can't keep track of your own child?" Jeremy's question came out in a roar. "Get the hell off my property!"

Jessica rounded the building to where Jeremy and Paz stood. They faced each other in a three-way standoff. Her phone rang. Alma. Jessica answered the call.

"Are you at the Wrights' property? You need to leave right now."

"We're looking for Lucía." Jessica spoke into the phone quietly, but she could tell the others overheard her.

"Lucía? Why would she be there? And what do you mean *we*? Is Paz with you?"

"It's a long story."

"Did you find Lucía?"

"We haven't been allowed to look for her."

"Do you have any reason to believe she's there?"

"No," Jessica said.

"Then get the hell out of there."

Jessica ended the call. "Paz, I don't think she's here."

She hated admitting defeat, especially in front of this asshole. But the car wasn't here, and evidently, neither was Lucía. Still, she wouldn't give up. "We can try Grace's house."

Paz seemed to waver and looked around the ranch. Finally, her spine straightened as if she'd made a decision. She pointed at Jeremy. "You better hope I find my daughter. And there will be consequences for how you took advantage of her."

Chapter 9

The drive back to El Paso seemed even longer than the drive to the ranch. Jessica didn't want to call Alma to find out how much trouble they were in. Paz sat beside her, silent but wringing her hands.

"Where else might she be?" Jessica finally asked. "And how far behind her do you think we are?"

"She probably drove right by us, and we didn't notice." Paz sighed. "I can't believe she just took off like that."

"Why don't you call the school and see if she's there?"

"I know my daughter. She's a crusader. If she thought her friend was in trouble, she'd do anything to help. Going to the Randolphs' is the right move."

"I hope she's not there. Grace's father seems more than a little off balance." It tightened Jessica's stomach to think about seeing that jerk again.

"That's why we need to go there first. If she's at school, she's safe."

Jessica stomped on the gas pedal. She wished she could teleport rather than drive through the traffic on the vast east side of El Paso. Her thoughts wandered to Nora. She hadn't seen her at the ranch. And what was that padlocked door about? Surely Jeremy hadn't locked Nora in the bunk house. Nora would have screamed to let them know her location. Wouldn't she?

Jeremy insisted she'd gone to see a friend, but what friends did she have after living out there on that isolated ranch? She'd probably met people who went through the rehab program over the years. Heck, Brother Bill might have even held some kind of services. She hadn't noticed a church on the property, but she could research it further.

Soon, she retraced the streets to Grace's home. They pulled to the side of the street behind Paz's white Camry.

"Thank god." Paz heaved a sigh of relief. "I'm going to kill her."

"She's trying to do the right thing." Jessica tried to reach for Paz, to slow her down or cool her anger, but she jumped out of the car too quickly.

Paz rapped on the Camry's window, and Jessica saw a head jerk inside the vehicle. Then Lucía opened the door and jumped into her mother's arms, crying. She carried the weight of all the bad adult decisions that had led to this trauma.

Jessica opened her car door at the same moment the Randolphs' garage door rose. Paz, Lucía, and Jessica stood together on the sidewalk by the time the door had risen enough to see the three family members inside.

Grace had a heart-shaped face and pale skin. Her light brown hair had been pulled into a ponytail, and she wore stockings and a long-sleeved navy dress with a white collar. She simultaneously looked like every shy teenage girl everywhere and like someone heading to church a full century before today.

The minute Grace's father saw them, his face turned red. He shoved his way past his daughter and stepped into the driveway.

"What the hell are you doing here?"

"Lucía was worried about Grace." Paz, a human shield, stepped in front of her daughter.

"My daughter is none of your business. Get the hell off my property."

"Technically, we're on the sidewalk. City property." Jessica had no idea why the comment slipped out, but it wouldn't make things better. The red in the man's face deepened, and he seemed to puff himself up into someone larger.

"Would you mind if Lucía talked to Grace, just for a minute?" Paz's low, smooth voice might have calmed the situation. It didn't work.

"No, you cannot talk to my daughter. She probably wouldn't be in this situation but for your daughter's bad influence. Your bad influence. You aren't even married."

"You asshole." Jessica had had enough of people calling out Paz because Lucía's dad was a jerk.

"Being married doesn't make you a good parent." Paz practically spat the words. "You need to be a good person to have a positive influence on a child. Jeremy Wright is not a good person. He took liberties with my daughter and probably with yours, as well."

"Mom!" Lucía's screech ripped through the air.

Grace started sobbing, and her mother pulled her into the house. Grace's father stepped forward until he was a few feet from Paz. "If you don't leave right now, I'm calling the police. I don't know why you, a woman of sin, think you can tell me what to do with my family, but I don't want anything to do with you. Take your slutty little daughter and this piece of trash and get out of here."

He waved a hand at Jessica when he made the piece of trash comment. It pushed her into a fury. "Oh my god. How is it horrible fathers like you are always crawling out of the woodwork? Will you just be rational for a moment? Lucía and Grace are two of the sweetest young women in El Paso. Jeremy Wright is a sleazebag. Don't send your daughter there."

But he was no longer looking at them. Instead, his attention had moved to his phone. "My name is Pete Randolph, and I'd like to report a case of stalking."

Holy shit. Had he actually called the police? That would be just like a guy to not understand the definition of stalking. "Come on, let's go." She pulled Paz's arm. Lucía quietly sobbed behind them.

"Yes, I need to file a police report." Grace's dad had his phone to his ear.

Paz turned to Jessica. "He can't actually file a report, we didn't do anything wrong."

"I know. But he's clueless. He doesn't realize people need to be protected from guys like him, not the other way around. We should go."

"What about Grace?" Lucía said through her tears.

"Honey, she's with her parents. They get to decide what is best for her. Come on. Let's go home." Paz wrapped her arm around her daughter and pulled her toward their car. "Thanks for your help." She nodded at Jessica.

"Anytime." Jessica hopped in her truck and drove around the block. She returned to Grace's street, parking several houses away. Soon, an SUV backed out of the driveway. Jessica followed it around the mountain that divided the city. She drove back through the east side of town. She followed the SUV down the lonely highway that would eventually lead to Carlsbad Caverns and other points east. When the vehicle turned off on the road toward Hueco Tanks and the ranch, Jessica turned around.

The entire drive back, she imagined that sweet-faced girl being locked in a bunk house. Whatever evils that ranch held, surely it wouldn't be hard to shut it down. Jessica had dealt with far worse. Drug dealers across the border in Juarez, fires, the threat of being shoved from a small boat into a vast ocean. She just needed to get to the right people.

She thought of Jaime Castro, the El Paso Police sergeant who'd lived beside her after her parents left town. He'd been her protector then, and again a few years later when she ran across a dangerous man looking to enter the drug trade in El Paso. Unfortunately, the police had no jurisdiction outside the city limits, and the ranch was far beyond that boundary.

She didn't know anyone in the sheriff's office, but Jaime probably did. She called him and left a message to call her back.

Out of things to do, she considered heading to the office to face the consequences of Jeremy Wright's phone call. But she'd already experienced so much drama in the young day.

Instead, she drove to Angus's work. The music program he ran for kids wouldn't officially open until later, but he'd likely be there getting ready for a busy afternoon of music lessons and band practice.

She grabbed a couple of black coffees from the Starbucks next door before knocking on the glass door of the music studio. She definitely needed more caffeine this morning.

When Angus saw her, his lips curled into a broad grin. She loved his smile, and how his face lit up when he saw her. She was damn lucky this man had waited for her.

"We're not open yet," he teased through the locked glass door.

"I brought coffee." She held up a cup.

Angus unlocked the door. "Bribery works, every time." He took the cups from her and set them on a nearby table. Then he turned and wrapped her in his arms. "I love when you stop by. Even when I know I probably won't like the reason."

"Yeah. I was hoping to talk through some stuff." She told him the story of the morning and watched concern, then anger, cross his features.

"Are you sure this is your battle? I know you want to save the world, but this guy sounds creepy."

"I need to figure out what happened to Nora. And I keep picturing Lucía's friend in a building padlocked from the outside."

"So, what's the next logical step?" he asked.

"The school needs to know about Jeremy Wright. I'm sure they have some kind of formal complaint process. And I want to find Nora. Other people must have been involved with Brother Bill and his organization."

"Those things sound reasonable. But please don't go out to that ranch alone." He reached out and stroked her cheek, his voice lowering to its sexiest octave. "I'm getting used to having you around."

She leaned into him, brushed her lips against his. She wanted to lose herself in his touch and shove her problems aside for a while. She'd perfected avoiding problems by having sex. Before Angus, that had meant an unfortunate series of one-night stands. With Angus, she'd learned to identify that twinge of panic when she locked her anxiety in a box and turned her attention to carnal pleasures. But that was the old Jessica who loved to disappear into the shadows. She'd promised herself to deal with her issues, bring them to the light instead of hiding them in the dark.

But how would she tell him she wanted to spend the rest of the day researching ways to get to Jeremy Wright, figure out what stank in his operation, and clean it out so he'd never lay another hand on a teenage girl? That work called to her, while the thought of returning to the office to face Alma and a stack of boring files made her want to flee.

Her promise to change her life, pursue the right career and stay with that one right guy had to win. Those decisions had entwined themselves in her mind. They defined the new Jessica, the one with a successful marriage and future. How on earth could she hold on to this new life when some buried part of herself wanted darkness and danger?

Angus broke their kiss and leaned his forehead against hers. "Hey, what's wrong? You seem a million miles away."

"I have to go face Alma."

"You do. It's going to be okay."

"The sheriff called the partners. What if they fire me? What if my actions make Alma look bad to the partners?" Her mind spun worst-case scenarios.

"I can practically see your brain working. Stop worrying about it. Go talk to Alma. You and I will deal with whatever happens."

"Yeah." Jessica looked into his brown eyes. She wouldn't burden him with her secret hope of getting fired in order to focus on something more important and exciting than legal work. Something that renewed her sense of purpose but risked her future.

Chapter 10

Jessica slunk into the office and made her way to Alma's desk, hoping no one who knew about the morning's events would see her. Most people ignored her, although she caught a glower from Saul Cohen, one of the firm's partners, when she passed by the glass-walled boardroom.

Alma glanced up when Jessica entered her office, then sighed and turned back to her computer. Jessica sat in one of the plush yellow chairs in front of her desk.

"I'll be done in a minute," Alma said.

Jessica rose and walked over to the sheet of glass that formed the exterior wall of the office. She looked out over downtown El Paso and into Ciudad Juarez. The Mexican city called to her. She'd worked there for years, doing real estate deals and related jobs. She'd gone to parties, concerts, and nightclubs there, back in her exciting earlier life. Exciting, but going nowhere.

Now she was on the fast track. So why did she want to escape this office and flee across the border to a time when she'd had to scrounge for a living? She had to get out of this funk.

"So, what the hell happened out there?" Alma asked.

"Paz hasn't told you?"

"She let me know Lucía was safe, but said she needed to spend time with her."

Jessica returned to the yellow chair. "Paz called me when she realized Lucía had disappeared this morning. Lucía had reached out to me about a friend she thought was in trouble—a fellow member of Jeremy Wright's Christian youth group. He is not a good guy, and that's not just my opinion."

"I don't understand." Alma's brow creased in confusion.

"He touched Lucía's breast, and who knows how far he's gone with Grace."

"What?" Alma's eyes widened with shock. "How long have you known this? Why didn't you tell me? He's our client." Alma stood, glaring down at Jessica. "She's my niece."

"I know." Everything Jessica said sounded so bad in the light of how things had turned out. "Lucía asked me not to tell anyone, especially you all. You remember high school—how excruciatingly awkward every-thing was and how you wanted to hide some things from your parents."

"Jessica, that's not good enough. Wright is our client. I need to know what's going on with him, even if you don't want to share Lucía's secrets. You tried to tell me something but let me assume it was your issue. Now, you've put me in an incredibly difficult situation. Did you know the sheriff called Saul Cohen directly—our senior partner? When he asked me why the sheriff had called him about you harassing one of our clients, I had no idea what to tell him. You left me completely in the dark."

The exasperation in her voice shamed Jessica. Alma had put up with a lot from Jessica over the years, too much. "I should have handled it differently. We should have called you on our way to the ranch. I'm sorry. By the way, Jeremy's a total creep."

"Stop. Do not talk about him in this office. Others in the office see him as a client, and we haven't given them a reason not to. I will follow up with Paz and Lucía. If there's something there, I'll follow up with the partners, the school, the police—anyone who needs to know. Thankfully, the firm's contract is finished, so you shouldn't have to work with him again." Alma shook her head and walked to the glass window.

"I'm sorry. I never intended to get you in trouble." She hadn't. Things had built up, then she'd needed to act.

"I can't control things I don't know about." She turned back to Jessica.

"I know. It won't happen again."

"Jessica, I need you to keep your head down in the office for the next few weeks. Sit in your cubicle and work on whatever I give you. You're a good paralegal, even if you complain too much. I'm trying to provide you with an opportunity here, and I think you're going to be a great lawyer. Can you keep your mouth shut and just do the work while I try to clean this mess up? I'll talk to Paz and then perhaps I can warn the right people so we never work with him again."

"Yes. I promise." For the thousandth time, Jessica reconsidered her dream profession. But she'd do anything to help Alma. After all, Alma had stood up for Jessica for years. Fortunately, she could get someone involved who would help.

***

On her way home that evening, Jessica made a detour to visit her favorite police officer, Sergeant Jaime Castro. She'd called him earlier in the day to set up the visit. She drove to her old neighborhood and parked in front of his house. The home she'd grown up in sat beside it.

For a moment, she wished they hadn't sold the house so her mom could move back in. But she'd needed the money for college and living expenses, and with her dad on house arrest—well, they had to live on something too. She'd have to find another solution for her mother. Besides, the home had a trike on the front porch, and she glimpsed a swing set over the back fence. The building had become a home again, something it had lost during Jessica's last two years living there.

Jaime opened the door before she'd made it up the walkway. He looked fit and happy, a combo she hadn't seen recently. "You look great. What's going on in your life?"

"Not much. I've just closed two cold cases and am getting a commendation from the mayor." A wide grin splashed across his face as he shared his news.

"Oh my god. That's fantastic! When? We should have a celebration." She started planning the festivities in her mind. Jessica hadn't known it until recently, but her parents had convinced Jaime to move in next door right before they left town. He'd always looked out for her, checking out any boys who stopped by when she was in high school and helping her out of a dangerous bind in college. She'd love to do something for him for a change.

"They've planned the ceremony for three weeks from now at the city council meeting. My partner is getting a commendation as well.

"That's awesome. Who is your partner now?"

"A guy named Clint Jones. He transferred into the force a few years ago from Phoenix. Says he didn't like the politics there, but he was already used to the desert."

"I'll say. Phoenix is so much hotter than El Paso. Can I plan something for you two?"

"Sure, that'd be great. But first let's talk about why you're here. You usually don't make social calls unless there's a problem."

The words stung, mostly because they were true. "Yeah, sorry about that. And yes, I do have another problem."

She explained what had happened with Lucía and Jeremy Wright, finally ending with this morning's episode and the impact it had on Alma. "I'm really worried about this guy. I think he's a predator, but I don't know what to do next. He seems to be friends with the sheriff. I sure don't want to cause any more trouble for Alma at the law firm, but I can't just walk away."

"No, you were never good at walking away. You do realize you have a tendency to go off half-cocked? In the police department, we solve our cases by doing research and understanding every angle of an issue. You tend to act first and ask questions later."

He didn't look angry, but his words still cut. "I didn't really have a choice once Paz said Lucía was missing. We had to do something."

"But you had your suspicions about this guy before then. Why didn't you call? I could have checked him out, especially since you think he threatened kids at the high school."

He was right. She should have contacted him. Did her desperation to do something exciting, to find meaning beyond her current job, cause her to bound off on her own without asking for help? She looked into his dark eyes. He'd led her into the kitchen and poured her a glass of his famous limeade, which he'd probably made just for her. She had to do better.

"I should have called you. I'm sorry. Lucía had wanted me to keep things a secret from her mom and aunts, but you could have helped. And you're right. I should have thought this out. I just had to act. I never do that anymore, I just shuffle papers."

He laughed, actually threw his head back and guffawed. "So, the lawyer path not meeting all of your needs?" he eventually said.

"It's not the way I imagined it. I don't think I want to work for a big law firm the way Alma does. There are so many boring cases for each one that's interesting." She held her hand up to stop any incoming comments. "I realize they aren't boring to the people going through the divorce or whatever I'm working on at the time, but they're all just about people arguing. I want to help people."

"While I think it's fantastic that you're getting a law degree, I'm not so sure you're cut out to be a lawyer. I mean, look at the jobs you've had. You managed commercial real estate deals in El Paso and Juarez. I remember when you were out in your car almost every day, scouring for new lease opportunities or showing clients buildings. Heck, even in college, you went and found one of the biggest nightclub owners in Juarez and convinced him to hire Angus's band. You traveled all over trying to find that Mexican bigwig's daughter. That was a pretty spectacular piece of detective work."

He stopped talking and let the words sink in. The glass of limeade sweated in front of her, but that didn't come close to matching her internal combustion. "Are you saying you think I should be a cop?"

"I would never tell you what you should do. But you've never been good at sitting in an office, and you've proven you're good at investigations." He crossed his arms and leaned back against the kitchen counter.

Her perch on a barstool at the island suddenly felt precarious. "But I've spent money on law school. I've studied so hard. I promised Alma." And she really hated the job so far.

"Keep working for Alma. Get your degree. Those are two important things that will help you no matter what you decide to do in the future. But keep your options open. Now let's talk about police work. What are the facts you've uncovered on Jeremy Wright?"

As she talked him through what she knew, she realized how little research she'd actually done. She hadn't looked into his past and hadn't researched Brother Bill or Nora nearly as much as she should have. She couldn't offer Jaime much beyond speculation and hearsay.

"You can do a little research," Jaime said, "But don't do any of this work at the law firm. You've already gotten Alma in enough trouble with her bosses. But if you wanted to do a little more research on your own time, let me know what you find out. In the meantime, I'll check into this guy from my end."

They agreed to talk again in a few days. Jessica left with a huge list of things she needed to do and a buzzing excitement about the future. She tempered that by reminding herself this was about a real young woman, two women, who might be in danger.

***

The second Jessica got home, she took her computer and a big glass of water to the front porch. Her talk with Jaime had motivated her. First, she wrote a formal complaint letter to the school district and emailed it to Paz for her approval. Then she researched Brother Bill Hardaway's organization.

She had to dig deep for information. A website showed photos of Brother Bill and his animals and touted the ranch as a haven for the downtrodden who needed to find the true path. She found no listings of clients, parishioners, or donors to the organization. Finally, she found a list of speakers from his funeral.

Nora had spoken at the service, as had Brother Bill's actual brother who'd come in from Tennessee. The final speaker was a man named Stan Setliff. Jessica looked him up on social media. Nothing. However, when she searched his name on Google, she came up with several Stan Setliffs, one of whom lived in Horizon City, a town east of El Paso. Bingo.

She called Stan's phone number, but it rang and rang without forwarding to voicemail. It seemed she'd reached a dead end unless she wanted to drive out there. She wondered what Jaime would do. She opened a map program and found a mobile home park at the address. If he didn't answer the phone by the weekend, she'd knock on his door.

Next, she turned to Jeremy Wright. He'd been introduced at a local church as a visiting minister two months earlier. Prior to that, he'd been at a church in Big Spring, Texas. From what she could tell, he'd been there for a few years. The main minister of that church had died several months ago, and Jeremy had spoken at his funeral.

It seemed odd that he would leave the church instead of becoming the main minister, not that she knew anything about churches or how their succession plans worked. She found the phone number of the dead minister. The obituary had mentioned a wife. Perhaps she had more information.

Jessica grabbed her phone and noticed it was after eight. Angus would be home soon, and it was after nine in Big Spring, thanks to the time zone change near Pecos. She'd try the minister's wife in the morning.

Instead, she used her phone to call the barbeque place at the turnoff to her street. The place had ice-cold beers, gigantic beef ribs, and the best potato salad and coleslaw Jessica'd ever had. She texted Angus to swing by and pick up their order on his way home.

She brought the computer back to life, happier and more excited than she'd been in a long while. She'd missed this feeling of searching for something, the perfect piece of property, a clue in a case. It was like she found a missing piece of herself in the hunt.

Chapter 11

Jessica watched in silence as houses eventually gave way to fields of alfalfa and onions. Each year, El Paso stretched a little higher up the mountain and a little farther along the agricultural land of the river valley.

She should be ecstatic. A long, hard week had ended, and she headed toward her two best friends' house for Friday night happy hour. Instead, her gut roiled, each mile squeezing her anxiety into a tighter ball.

She studied Angus as he drove, one relaxed hand on the wheel, the other resting on his thigh. "Hey, let's not go tonight. Why don't you and I do something together instead. We can drive up to Chope's and have dinner in the bar." She hoped referencing his favorite Mexican restaurant with its detached biker bar would tempt him.

He glanced at her with concern before returning his eyes to the road. "We've got a dozen avocados worth of guacamole in the car."

She craned her neck to look at the back seat floorboard where the vat of guacamole lay nestled in a towel to protect it from sudden turns and stops. A case of Shiner and two bags of tortilla chips occupied the trunk. Jessica sighed.

"You worried about seeing your mom?" Angus asked.

"Not worried so much as I feel like she's invading my space." Why did she have to sound like a whiny teenager? "It's not that I don't want to see her. It was just better when we saw each other every once in a while. I've tried, Angus, I really have. But every time we're together there's so much turmoil."

Angus slowed the car, then eased it off the road next to an irrigation ditch. A flock of red-winged blackbirds rose from the reeds beside the ditch and flew away. He turned to look at her. "I'm not going to force you to go, but I think you should. Not for your mom, but to show Luz and Sarah how much they mean to you. Think about the position they're in. They feel obligated to help your mom. Don't let them lose you over this."

Something in her gut unhitched, and with it tears came to her eyes. She prided herself on rarely crying, but his words hit her like a drug, or a smooth shot of tequila. She needed to hang on to the people who mattered. "You're right. Whatever is going to happen with my mom just needs to play out. I can't let it get between my friends and me."

"If you need me to run interference, just let me know." One side of his lips crooked up in a grin.

"Angus Delgado, you are the best man I ever married." She leaned forward to kiss him. But for the seatbelt and the traces of trepidation about the evening, she'd have run her hands all over him. Instead, she ran one hand up his inner thigh.

He clasped his hand over hers, moving it to safer territory. "Let's go. You can face your mom, but there's only so much I can take and still make it to the party."

***

The patio with its twinkle lights and view of the mountains as they tinged magenta in the last rays of the sunset welcomed them to happy hour. Sarah stopped arranging food on a long table and swept Jessica into a hug.

"I miss you so much. You have to visit more often," Sarah said. She took the bowl of guacamole from Angus and hugged him as well.

"Angus! Jessica! I'm so glad you're here." Clarice Watts darted out from the house, her arms wide, looking for hugs.

I'm the one who's supposed to be here. Jessica kept the uncharitable thought to herself as Angus hugged her mom then asked how she was settling in.

Jessica glanced at Sarah and thought she saw a cloud pass over her face before she caught Jessica's gaze. She quickly rearranged her features into a smile.

"Hey, Mom," Jessica said as her mom wrapped her in a hug. She pulled away quickly.

"How is work going? Have things gotten better?"

Jessica looked at her mom, confused by the comment. Jessica hadn't mentioned her dissatisfaction with her job to her mother, and she certainly hadn't talked to her about this terrible week.

"Oh, I overheard Luz talking to Paz on the phone. I'm sure everything will be fine." Her mother patted her arm, oblivious to the emotions racing through Jessica.

"Jessica, can you help me in the kitchen?" Sarah asked.

"Oh, let me help." Her mom sounded almost giddy with excitement.

"Mrs. Watts, would you help me get the chips from the car while I bring in the beer?" Angus asked.

Thank you, Angus. Jessica didn't speak the words, but hoped her gratitude showed on her face. She and Sarah slipped into the house before her mom could protest.

"Luz," Jessica said, reaching for her friend.

"Good to see you. You have got to stop by more often." Luz gave her a firm squeeze. "Here, stir the queso." Luz handed her a wooden spoon and pointed to the Crock Pot on the counter.

"How are things going with my mom?" Jessica asked.

"They're good." Luz poured tequila into a pitcher of margarita mix. She looked up at Jessica, eyes twinkling. "Although, we might need a little extra tequila tonight."

"I think what she's trying to say is that if your mom's going to move back to El Paso, we need to figure out a permanent solution for where she'll live," Sarah said.

"Yeah, she mentioned my old place, but I didn't think it would work." Jessica had appreciated the single-room studio and tiny bathroom and had hung on to it much longer than she should have.

"I don't think that place would work for most people," Luz said. "Especially not an artist. She likes to paint on the patio. At all hours." The smirk in Luz's voice didn't show on her face.

Jessica looked to see Sarah's reaction. "So, Mom's settling in here?" she prompted.

"It's fine. We're happy to be able to help," Sarah said. Her sigh told the rest of the story. "I'm not sure what the long-term solution should be."

Heat rose to Jessica's cheeks in a mini panic. Her mother did not have enough money to purchase a home. Would an inexpensive apartment do? She wanted to avoid the solution staring her in the face. "Angus thinks we should offer to take her in."

"Oh, hell no." Luz's quick staccato response surprised Jessica.

"Yeah, I don't think that's a good idea either," Sarah said. "Your mom needs a lot of attention right now. She's struggling to get beyond your dad's death and figure out the rest of her life. Counseling might be helpful. You and Angus need your space."

"For what?" Angus asked, coming in from the patio.

Jessica strode to him, grabbed the back of his neck and pulled him into a savage kiss. She felt him resist for a moment, then he wrapped his arms around her. "For that."

"Gross. Would you two take it outside? Or maybe back to your old place?" Luz pretended to be angry, but Jessica saw the repressed grin. "But yeah, having someone else around all the time can get a little old."

"What did I miss?" Angus asked.

"Nothing, I'll fill you in later," Jessica said in a whisper as her mom walked in.

"Guests are starting to arrive." Clarice's excited voice filled the room. "Including some special visitors I invited. Can a few of you come out to the terrace so I can introduce you?" Her mom almost bounced with excitement as she waved them toward the patio.

Jessica noticed a questioning look pass between Luz and Sarah before Sarah followed her mom out the door. "Let's go see," Jessica said, tugging Angus's hand.

A few regulars stood near the food table. In the center of the patio stood a new couple. The tall, husky man looked vaguely familiar. His square jaw and stern face reminded her of someone she'd seen on TV, but she couldn't place him. A short blond woman with a chin-length bob stood beside him and smiled broadly at Jessica's mom as she approached.

"I'd like to introduce you to one of our hosts tonight, Sarah Gooden." Her mom gestured toward each person as she introduced them. "Sarah, this is Robin and Dick Saunders. And this is my daughter Jessica and her husband, Angus Delgado."

"Dick Saunders, you used to be mayor, didn't you?" Jessica asked.

"I did, although it's been a few years." His smile didn't reach his eyes, but he gave the hearty handshake of a politician.

"Has Clarice told you the big news?" asked Robin.

"No," Jessica and Sarah said in unison. What was her mom up to?

"Well, I own the Robin Saunders Gallery, and we'll be exhibiting Clarice's art. I've already sold a painting to a collector in Dallas, and I'm planning an exhibition for next spring."

Jessica congratulated her mother, as did everyone else. Visions of the extraordinary paintings flashed through Jessica's mind. When she'd discovered them on her first trip to Fort Davis, she'd been struck by how they seemed to mirror the inside of her soul. The colorful desert landscapes looked as much like shattered glass as oil on canvas, both beautiful and broken. If she could have afforded it, Jessica would have hoarded each picture and never let them go. The paintings proved she still had a connection to her mother.

But having gallery representation might mean enough money for her mother's living expenses. They both needed that type of independence.

"She sold my painting for $2,300. I've never gotten that much before." Jessica's mom clapped in excitement.

"That's impressive. Congratulations." Angus made the comment, but Jessica completely agreed.

Jessica studied her mom. She looked more than happy. She looked proud. She probably didn't like begging for a place to stay. Jessica would hate that. Maybe she needed to step back and wait for her mom to figure out her life instead of worrying about ulterior motives for every move and phone call.

"You all should come by the gallery as soon as I've got some of Clarice's work up," Robin said.

Sarah immediately agreed. Jessica and Angus glanced at each other, remembering the last painful time they'd gone to see her mom's works. When Clarice stood them up.

Perhaps Jessica needed to let that one go. Besides, Dick Saunders was more than just the ex-mayor, his position on the school board made him responsible for Jeremy Wright's program at El Paso High.

Jessica studied the man. Tonight, he smiled and shook hands with people on the patio, but she'd seen him before at chamber of commerce meetings where arrogance had wafted off him. Was he the reason Jeremy had connections to the sheriff? She wanted to learn more, but not here. Not at Luz and Sarah's and not when her mother had invited him. Here, he blended in with the crowd the way a rattlesnake blended into the desert rocks. She promised herself to tread carefully.

Chapter 12

Jessica's cell phone pulled her from bed again, on a Saturday, no less. She should probably turn the damn thing off at night. When she didn't recognize the area code, she almost didn't answer, but something about it looked vaguely familiar.

"Hello." She tried to sound crisp, but frogs scarred her voice.

"Hello. I'm looking for Ms. Jessica Watts. This is Mrs. Harris, returning her call."

"This is Jessica," she said, stalling for time. Suddenly, it hit her. Mrs. Harris was the pastor's wife in Big Spring. Jessica had left a message for her after she'd found her number but had never gotten a call back.

"Thank you so much for returning my call." Jessica shuffled out of bed, closing the door behind her. Hopefully, Angus would get a little more sleep.

"Of course. I apologize that it took so long. I was visiting my sister in McKinney yesterday. It's been lonely here since Drew passed away."

"I'm very sorry for your loss. From what I've read, he was beloved in the community."

"Yes, he was, and he passed far too soon. How can I help you?"

"I hoped to talk to you about Jeremy Wright. He's recently relocated to the El Paso area." Jessica held her breath, hoping the woman would respond and shed some light on the pastor.

"Is that where he is? I wondered why he disappeared so quickly."

Yet one more odd thing about this guy. The woman on the phone seemed like the grandmotherly type, and loneliness laced her voice. She sounded like she missed Jeremy, although it could just be the sadness from losing her husband. Jessica probed deeper. "He and his wife have bought some land out here in the desert. I'm surprised he didn't tell you."

"Well, I am too. He seemed extremely distressed about Drew passing away. It was a horrible time. Drew was like a father to Jeremy. I thought he'd want to stay here and lead the church. Perhaps, without Drew, well, it's impossible to imagine this church without him. Our flock is truly lost." The woman sighed on the phone, her breath rattling.

Jessica pictured a gray-haired lady trying to hold back tears. "I'm so sorry." The pang of her father's death and not enough time with him pierced her.

"The Lord will get us through it. I'm glad you called and told me what became of Jeremy. I guess it's a good thing that Emmy is with him." The woman sighed heavily.

"You guess?" What a strange comment.

"Yes, I've known that child since the day she was born. Beautiful, and pious, but a strange one."

"What do you mean?"

"Oh, I don't know. It's probably not my place to talk. She always seemed like such a good girl. But when she found out Jeremy had joined our church, she set her sights on him and wouldn't let anything get in her way. I shouldn't really talk about it."

"No, it's okay. I appreciate your honesty. They were clients of the law firm I work for. They came to us when they needed to acquire the ranch."

"You said earlier that they bought a place? That's a surprise. I didn't know they had the money. A preacher's salary isn't much, and Lord knows our church hasn't been doing well lately. I found that out after Drew died."

"Believe me, they got a hell of a deal."

An angry "Hmph" came through the phone, followed by a long pause. The woman's raspy breath crossed the hundreds of miles between them. "Why are you calling me, young lady?" Mrs. Harris asked, her voice now tinged with suspicion.

Jessica couldn't believe she'd blown it. She probably shouldn't have said hell. She had to save this. "I found them intriguing. Especially Jeremy. He's so young and seems so devoted to God. That's something that is missing in my life. I'm interested in attending services, but I wanted to learn more about them first." Jessica paused. She hated lying to this woman but needed more information. "I find it hard to trust people, so I wanted to talk to someone who knew him. He does seem special."

"Oh, honey. You aren't the first woman to ask about him. He's an attractive young pastor, but he is a man of God. And if I were you, I wouldn't cross Emmy Wright."

Jessica hadn't expected Mrs. Harris to chastise her, but she'd pushed her story a little too far. No reason to stop now. "Is Jeremy from Big Spring too?"

"Oh, no. He's from Pecos. He used to work for The Way, that's how we originally met him. He visited us as one of The Way's teen clergy members. He'd speak to the youth groups at the high school, and he'd stay with us. Such a wonderful young man. If you see him, please tell him hello for me."

"I will and thank you for your time." Jessica ended the call, then filled two mugs with coffee from the pot brewing during the call and took them into the bedroom.

She set the coffees on the nightstand, then crawled back into bed and snuggled against Angus's lean body. He threw an arm over her and pulled her close.

"Hey, babe." She ran her free hand up his long warm back, hoping to wake him enough to talk.

He grunted and pulled her closer. She definitely felt part of him waking up.

"I think I'm going to stay home today and do a little research instead of going into the office with you. I may drive out to Horizon City to check on something." Saturdays she usually managed the books for Angus. It was a great way to save money, and she was proud of how quickly the business had grown.

Angus opened one sleepy eye and looked at her. "Is this about that Jeremy Wright guy and Lucía?"

"Well, yes. It's not really about Lucía. I'm just doing some background research on him. Jaime recommended it. I also want to visit this guy who was at Brother Bill's funeral. Perhaps that's where Nora is. I really feel like I let her down by not talking to her when she called, and I just want to make sure she's okay." Next, he'd chastise her, but she needed to be honest with Angus. This one thing, out of all the things in her life, needed to work. Without Angus, life had no meaning. It had taken her years to realize that. She'd often walked the crooked path, but Angus was her straight line.

"I thought you weren't supposed to work on that. What about your job? And Alma?" He'd separated from her slightly, and his brow wrinkled with concern.

"I know. But I'm worried about Nora. If she's with this guy or he knows where she is, I'll feel better. I am also still concerned about Jeremy. Jaime seemed concerned as well. He's going to look into him, and he said I should focus more on background research and not go off half-cocked again. I promise I'm not doing any of this on work time."

Angus grinned. "Half-cocked?" He pressed into her.

"Are you twelve?" But she couldn't keep from giggling, more from relief at the change of subject than the terrible joke.

"Just don't get Alma into trouble."

"I promise. Now tell me more about this cock thing." She rolled herself on top of him and erased everything from her mind except the man beneath her.

***

Jessica took the loop road that followed the border of Texas, first along the New Mexico border, and then hugging the river with Juarez, Mexico. The raised highway gave her a view of the University of Texas at El Paso on her left, and multicolored Mexican houses built right up to the river's low levee on the right, just a few feet away.

As she traveled further, the road and the river split the two down-towns. Finally, she drove down a long stretch of highway with homes on the US side of the border and manufacturing facilities dotting industrial parks in Mexico. She knew each of those parks from her days in real estate. She'd made a good living for a while, but the vagaries of global economics made it hard to recover from a couple of lean years. She'd expanded her business into delivering documents and other materials by using her numerous contacts on both sides of the border.

She'd liked the challenge of finding clients and matching them with the perfect building. Sometimes, she helped U.S. companies find Mexican partners to design or manufacture their goods. Being the person who made those connections empowered her. But the lack of a regular paycheck, any stability at all really, wore her out.

When she finally took that last job, finding the daughter of an enormously wealthy and extremely shady Mexican businessman, her future seemed bleak. She'd never done a job like that, hunting down a person instead of a building or paperwork. She'd done it for the money, but also because the parents seemed to care so much about the missing woman, unlike Jessica's own. When that deal went south, she'd cut Juarez from her life the way she'd cut out her desire for thrills.

She had located the missing woman, but it turned out she didn't want to be found. Unfortunately, someone who did want her found followed Jessica's trail and turned a job into a disaster. Jessica barely escaped with her life.

After that, law school and working for Alma became her respite. She'd get a regular paycheck, would set herself up for a career helping others, and would stay out of danger.

And she had. The lure of learning Jeremy Wright's secrets and the potential of stopping him dipped a toe back into the water of that earlier chaos. It taunted her, pulling her into its web in the most irresistible way. She told herself if this Stan person couldn't help her, if Jaime didn't find anything, she'd walk away and be glad Lucía had escaped relatively unharmed. She tried to believe the lie.

She turned north into Horizon City. As a girl, she'd gone to horse shows there, during the brief time her rodeo champion mother had convinced her to ride. Back then, it really had been a town on the horizon, with a wide swath of desert separating it from El Paso. The larger city had grown in the intervening years and had consumed Horizon City whole, like a snake eating an egg.

She found the trailer park near the freeway and turned into the narrow drive with dilapidated mobile homes lined up on either side. Four trees, giants for this arid landscape, must have been planted long ago. Two of them had branches arching over and shading some of the homes. The others, a palm and an Italian Cypress, provided only a slim line of relief from the burning sun.

GPS led her to a dingy white mobile home with rusting seams that provided a counterpoint of color. She guessed the home had been manufactured long before her birth. It had rickety stairs heading to a landing decorated with a half-dead potted plant. A faded Dallas Cowboys tailgate chair sagged next to the landing. She pulled partway into the drive, a dusty dirt bike its only occupant. She wondered if Stan had gone out, but the tire-rutted space did not look freshly used.

Stepping out of her truck, she noticed curtains swinging in a different mobile home. These metal boxes had eyes. She squared her shoulders, walked up to the trailer, and knocked firmly. Nothing.

"Mr. Setliff. Are you home?" she asked, knocking again.

"Just a minute." The voice had an East Texas twang.

She recognized the man who opened the door from the photo of Brother Bill's funeral. Slim and tall, he wore faded jeans that matched his washed out hair and lined face.

"What do you want?" he asked, stepping onto the landing and shielding the inside of the trailer with his body. Not that she wanted to go in there.

"I'm looking for Nora Riggs. I was hoping you knew where she was."

A look of confusion passed over his face. "Why are you here? She's at Brother Bill's. He left everything to her."

"She's not there anymore. The people who are buying the ranch from her said she'd gone to visit friends."

"What do you mean, buying the ranch? She'd never sell that place. It meant everything to her." He shook his head as if he didn't believe her.

"And just about the only friend she has left is me, so I'm not buying your story."

He looked increasingly distressed. Jessica wanted to learn more but needed a safe place to talk to him. "Hey, can I buy you a cup of coffee? I only met Nora once, a few days ago. I really liked her and I'm just trying to find out where she went. I think it would help if we talked about it."

Stan looked around the mobile home park, seemingly undecided and perhaps hoping someone would come along and tell him what to do. Finally, he inhaled, then exhaled deeply. "Fine."

Once in the truck, she asked if he had a favorite coffee shop. She certainly didn't know any places way out here.

"The Flying J near the freeway is good."

An enormous truck stop along Interstate 10, Jessica expected the Flying J to have mediocre coffee. Instead, she was given a cup of strong, black jet fuel with a hint of chicory. For someone who had worked at Starbucks and preferred moody, off-the-beaten-path coffee shops, drinking java under the glare of bright lights and with all the atmosphere of a 7-Eleven seemed wrong.

They sat at a gray vinyl booth and watched people order everything from pizza to breakfast sandwiches, coffee to beer. The odd little slice of America had a relaxing effect on Stan, who sat back in the booth and sighed almost wistfully as he took his first long sip of brew.

He fixed her with pale blue eyes. "Now, tell me everything you know about Nora."

She tried, but he constantly interrupted her. When she mentioned Nora's sadness at getting rid of the animals, his face visibly reddened, and his eyes became glassy with tears. "Nora would have never let those animals go. She loved them more than anything."

"That's what it seemed like. Can you help me understand who she is and why she might have entered into this deal? Why would she want to leave the ranch when she owned it free and clear?"

He shook his head. "It doesn't make sense. The ranch, the animals, they were all she had. When I talked to her after Bill died, she said she was going to take some time and figure out what was next."

Stan hung his head. "I loved her. I told her I loved her. It was too soon." His voice had gone small.

Jessica pondered the revelation. "I thought she was with Brother Bill."

"She was. But I still loved her. You couldn't be around her and not love her. She'd been through so much." He finally looked up, not hiding the pain on his face. "Nora had been abused from when she was a child. She'd practically grown up on alcohol and drugs. She told me she'd been using since she was twelve. Most people don't make it when they grow up like that. But she had so much goodness in her that she quit using once she found her family at the ranch."

"That's where you met her?"

"Yes. I had my own problems with drugs. Unlike Nora, it was all my own fault. I started out looking for a good time, and then a better time. I was the guy you've read about, stole from family and friends, lost everything. Who knows where I'd be if I hadn't found Bill and the ranch?"

"Are you from this area?"

"No, Beaumont. But I moved here in high school. I stay in Horizon City now. No one in El Paso wants to have anything to do with me anymore." He sat silent for a moment, seemingly lost in the man he used to be. He sighed heavily, then looked at Jessica. "We're not here to talk about me. We have to find out what happened to Nora. She would have told me if she were going to leave the ranch."

"Why?"

"Well, because she literally didn't have anyone else. She didn't know her dad. Her mom passed on several years ago, and she'd never go back to the people she used with. She's been out at the ranch just over seven years now. It's her life."

"When I talked to her, she seemed sad about losing the animals, but it definitely didn't seem like she wanted to fight to keep the ranch. Do you think she needed the money? She mentioned the taxes she'd owe." If so, she could have probably gotten a better deal than the one she took. Although, it might take a while to sell a place so far out in the desert. Maybe the Wrights just came along at the right time.

"I know Bill didn't have a ton of money, but he kept some cash in a safe in the main house. People also donated to the church's treatment center. He'd just built new barracks, but I'm sure he raised the money for that before he started them. Bill didn't trust the government, and he didn't believe in being in debt."

"None of this makes any sense."

"We have to go out there. I know Nora is still at the ranch. I just know it." Stan slammed his coffee cup down, causing a few drops to splatter onto the table. He suddenly seemed nervous and jumped out of the booth and looked around.

"Is everything okay?"

"I need to walk around." He grabbed his coffee and headed for the door.

Jessica scrambled after him. He took off across the parking lot, passing her truck and heading to a line of semis parked along the perimeter.

"I don't think she's there." Jessica panted after finally catching up with him as he stared northeast. The direction of the ranch. "The last time I was at the ranch, the people who bought it said she'd left."

"She wouldn't have taken the money and gone. She just wouldn't have."

Jessica wondered what made him so sure. And there was another problem. "She didn't have the money from the sale yet. She agreed to lease the ranch to Jeremy and Emmy Wright for a small amount. They had the right to purchase it from her, again at a discount rate, whenever they were ready. They haven't exercised the purchase agreement yet, so all they've paid is the first month's rent."

"I don't understand why she would make that deal. Brother Bill left her the ranch so she'd be safe and protected. Do you think they've done something with her?"

The sick feeling that roiled Jessica's gut when Lucía first told her about Jeremy Wright returned. Something was wrong, and she needed to fix it. "Honestly, I don't know what's happened."

"Let's go out there. Right now. I need to find Nora." Stan fidgeted, looking completely wrung out. Jessica wondered if his addiction still haunted him.

"I can't go back there." A part of her wanted to return to the ranch and find the truth. But she'd made promises to toe the line this time. She explained what had happened the last time she visited the ranch. "This guy means business. He called the sheriff and got him to threaten my job."

"What the hell is he doing out there?" Stan's agitation cranked up a notch.

"The wife told me they're starting a home for wayward girls."

"What does that mean? I can't imagine Nora being involved in that."

"Actually, she was excited about it. She said she wished she'd had a place like that when she was young."

Stan stilled and didn't speak for a long moment. "Yeah, I can see that. But still, there's something wrong. You can't go out there, but I can. There's just no way Nora would have left. Not without talking to me."

Chapter 13

Jessica drove home in a funk. She had done a lot to screw up her life, but fortunately, serious drug use wasn't on the list. When she'd needed some kind of hit to make her feel alive, tequila and men had done the trick. Looking back, she regretted the time she'd wasted. Did Stan feel that way? Did Nora?

For years, she drank to get drunk and go home with a stranger. She'd known Angus then, loved him even, but she'd convinced herself he needed to end up with anyone but her. But in her darkest moment, she couldn't live without him. He made her better. And he seemed to feel the same way.

Since she'd restarted the relationship with her parents, Angus had been by her side. They'd married in Fort Davis less than a month after Jessica started communicating with her parents again.

She wanted to repair the damage of years without contact. That had damaged her as much as the abandonment. With her father, it had been easy. His stroke limited their ability to rehash the past. He seemed grateful just to have her there.

Her mother wavered between meddling and completely withdrawn. She'd call and text every day, then not be there when she'd promised. Jessica didn't know how to deal with it, and often chose not to. She told herself it was self-preservation.

Now her mother's move to El Paso had Jessica wanting to shove her back to some unknown corner of Texas. Or Jessica might flee to Roatan. She'd first visited the island off the coast of Honduras while trying to find the missing woman. She returned with Angus for her honeymoon, a generous gift from the Rey sisters.

Although tempting, escape wasn't an option. Her life, Angus's life, was baked into the El Paso desert. She'd have to figure out how to deal with her mother.

Jessica turned onto her street and noticed a navy minivan in the driveway. Her mom's minivan. God damn it. She kept her eyes on the road in front of her and kept driving. She'd seen her mom sitting on the front porch in her peripheral vision. When she got to the stop sign at the end of her block, she idled there.

She had to turn around. Her mother had surely seen her. Jessica had spent the past twenty minutes thinking about her mom. The eerie connection that had conjured her into the front yard scared Jessica.

She took a few deep breaths to calm down. She was Jessica Watts. She'd faced down one of the most dangerous men in Juarez and lived to tell about it. She'd survived on her own from the time she was sixteen. She would not let a single woman paralyze her. She turned the truck around.

"Hi, Mom. What's up?" She walked up the porch stairs and sat in Angus's chair, since her mom was in hers.

Tears silently dripped down her mother's face. "I saw you drive by. Will you ever quit hating me?"

"It's not hate." Not entirely. "You just surprised me. I'm sorry. Why don't you tell me what brought you here?"

The words didn't help, and the tears didn't stop. Worse, her mom's hands began to shake. Jessica watched her mom tightly grip the armrests. Jessica had used that same tactic to keep from showing weakness. She gave her mom time to compose herself.

"I don't know what to do." So much for composure. Her mom's voice trembled along with her hands and her body shook with sobbing. "I am completely lost. "Joe is gone, and I don't know how to live without him. I have never once lived on my own."

Jessica's heartbeat slowed as her mother's loss seeped into her. She reached for Clarice's hand, pried it from the armrest.

"The house is full of memories of Joe, and that's both good and bad. And he was the one who had to be exiled anyway, not me."

Jessica dropped her mother's hand. "You're right. Leaving was entirely your choice." Unlike Jessica, who'd had no choice at all.

Her mother sighed, and Jessica heard the anger in it. "Do we really have to rehash this tired old argument? I left. I was a bad mother. I should have come to see you. There is absolutely nothing I can do to change the past. I wish you'd quit living there."

"I'm a little more worried about where you're going to live in the future right now." Jessica couldn't keep the edge from her voice.

Her mom seemed to shrink from the comment. "Me too." The anger had fled her voice, leaving it small and unsure.

"Angus says we should take you in. You know, family and all."

"Angus is a really good man."

They sat in silence, gently rocking in the chairs. Jessica didn't know what to say. Some daughters might generously open their homes to their moms. But Jessica didn't want that stress on her marriage. That relationship, she wanted to protect with every cell in her body. But what would Angus think of her inability to forgive, her unwillingness to open up to this woman and be vulnerable?

"What do you want?" Jessica finally asked. "Not from me, but from El Paso? From the future?" The question seemed like the most reasonable way forward.

"I want to paint. I want to have a social life again, but slowly. I'm out of practice."

"You mean like the Junior League and stuff you were involved in before?"

Her mom stopped rocking and looked at Jessica. She could almost see the steel coiling in her mom's spine. "No. Never. Those 'lifelong friends,'" Clarice used air quotes, "turned mean and spiteful. That hurt me almost worse than your dad breaking the law."

"Most of my friends dropped me, also," Jessica said. "Although it was high school, so there was all kinds of drama."

"I'm really sorry to hear that."

They quieted again, rocking and staring out into the front yard with its straw-yellow Bermuda grass. Birds bounced around the branches of a gnarled Mexican Elder tree. The valley always smelled like hay and horses to Jessica. Today, she also caught the scent of her mom's jasmine perfume.

"I don't want to my welcome at Luz and Sarah's. They'd never kick me out, but I think it's been a bit of a grind having me there. They've been great therapists, helping me deal with losing Joe and trying to plan a future, but it was a lot to lay on them. I'm hoping Robin Saunders can sell a few more paintings for me. I figure I'll need five to ten thousand to tide me over until the house sells. After that, rents are so affordable here that I should be okay."

Jessica stood and reached for her mom's hand. Part of her, the skeptical, loner part, recognized the idiocy of her action. Some other part of her, the part connected to the good in Angus, acted anyway. She led her mother inside and showed her the small extra bedroom.

"I'm not promising anything long term, but you can stay here when you need to."

"Thank you, I really appreciate that." The tears had returned to her mother's eyes, and she wrapped her arms around Jessica in a fierce hug.

***

Clarice's visit motivated Jessica to go to the store and buy two thick steaks. By the time Angus came home, potatoes baked in the oven, and she'd cleaned and warmed the grill and seasoned the meat. She waited on the back porch, sipping a beer, her dog Tela at her feet. Two shot glasses filled almost to the rim with her favorite white tequila balanced on the table beside her.

She heard Angus pull into the driveway, then tramp through the house, calling her name. He finally opened the screen door to the back and took his time looking at her preparations.

"Well, this news has to be really good or really bad." He sat beside her and lifted the bottle of tequila. "Don Rico, you got out the good stuff." He took one shot glass and she the other, and they clinked them.

Too delicious to be thrown back in one gulp, Jessica sipped the liquid, letting the smooth taste heat her throat. She finished it after a second, pleasurable swig, its warm courage flowing through her.

"So, what's up?" he asked.

"Well, I went to see that guy I told you about. He's super fidgety. I almost wondered if he was using. But he seems to really care about Nora and doesn't think she'd ever leave the ranch."

Angus started to say something, but she raised a finger. "But that's not why we're having steak for dinner. When I came back home, my mom was sitting on the porch waiting for me."

"Ah. That makes more sense." Angus opened the bottle of tequila and filled each of their glasses halfway. "Let's hear it. Did you guys argue?"

"No. Kind of the opposite. I felt really sorry for her. She seems lost. Somehow, I invited her to stay with us." She downed the second shot of tequila, faster this time. She wished the elixir had the power to turn back time so she could take back her offer. Their house was so small, just a thousand square feet. Too small for three people, especially when, at times, she barely tolerated one of them.

"Did she accept?"

Angus's concerned look surprised her.

"I thought you said this was a good idea."

"I said we had an obligation to take in family when they needed us. I definitely don't think this is a good idea. I mean, just the prospect of it has you downing tequila and grilling steaks in the backyard. Not that I don't appreciate that."

Jessica thought back to her mother's tears. "She's really broken right now. I think she's lost without my dad, and I sure can't blame her for not wanting to stay in Fort Davis. She says she needs five thousand dollars to get back on her feet. She'll have that if the house sells, or if she makes enough on her paintings. But there's no telling how much time either of those things will take."

Jessica stood and walked to the grill, grabbing the long metal brush to clean the grate. She'd cleaned it once, but if she stayed next to the tequila, she'd down the whole bottle before she stopped.

"I wish I could just give her the five thousand." Angus got up and took the brush from her hand. "I'll handle this." But he didn't. Instead, he set the brush down and wrapped his arms around her, pulling her into his chest.

Jessica closed her eyes and sank into him. She wanted this. Just the two of them. How awkward would this moment be if her mom lived here too? If they hadn't bought the house, then they could front her mom the money. Of course, if they hadn't bought the house, they wouldn't have a place for her to live.

"Maybe we can put off expanding the business."

A chill slid down her spine. "No. Expanding the music school to the Eastside makes sense. Your business partner agrees, and you've already got a waiting list."

Angus's music school for kids had taken off, and they already had more kids than they could handle at the original location. Expanding made sense, even if they had to take out a business loan to soundproof the new space and buy new equipment. They'd pay that off in just a few years, and then the business would be lucrative.

"I still worry that we're expanding too fast. I hated having to secure the loan with your salary." Worry lines crossed his brow.

"Don't worry, it's not like Alma's going to fire me." But she had gotten Alma in a lot of trouble this week. And she still wanted to drive into the desert and find Nora and take down Jeremy Wright. Things were so much less complicated when she'd only had herself to worry about. But the new version of Jessica had tied herself to new responsibilities.

Chapter 14

J aime Castro's name flashed on Jessica's phone's screen. "Yeah," she said, her voice groggy from the late night.

"Are you seriously just getting up? It's eight-thirty." Jaime teased her, although she heard the smile in his voice.

"It's Sunday. Why are you up so early? Did you start going to church or something?" She ribbed him back. Angus moaned beside her and pulled a pillow over his head. Jessica slipped out of bed and pulled on a robe as she wandered into the kitchen to start the coffee maker and let the dog into the backyard.

Jaime chuckled. "No church here. Only midnight mass on Christmas. My mom would kill me if I missed that one. Speaking of religion, I did a little follow up on your boy Jeremy Wright."

"He's not my boy. But thanks. What did you find?"

"He grew up in Pecos. Before he moved to Big Spring, he worked as a youth counselor for The Way. Have you heard of them?"

"They're a religious group, right? Like a church or something? The pastor's wife in Big Spring mentioned them."

"Exactly. They've got a big mega church in the Dallas area. He reported to the Lubbock office and had something to do with the high school programs in West Texas. That's probably why he's involved with the high school program here."

"Okay. Anything interesting?" She doubted Jaime had called her just to talk about this guy's former jobs.

"I didn't find anything official. There were a few rumors, but they never went anywhere. And they're not going to."

"What do you mean?"

"This guy has some powerful friends. When I started asking questions, I was quickly told to back off."

"By whom?" It didn't make sense. But it also didn't make sense that Jeremy had been able to call the sheriff and get him involved.

"By my boss. And his boss. I was given assurances that he is a model citizen. This guy has friends in high places. I don't think it's the kind of thing you should get involved with."

Jessica sighed, trying to push the frustration out with her breath. "Listen, Lucía is worried about her friend. We can't just drop this."

"You mean the friend whose parents have probably voluntarily enrolled her in Jeremy Wright's program? Parents get to decide what to do with their kids. Do you really want to be out there second guessing them?"

"Maybe? What about Nora Riggs, the missing woman?"

"You mean the one you were told was visiting friends. The one you barely know who has no reason to check in with you?" The way he said it insinuated she was grasping at straws. Perhaps she was.

But her gut told her she had something to uncover. "Can you tell me anything about the cases that might have been filed against him?"

"I didn't really get that deep before I was asked to stop. Jessica, I have to advise you to step away from this one. It's already gotten you in trouble at work, and that's something you don't need. Alma put her trust in you, and you don't want that to look like a mistake."

"Grrr. This is so frustrating. I just want to do something good, and my instincts say there's a problem with this guy."

"If you want to chase bad guys, become a police officer. Right now, you're a paralegal, and your job is to help Alma."

"You're right." She sighed again, in acceptance this time. She and Angus had just talked about how they needed her salary to expand his business. Thus, she needed to behave and focus on the straight and narrow, something especially hard for someone who'd grown up finding her own winding path. "Thanks for looking into it."

"Anytime. And don't worry, I'll keep my eyes open, just in case."

"Appreciate it." She hung up the phone and took coffee to Angus.

She slipped back into bed, sitting against the headboard and looking at her phone. Jeremy grew up in Pecos. She'd driven through there on her way to Dallas. It was exactly a third of the way through the trip. It was also the location where the desert changed, turning into the vast Permian Basin, a grassland that stretched two hundred miles or so, before morphing into the slightly lusher land of east Texas. The Permian Basin looked dry as a bone but hid millions of gallons of viscous Texas crude oil beneath its parched surface.

Oil rigs, some cranking up and down like crazed dinosaurs, others still and rusting to dust, lined the entire drive. The desolate country seemed to last forever. A kid might grow up with some weird ideas way out there.

She looked up the population of Pecos on her phone. Just twelve thousand people. A small town. She wondered how many people there knew Jeremy Wright. Perhaps he still had family there. She searched his name but didn't come up with any other Wrights. Was it worth a two-hundred-mile drive to learn more?"

She set her phone aside. She shouldn't be looking into this. If only she could get that nagging feeling to go away. She slipped down into the covers, snuggling up against Angus's warmth. He groaned, but rolled toward her and pulled her close.

Her phone rang again. Damn it. She rolled to the side of the bed and recognized the number. She thought about letting the call go to voicemail, but she wouldn't get back to sleep. She got up one more time and took the phone into the living room before answering, bringing her coffee with her.

"This is Stan. Stan Setliff," she heard after she said hello.

"Stan. Nice to hear from you."

"I, I wanted to call you. I went out there yesterday the way I said I would."

"To the ranch?" She tried to make her voice calm. He sounded even more agitated than before.

"Yes. I went out late in the afternoon and talked to that Jeremy Wright guy you told me about. I told him I wanted to see Nora. A woman stood in the doorway, and he came down the steps to see me. He told me Nora was gone, just like you said."

"I expected that." She wondered if there were other Stans out there. People who would eventually worry about Nora. She tried to keep her concern in check, remembering her earlier conversation with Jaime.

"He said she'd gone off with her friends, but I told him I knew all of her friends. I was one. And she hadn't contacted me or anyone else she knew."

"Then what happened?" Jessica couldn't resist the story's draw.

"He got real blustery, telling me he had no idea who her friends were. He said I might not be such a good friend if Nora hadn't gone to see me. But his wife, she started getting real nervous. Her face turned pink, and she half hid behind the door. Believe me, I've seen that kind of guilty behavior lots of times."

Jessica wondered about the comment. He'd admitted to being a junkie. That probably prompted all kinds of suspicious behavior.

"She kept looking out beyond the barn, where the trailers are. There's something going on, and I don't like it. I think they've got Nora trapped out there. I asked to look around the property for her, but he told me I was trespassing. Said he'd call the sheriff if I didn't leave."

"Same thing he told me," Jessica said. "And he did call the sheriff."

"Yeah, I figured he'd do it. I don't like him. There's something wrong there. Something else had to be going on for Nora to sell him the property."

"So. What are you going to do now?"

"Well, that's not the end of the story. I left, just like the guy told me to. But as I was riding out, two big Suburbans came speeding down the road and damn near ran me over. As soon as it felt safe, I pulled my bike into the desert and hid it. Then I hiked back to where I could see the house. I thought they might have Nora with them."

This guy had balls. "Did they?" she asked.

"Not that I saw. By the time I got close enough to see anything, they'd all gone inside. I waited until they came out. First came two Latina girls, maybe ten or twelve years old. They were with the blond woman I saw earlier. Then came four guys who looked like cowboys. Jeans, hats, lean muscles. They were probably my age, late forties."

Jessica would have pegged Stan at least a decade older. Hard life.

"Then came that Jeremy guy," Stan continued. "He shook their hands and clapped them on the back like they were the greatest guys in town. Completely different from how he treated me. The guys got back in their vehicles and drove away."

"Wait, they left the girls?" Jessica asked.

"Yeah. The woman took them to one of the barracks Brother Bill constructed for the rehab people to stay in."

That seemed like a sinister turn of events. Why would four men show up with two girls? That didn't sound like normal parental consent.

"We need to go back out there and look for Nora," Stan said.

"But you said she wasn't there."

"Listen, I know Nora. She has no place else to go. She has to be there. The woman, that guy's wife, she knows something. I think they're keeping her prisoner there. We have to go find out." He practically shouted into the phone.

That seemed like a huge leap. Being freaky around young women and actually kidnapping an adult were two entirely different things. Nora knew the ranch and could probably take care of herself. Besides, Jessica shouldn't go out there at all, and given how worked up Stan was, he wouldn't be a good partner.

"I think we need to slow down," she finally said. "We have no idea if anything has happened to Nora, and I can't go back out there anyway."

"You have to. You have to help me find her." He sounded so desperate.

"Listen, I might lose my job if I go back out there. And honestly, I don't know Nora at all. Maybe she does have friends you don't know." Despite her words, Jessica's worry pulled at her.

"We can go at night," Stan said. "Nobody would see us. The guy didn't have a dog, and I know my way around the property. I lived there for years and worshipped with Brother Bill for a decade."

Jessica turned the proposal over in her head. So many things could go wrong. If Jeremy caught them, she'd certainly lose her job. Not to mention they might get shot for trespassing. She hadn't seen him with a gun, but every rancher had one.

If she went, she could tell Lucía she'd checked on Grace. The only positive in a sea of negatives, it didn't overcome the responsibility she had to Angus and Alma. She had to act like a grownup now. A couple of years ago, she'd have gone in a heartbeat. But her life had changed.

"Stan, I just can't do it." She'd let him down. Part of her wished she'd never contacted him. He wouldn't know Nora had disappeared, and she wouldn't feel guilty about not doing more.

"You have to." He had a coughing fit, as if he'd choked on despair. "I've only got the motorbike, and it makes too much noise. They'd hear me coming for miles. Please. Just drive me out there. You don't have to go in. I'll hike in from the gate."

Curiosity and her desire to help him battled with the amount of trouble she might get in. How bad would it be? "What's your plan?"

"I just want to take a look at the trailers. If she's not there, I can double-check the barn and the barracks. We need to find out if she's okay."

"Won't everything be locked?" Jessica kept asking questions, kept telling herself she hadn't made a decision. But she had. This guy cared about his friend. Jessica had met and liked her. If she could help Nora, it would have more meaning than a thousand divorce cases.

"Nah. You don't allow junkies to have locks. It was one of Brother Bill's rules."

"You want to go tonight?" She shouldn't have asked, wanted to kick herself as the words fell out of her mouth.

"Yes. Pick me up at my place at seven. It should be dark enough by then. Thanks." His quick voice sounded relieved.

"I'll try to get away." She spoke the words, but he'd already hung up. She dropped her forehead into a hand. What had she gotten herself into?

She headed into the kitchen for more coffee and heard the shower turn on. How would she ever explain this to Angus? He'd probably understand. If only he had heard how desperate Stan sounded. Angus always wanted to help people. Still, he wouldn't approve. He wouldn't want her to risk getting Alma in trouble or have her jeopardize her job. Why had she agreed to this?

Jessica panicked. She needed time to figure out how to explain what she'd agreed to. She considered calling Stan back, telling him no. She rinsed her cup at the sink instead of getting more coffee. Then she slipped into the bedroom, threw on a pair of jeans, and grabbed her keys and wallet. She scribbled a guilty note to Angus saying she had errands to run. As she closed the front door, the shower turned off.

Chapter 15

Jessica hated running away from problems like a child. But she had to follow her gut. Something wasn't right on Jeremy's ranch. His behavior with Lucía, Nora's disappearance, the arrival of two girls. And who knew what had happened to Grace? Too many things pointed to trouble.

That included all the warnings to stay away because of Jeremy's important friends. She drove through the El Paso streets, no destination in mind, her thoughts churning. Corruption hid in powerful places. She'd seen that searching for Velasco's daughter in Mexico, wondering if the woman had died or chosen to escape. Jessica had barely survived that case, and it changed her. Perhaps, sometimes, you had to stray from the straight path.

She found herself driving over Trans-Mountain, the four-lane divided road that climbed between the two tallest mountains splitting El Paso. She stopped at a rest area with a view to the east, where she overlooked the Fort Bliss Army Base and peered into the rest of Texas. On such a clear day, her view probably encompassed Jeremy's ranch. She would do this one thing tonight. She'd help Stan try to find Nora. If Nora wasn't there, if no sign existed of Grace or the other girls, she'd leave it alone and never look back.

If she and Stan uncovered something unsavory, she'd tell Jaime. The ranch lay far outside of the El Paso City limits and his jurisdiction. And even though important people wanted it to stay hidden, if something were truly wrong, Jaime would find a way to handle it. He became a police officer to help people, and he'd never turn his back on someone in need.

She drove down the winding road on the east side of the mountain. The Army base spawned auxiliary businesses like military surplus and combat supply stores. She stopped at one of these, not for one of the hundreds of guns or knives they sold, but for a flashlight. A wealth of knowledge, the guy behind the counter asked her about her plans.

"I'm going to do some exploring in the desert at night." It sounded crazy, but he might suggest something useful.

"By yourself?" he asked, his eyebrows sliding up his forehead.

"Maybe." That sounded better than trespassing with an ex-drug addict she barely knew.

"Might I make a suggestion?" The man's gentle voice contrasted with his burly six-foot, six-inch frame and wild red beard.

"Sure."

He unlocked a glass case and took out what looked like a regular, if heavy duty, flashlight. "This is the Guard Dog Diablo, and it's got a couple of extra features to keep you safe. It works like a regular flashlight, but it's heavy and can be used in a fight."

"Okay . . ." She couldn't imagine winning hand-to-hand combat with a flashlight.

"But most importantly, it's got a stun gun setting." He clicked a couple of buttons, and the device in his hand crackled and shot blue light.

"Holy shit. That's not what I was expecting." Was this guy crazy? "Actually, I kind of wondered if there were flashlights that could help you see in the dark, but where others wouldn't see you."

"Sure, we've got blue light flashlights." He grabbed another flashlight with a cobalt instead of a clear covering over the light.

Jessica expected questions about why she needed something that would obviously allow her to sneak onto someone else's property, but he didn't seem concerned.

"I'll take it," she said, handing him back the lightweight blue screen flashlight. "And I'll take the taser one as well."

***

She returned home midday to an empty house. Angus had likely gone to work, or perhaps had met up with a friend or two to jam. She hoped he'd get his band back together. They used to play all the clubs in El Paso and Juarez. For some reason, growing up had meant putting the instruments away except for the odd Sunday afternoon.

She longed for him but appreciated the delay in spilling her upcoming plans. If only doing the important thing meant more to everyone else than doing the responsible thing. Responsibility shackled her to the mundane. She wanted meaning. That's what tonight was about.

Jessica picked up her phone and found Paz's number. "How's Lucía?" she asked.

"Honestly? She's depressed. And worried about her friend."

"I'm really sorry to hear that." The conversation lulled.

Finally, Paz spoke. "She's mad at everyone right now. I think she's mad at me for not doing more. She's furious with Grace's parents. She's angry with herself for thinking Jeremy Wright was a good guy. I really wish I knew what was going on with him. Something tells me he's far worse than he appears."

"I completely agree," Jessica said.

"I sent the letter to the school, but there's nothing else we can do. You know that, right? I'm a single parent who needs to put a smart girl through college. I need my job."

Jessica sighed, trapped. "I know. It just seems so wrong."

"This guy's time is coming. I promise someone will figure it out. Why don't you come by for dinner soon? Lucía would love to see you."

"That sounds great. I'd love to see her too." Jessica hung up the phone, more sure than ever about her decision to return to the ranch.

But she did need to come clean to Angus. She shouldn't have left in the morning without letting him know about Stan's call. He'd understand, or at least she'd have to convince him.

She texted him. "When RU coming home?"

Three dots quickly followed. "Watching Cowboys with Dad. Mom says dinner at 6:30."

Shit. She'd forgotten Angus's parents had invited them over for dinner. His two sisters and their families would be there as well. In that big, noisy family, no one would miss Jessica. She dialed the phone.

"Hey, can you give my regrets to your mom?" she asked when he picked up the phone.

"What's going on? I thought you wanted to come for dinner."

"I did. I do. It's just that something came up. You remember that Stan guy I told you about? He's incredibly upset about his friend Nora being missing. He seems really down on his luck. I thought I'd take him some dinner and some groceries. Maybe I'll do a little research on my laptop and see if I can find any background info on the woman." She hated how the lies rolled off her tongue as if she lied to him every day.

"Are you sure? I mean, my parents would really like to see you. And I haven't seen you all day."

"I'm sorry. I promise I'll make it up to you." She would. Somehow.

Chapter 16

S tan waited outside his mobile home when Jessica pulled into the driveway. The sky had turned deep indigo, and only a sliver of a moon shone above the eastern horizon. The night invited danger.

Stan jumped into the front seat and started fidgeting. As she backed out of his shallow drive and headed down the center aisle of the mobile home park, he adjusted the direction of the vents, moved his seat forward, then back, played with his seatbelt.

She almost told him to stop, but she opted not to say anything. She needed to get this done and go home, back to the world of adulting.

It took forty minutes to drive to the ranch. He tried to engage her in conversation, but Jessica kept to one-word answers. Her tension filled the truck and seemed to affect Stan as well. He slowed, then stopped his constant movement.

When they reached the gate, she switched the headlights off, then turned into the drive.

"You can drop me off here," he said.

"No, I'll go in a little farther."

"There's not really a place to park farther in."

She barely heard his quiet voice above the rattling of the wheels. She slowed the truck until the road noise abated. "We'll just have to park on the side of the road. It would take too long if you had to hike all the way in."

"Well, okay." He seemed almost forlorn. She wondered if he realized this was a mistake.

"I'm going with you. It will be faster that way. You can check the trailers and the barn, and I'll see what's up with the barracks."

"Are you sure? I thought you were worried about getting into trouble."

She blew out a long breath. "I am worried about that. But I'm worried about Nora, and this girl Grace, and the two girls you saw. Something's wrong, and I couldn't live with myself if I didn't look into it."

After a day of ruminating, that's what it came down to. She couldn't walk away. She'd owe Angus an explanation for that.

She'd studied the ranch on Google Maps and had seen a place where the drive widened about a mile from the ranch house. She pulled over as far as possible without sinking into the soft desert sand. One deep breath, then she cut the engine.

"We should walk along the road a little longer," Stan said. "The loose sand is hard walking. Plus, we'll leave fewer footprints on the road."

He took off before Jessica had shut her door. She quickly debated about the flashlights. She took the one with the blue light and left the taser in the truck. Tonight, they searched for a woman, not trouble. They had both dressed in black, the attire of crooks not saviors, but she did not want to get caught.

She estimated the walk should take twenty minutes, but time seemed to slow. A coyote howled, sounding young and on the prowl. A common sound in the desert, Jessica often heard whole families singing late at night, using their special blend of yips and wails. Tonight, a lone voice echoed across the desert, in either welcome or warning.

She wondered what other animals watched their trek. They'd left the road when they closed in on the ranch buildings. Mountain lions likely prowled nearby, hoping to feast on Pronghorn antelope. She feared snakes the most. They wound their way through mini dunes of sand topped with rocks and sage, the perfect hiding places for the rattlers that owned this land. But, of course, humans held the master predator slot. If someone had seen their trek from the car, the exercise would end before began. A chill colder than the desert night ran up her spine.

Finally, buildings darker than their surroundings appeared. Jessica and Stan crouched behind a sage-topped mound of sand.

"I'm turning this off," Jessica said. She flicked off the blue flashlight and slipped it into her back pocket.

"I'm going to work my way over to the trailers." Stan's fidgeting had ceased. She could feel the calm purpose underlying his motions. "It's farther away, so they're less likely to hear me. The barracks are close to the house. Be careful." With that, he disappeared into the night.

Jessica wished they'd talked longer, had made a plan for when and where they'd meet once they'd finished. Instead, he'd left her on her own. She spied the two dark humps that made up the barracks. She had no place to go but forward.

She crept to the nearest building. No light escaped through a window, and no sound escaped the wood paneling. Standing next to the mass made the night darker. An owl hooted in the distance. She walked around the corner, circling the building, keeping her steps light in the hardpacked sand.

Jessica had no idea how to determine if the building had occupants. If she knocked on a window, the noise might wake more than those inside. Perhaps she'd try whispering. While newly built, the buildings didn't seem tightly constructed. Maybe Brother Bill and his flock had built them without contractors. She doubted the building had seen permits or inspectors.

When she reached the front, the side that faced the ranch house, she noticed the padlocked door. Surely the building was vacant. No one would padlock a human inside. That would turn a fire or other disaster deadly.

She tiptoed up the steps to investigate the lock. The heavy chain had been looped through the door's handle and secured to a metal loop beside the door. She lifted the weighty lock. It required a key. The ice-cold metal felt like a death sentence. She dropped the lock, and it thunked against the wooden door. Jessica scrambled off the steps and darted around the side of the building.

Leaning against the wood, Jessica tried to fade into it. Her haggard breath was the loudest thing in the night. By the time her breathing slowed, she'd convinced herself no one had heard her. She still had one building left. "Grace," she whispered lifting herself from the side of the building.

"Hola?" a voice so small it might not have been real reached her.

In the next second, lights flooded the space between the ranch house and the barracks. In the distance, she heard sirens. Panic rushed into Jessica's bloodstream. She ran for the desert.

"Stop!" a voice shouted through a loudspeaker. Despite the distortion, she recognized Jeremy.

Her shoe caught on a root or a rock, and she slammed into the sand. She hoped the barracks hid her from sight.

"Turn yourself in. You have nowhere to go. The sheriff's deputies have already found your truck, and they'll be here in seconds. There is no escape."

She lay in the sand, not moving for fear of being seen. The harsh country limited her options. She doubted she'd make it back to civilization with no water. The mountains would provide better markers than a compass, but miles of stark, empty land lay between here and safety.

The sirens grew louder, and soon she heard wheels on gravel. Jeremy must have somehow seen them drive in and called the sheriff's office some time ago for them to be so close. A ferocious engine approached, then died. A car door opened. She heard voices speaking unintelligible words, then a new voice took over the loudspeaker.

"Come out with your hands up."

Jessica wanted to barf and wished she had made different decisions. Over and over again, people had warned her to stay away from the ranch. Yet here she lay, covered in sand and about to encounter some of the most serious trouble of her life. Her work colleagues, her friends, her husband, they'd never understand why she'd come and why she hadn't told them. Had she not trusted them or not trusted herself? Did it matter?

She pushed herself to her knees, spitting grit from her mouth. Then she put her hands up and rose.

"Well, look who we have here," Jeremy said with a sneer in his voice.

"Do you know her?" asked a man in the patched-filled gray shirt of an El Paso Sheriff's deputy.

"That is Jessica Watts. This is the second time she's trespassed here, and I talked to Sheriff Lee Burns about it last time. In fact, he called the law firm she works for, and they promised she'd quit bothering me. I don't know what her problem is, but I want her permanently off my property."

Another SUV with the sheriff's logo rolled to a stop and disgorged two additional men.

"Are you here alone?" the deputy with the bullhorn asked.

Jessica froze. She wondered if Stan could make it back alone.

"Search the property." The first deputy commanded.

"No need." Stan walked into the light, his hands up.

"You?" Jeremy sounded incredulous. "This is another person I told to stay off my property."

"There's a girl locked in that padlocked building," Jessica said, pointing toward the barrack where she'd heard the voice.

"Yeah. And my friend is missing, and the last time anyone saw her it was out here."

"Hands up!" yelled the deputy. "Both of you get down on the ground and keep your hands behind you." One of the deputies approached Jessica, patted her down, and handcuffed her hands behind her. Out of the corner of her eye, she saw another deputy doing the same to Stan. Suddenly, the man who'd handcuffed her jerked her to her feet. Her shoulders screamed in pain. He shoved her forward, toward one of the SUVs.

"I can walk on my own," she said. "Are you going to look for the girl I heard?"

"You have the right to remain silent, and I highly encourage you to do that." He gave her another shove before reading her the rest of her Miranda rights. When they reached the vehicle, he pushed her into the back seat. Damn. She didn't want to think about the kind of trouble she was in.

She watched as they loaded Stan into the second vehicle. That car sped off, while the remaining deputy spent several minutes speaking with an animated Jeremy.

Jessica looked again at the barrack where she'd heard the voice. Who was in there? How many were there? Was Grace one of them? She had way more questions than when she'd started the night, and fewer resources for getting them answered.

On the drive back to El Paso, she tried to talk to the deputy about the voice she'd heard. He reminded her about staying silent, and she took his advice.

At the sheriff's office, she saw Stan again briefly as they processed her. She wanted to talk to him, to find out if he'd learned anything, and see if he was okay. He ignored her glance and stared silently ahead.

It seemed to take hours for them to offer the one thing she wanted, her phone call. Her heart told her to call Angus and spend any time they gave her apologizing. Instead, she called Alma. She needed to give her a heads up about what she'd done because it might affect Alma's career. She wondered if the deputies had notified Sheriff Burns and if he'd already called the law firm's main partner.

"Jessica, what's going on?" Alma asked the moment she got on the phone.

"I did something really bad, and I've been arrested."

"No." The word came out almost as a grunt. As if Alma had spent her life waiting for this punch in the gut.

"I'm sorry. I went back out to Jeremy Wright's property. It's a longer story than I have time to tell right now. I know the partners will be angry, and I understand if you have to fire me. I caused this problem."

"Jessica, how could you do this? You know better. I warned you." A heavy sigh emanated through the phone line.

"I know. You're right. I really screwed up. I'm sorry. I'm so sorry. I know it sounds crazy, but I thought I was doing the right thing." Regret seared its way through her belly.

"Let me call my mom to come stay with the kids and I'll get down there and bail you out." Alma sounded resigned.

"Can you do one more thing for me? Will you call Angus?"

***

A few hours later, Alma led her from the jail. She'd asked Jessica to say as little as possible while she worked on getting her out. Once they released her, Alma drove her to a diner near downtown. Angus sat in one of the booths, eating a stack of pancakes.

Alma slid into the seat opposite him. Jessica stood, open mouthed, afraid to move forward.

"I'm so sorry," she finally said.

"You lied to me." The calm of his voice didn't match the hurt on his face.

"It was a partial truth." She wanted to kick herself. "Yes. I lied to you. I'm sorry."

"Why?"

She slid into the booth beside him. "It was important to me to find out what was going on out there, and I didn't think you'd understand."

He stayed silent, just looking at her, as if waiting for a better explanation.

"I did go see Stan, the man I told you about. He is convinced something bad happened to Nora. He's sure she wouldn't have willingly left the property. We went to look for her."

"How long did you have this planned?" His words stayed cold.

"All day. He called me before you woke up. It took me a while to decide to go with him, but it didn't really feel like a choice. It was something I had to do. There's something wrong out there. He said two girls were dropped off at the ranch the first time he went out there. I'm pretty sure I heard one of them. She was in a padlocked building they call the barracks."

Angus looked from Jessica to Alma.

"I spoke with Stan at the jail," Alma said. "He didn't find Nora, but he said all of her belongings were still in one of the trailers."

"You weren't able to get him out of jail?" Jessica's words fell flat onto the table.

The waitress arrived. "I'll have what he's having," Alma said, nodding at Angus's plate.

"Me too," Jessica echoed.

Once the woman left, Alma continued. "Stan has quite the rap sheet. Lots of prior arrests for possession, burglary, and a few other charges. I'll get him out when I can, although I'm not sure why. By the way, I'm not doing any of this on behalf of the firm."

"I didn't know about his prior arrests." Jessica burned with embarrassment. She must seem ridiculous to these two. Not only had she broken her word and done something monumentally stupid, but she'd also partnered with a recovering drug addict with a criminal past.

"I understand how badly I've screwed up," she said. "But I can't help thinking about Nora and Grace and those girls. They call it a home for wayward girls, but there's something bad going on, and I can't just ignore it."

"Jessica." Alma's voice cracked with anger. "You do not have the right to tell people how to raise their children. As for Nora, she's an adult and you have no proof that anything is wrong, just an idea. Regarding the girls, I don't know that we should trust what Stan says. Perhaps you just heard something out there. I will ask the sheriff's office to look into it, since I doubt they'll take your word for it. They've had to go out there twice to get you off his property, and they told me they think you have it in for the guy."

Jessica sat and let the silence draw out between them. Alma was right. No easy solution existed.

The waitress set plates loaded with pancakes on the table, then returned with full mugs of coffee. Jessica shoveled food into her mouth to keep from saying anything stupid.

"I probably can't save your job. I'm really sorry about that." Sadness emanated from Alma's dark eyes.

"I understand. I hope I haven't hurt your career with this stunt." Jessica knew this possibility existed, but she'd acted anyway. How did you tread a path between wrong and right? How did you pursue justice when it hurt the people around you?

"I'll get through it," Alma said. "And if the sheriff finds out this guy really is bad, well, the firm doesn't want to do business with people like that. In the meantime, I'll ask around and see if I know anyone who needs a paralegal."

"Thanks. I can always go back to the coffee shop." Such a long way back. She'd worked there in college and had embarked upon two careers since then. How ridiculous to be thirty years old and be going back in time.

"I sure wish I hadn't signed that lease for the property on the Eastside already." Angus's words rang with frustration.

"I can get you out of that if you'd like," Alma said.

"Yes. I better do that. We can't make it on just the income from the one store. Thanks." Angus pushed his plate away, only half the pancakes gone. "I'll take you home whenever you're ready." He looked at Jessica, but there was no compassion in his voice or on his face.

"Yeah, I better get going too," said Alma. "I need a quick shower before I go into work. It's going to be a long day."

Alma left twenty-five dollars on the table. She looked at Jessica, her face grim, then she turned and left the restaurant.

"Thank you," Jessica called out as Alma walked away.

"We better go get some sleep," Angus said. She hoped she'd heard exhaustion and not disgust in his voice.

"I'm really sorry, Angus." Jessica turned to him, trapping him in the booth even though he wanted to leave. "Are we okay?"

"I don't know."

She deserved that. She'd pierced his dream about expanding his business and broken something between them. And she had no idea how to make it up to him, or how to get her life back.

Chapter 17

Jessica rolled out of bed Monday morning at her usual time, despite the exhaustion from the night before. She made the coffee, dressed, and sat at the kitchen table waiting. Eventually, Alma would call her with news about her job or Angus would wake up and they'd talk.

They'd barely spoken on the drive home last night, and he'd gone straight to bed. His hulking anger inhabited their bedroom, and she'd tossed and turned during what remained of the night.

Jessica searched for jobs while she drank her coffee. She might try to get a real estate job, but she had specialized in commercial real estate in Juarez, and she wouldn't return to that city for the foreseeable future. That last deal gone wrong had almost gotten her killed. Last night's deal gone wrong might end in jail time.

Selling houses in El Paso ranked dead last in jobs she'd consider. Catering to whiny couples who wanted spa master bathrooms and man caves held even less appeal than divorce mediation. Alma might come through with someone who needed paralegal help, either that or she'd return to Starbucks. They always needed help, and at least there she'd get healthcare.

Shit. She and Angus had enrolled in the law firm's healthcare plan, her most important employee benefit. Not only would they lose her salary, but they'd also have to find new healthcare. She'd dug herself into a giant hole and had zero to show for it. No one knew where Nora was, no one seemed to care about the person she'd heard in the barracks, and there'd been no sign of Grace. Not that Grace was her problem.

Eight o'clock came and went. Jessica called the sheriff's department to find out about her vehicle and was given the number of a towing company.

Before she could formulate a plan, Alma called. "You are on thirty days unpaid leave. You are not to come into the office, and you are not to work on any of the firm's official business. A determination about your future at the firm will be made at that time."

"Wow, how did you swing that? And does that mean I'll be covered by the firm's insurance during that time?" She crossed the fingers on the hand not holding the phone.

"Yes, you still have insurance. I figured that would be important to you. The only reason you're not fired is because I convinced the partners that something hinky might be going on out at the ranch, with the seller disappearing and the buyer adamant that nobody visit the property. It's unusual, and our partners don't want to end up as the defendants of some future lawsuit. I must stress, though, that this is just a temporary reprieve. They're not happy with you or with constant run-ins with the sheriff's department."

"I completely understand that. Thank you. Thanks for bailing me out last night and thank you for everything you've done to preserve my job. I know there's no way to repay you, at least right now, but I hope to someday." She'd been in this woman's debt since she was sixteen, and it didn't look like that would end anytime soon.

"Don't worry about it. You're about to start a new semester. Try to get ahead in your studies, and I'll let you know if I find anyone looking for a paralegal."

"Thank you."

Jessica expected Alma to hang up, but she didn't. Tension seemed to pour into Jessica through the phone as the silence continued.

Finally, Alma spoke. "You have to clean up your act if you're going to be an attorney. Especially in this town. With your dad's reputation and all. Please stay out of trouble."

Jessica heard Angus get out of bed and walk to the bathroom. The beautiful old pine floors in their home groaned with each footstep.

"I'll do my best." Jessica doubted her best would be enough. It never was. She ended the call as Angus walked into the kitchen. On to the next problem.

"Hey, I made fresh coffee." She handed him a mug. He looked at her but said nothing.

The aroma of coffee wafted through the small kitchen as he poured. Its strong, homey smell gave her courage. "Could you take me to the vehicle impound lot before work today? I need to get my truck."

He finally looked at her but raised his mug and drank before speaking. It pained her to watch him struggle to keep his emotions hidden, but the hurt showed through his eyes. "I can't take you. I need to meet with the realtor on the east side of town and see if I can get out of the contract I just signed for a second location."

His dreams, their dreams, crashed down around them. She struggled to inhale through the pain she'd caused him.

"I'm really sorry," she said, for what felt like the hundredth time in the past twenty-four hours. "I'm not fired yet, so we still have health insurance for another month."

"Well, that's better than I expected." His voice was flat, and he turned back toward the bedroom.

"Angus. I know I screwed up. We need to talk about this."

He turned back to her, pure anger on his face. "You lied to me. After all we've been through, how could you think lying was okay?"

She'd hurt him so many times in the past, and she'd sworn she wouldn't do that again. But of course, she had. "I don't think lying is okay. I just got caught up in what was going on out there and didn't tell you the truth about what I was doing."

"That's lying, Jessica. Not telling the truth is lying. We specifically talked about you not getting Alma in trouble at work, and that's the first thing you did. You don't care about anyone but yourself. I thought you had changed, but all I see is the same old Jessica." He turned and stalked back to the bedroom.

Sadness about how she'd upset him pinned her to the couch. Even Tela cowered in a corner, a paw over her snout and eyes scanning the room for the next harsh word. Jessica patted the space beside her and gently called the dog over. Tela crawled up, and Jessica wrapped her in her arms and buried her face in soft fur.

She didn't call her mom until after Angus had left. She couldn't believe she needed to beg a favor from her mother, but Jessica doubted Clarice had plans for the morning.

When she told her she needed assistance, the glee in her mother's voice almost made Jessica hang up the phone. But she needed her truck far more than she needed her pride.

***

Her mom picked her up thirty minutes later, and they began the long trek east to the impound lot. Jessica told her the barest bones of the story. She'd been out to the ranch to investigate a missing woman with the woman's best friend, and her truck had been towed. Her mom would likely hear the whole story soon. They knew all the same people.

Jessica had finally gotten her mom to stop asking questions when the phone rang. Stan.

"I'm surprised to hear from you," she said. "Are you out of jail?" Jessica noticed her mother's head swing toward her at the question. "Eyes on the road, Mom."

"I got to see a judge first thing this morning," Stan said. "I was surprised how quick it was. I think the jail is overcrowded and they're trying to get nonviolent offenders out of there. They let me out about an hour ago. I'm headed home."

"Do you need a ride?"

"Nope. I'm on the bus already. I'm sorry I got you into trouble last night."

"I knew better than to go out there. It was a big mistake."

"Listen, I'm more worried than ever. One of the trailers had Nora's stuff in it. I mean everything. Her clothes, her wallet. Everything but her phone. She wouldn't have left that stuff if she'd moved out or gone to visit someone."

Jessica would not get drawn back in. "I don't know what to tell you. I don't think we can do anything else. Alma will follow up with the sheriff's office. Maybe they'll find something."

"After last night, I can't say I trust the sheriff. I hoped maybe you'd heard her in the barracks. I checked the barn, and she wasn't there."

"I only got to check one of the buildings before I was caught. I heard someone say 'hola.' It sounded like someone young. It wasn't Nora."

"She could be in the other building," Stan said. "I heard you tell the deputy they'd padlocked the doors. She might be a prisoner."

"Stan, I appreciate your concern about Nora. She's an adult, and she seemed very capable. As I said, Alma will have the sheriff's deputies follow up on the voice from the barracks. I think it's likely that she did go visit someone else." Jessica couldn't convince herself of that, but she needed to step away from this mystery.

"Well, I can't give up. I don't know what I'm going to do next, but I have to try to find her."

"But you can't. You're already in trouble." This had to stop. There must be a better way to find Nora and figure out what the Wrights had going on at the ranch.

"I've got two weeks before my court date. Chances are, I'll do jail time after that. I need to find out what happened now."

"Why will you do jail time? Trespassing is just a misdemeanor." Alma had told her she'd likely get a fine, but nothing else. Jessica's mother huffed and looked at her again.

"I've got prior arrests, like more than two strikes against my record already. They'll likely put me away for a while. Texas has gotten a lot stricter about jail time lately."

Shit. None of this seemed fair. "I don't know what to tell you. I'm headed to pick up my truck. I can't think of anything else I can do to find her."

"We need to learn more about this Jeremy Wright fellow because there's something really wrong with him. Nobody innocent would behave the way he does."

"Well, I agree with that," Jessica said. "Let me know if you think of anything. I'll do the same. Thanks." She hung up after reluctantly promising him she'd stay involved. She could kick herself. Although from the agitated way her mom drove, Jessica had more to worry about than her promise to Stan.

"You're not being straight with me. Tell me what's going on," her mother said after Jessica ended the call.

"Last night was a really long night, and today's turning out to be an even longer day. I just can't talk about this anymore."

Clarice drove in silence for a few blessed moments, probably processing what Jessica had said.

"Well, you have to talk about it," she finally said. "Were you in jail last night? What the heck is going on, and who were you talking to?"

Jessica sighed, the never-ending saga continuing. "I was arrested for trespassing last night. There are women missing. The man on the phone and I tried to find one of them."

"Oh, Jessica!" Her mother's high-pitched voice rang with anguish.

"It's not that big of a deal." Although it was. Clarice started crying, her face turning blotchy pink. "Mom, pull over."

They sat in a 7-Eleven parking lot, her mom inconsolable. Jessica tried to explain that it was just trespassing, and Alma thought she'd get off with a fine at the worst.

Clarice wailed back. "I can't have you in trouble with the law. I can't have you going to jail or ruining your life in some Texas backwater."

Oh, shit. Her father. Her mom had been through this before. Although, his crime was totally different. He'd tampered with evidence in a case by deleting files, allegedly to protect his employees. He'd been tried, found guilty, and sentenced to house arrest. Threats from some of the bad guys in the case caused her parents to move to Fort Davis, a small town in West Texas. Clarice had exiled herself to take care of her father. No wonder run-ins with the law scared her mom.

"This is totally different. I'm not like Dad." She kept her voice calm and gently placed her hand on her mom's shoulder.

Clarice erupted in rage, swatting her hand away. "I don't want excuses. I bought so many damn excuses from your dad. Breaking the law is breaking the law. I'd think after everything you'd been through that's the one thing you'd stay away from."

The anger and screaming stunned Jessica to silence. Man, this day just got worse and worse.

After a minute, Clarice's ragged panting slowed. She sucked in a huge breath, seemingly stealing all the air from the minivan. "You will not relive your father's life. You will not be arrested. You will not go to jail. What do I need to do to keep that from happening? I can't take this again. I truly can't take it."

"Well, I've already been arrested, so you're too late for that one." The comment wouldn't help, but what else could she say?

"This will kill me."

"Mom, this has nothing to do with you. I was trying to help someone."

"That's exactly what your dad said."

Jessica let the silence stretch. She was not her dad. "I was just a kid when all that went down with Dad. Nothing about him drives any of my decisions. A woman is missing. I met her. She was in a lot of pain the first time I saw her. She'd just agreed to sell the property where she'd lived for years along with most of the animals she loved. Then she vanished. I reached out to a friend of hers, and he said she'd never leave, at least not without letting him know."

"Honey, you don't have to get involved in other people's problems."

Jessica looked into her mother's blue eyes, still tinged red from crying. "I want to spend my life helping people who need it. When I was there last night, I heard someone inside a padlocked building. I think it was a girl. There's something very bad going on there."

"Shouldn't the police investigate something like that? Why do you need to be there?"

"I tried to tell the sheriff's deputy who arrested me, but he didn't seem to care. I talked to Jaime Castro about some of this, but his boss stymied him." And where did that leave her? Frustration steamed through her.

She wanted to do the right thing, but she couldn't get into more trouble. She didn't even know how to resolve the problems she already had.

Her mom sighed, then pulled a tissue out of the center console and wiped her face. She turned the car on, then sighed again and turned it off. "I think it's wonderful that you want to help people. But you have to find a way to do it that won't ruin your life."

Her mom reached over and squeezed Jessica's hand so hard it hurt. "You are a lot more like your dad than you think. He always wanted to help people too." She bit her bottom lip. "But he also had no self-preservation gene. It ruined his life. It ruined my life. I don't want the same happening to you and Angus."

Now Jessica wanted to cry. She never wanted to hurt Angus, yet she already had.

"Let's go get your truck." Her mom started the engine again and drove out of the parking lot.

Jessica had to find a new way forward. She would not repeat her father's mistakes.

Chapter 18

Jessica returned home to an empty house. She texted Angus to let him know she'd retrieved her truck. No response. She asked when he'd be home. Who ever thought she'd play the role of nagging wife? But she didn't want his anger to fester. They needed to talk it out.

He finally texted, "Going to Robbie's after work."

Fine. He couldn't avoid her forever.

When he'd accused her of lying, it had taken her aback. She'd done a lot of shitty things over the years, often to Angus. But he was right, she'd never lied. She'd never let herself care enough about anyone else or what they thought to bother lying.

Now, she snuck around and told half-truths so she wouldn't hurt him or anyone else. That didn't say a lot about her character. She needed to be better than that. If she truly believed her actions would help someone, she should be proud. And brave enough to admit it.

Surely Angus understood that. He spent his days helping children learn musical instruments and then encouraging them to play in a rock band. She loved how those kids transformed from shy and scared to rock and roll badasses. They gained confidence, and even when they didn't hit a set one hundred percent, they played better each time. They saw their improvement, as did their teachers and band members, and it was enough.

Why did Jessica always journey alone? It had been that way since her parents, and most of her friends, abandoned her. Everyone except Alma and Angus. She brought herself back to Angus's comments that morning. He'd been upset about her lying and about her getting Alma in trouble at work. He was right. She had to do better by the two people who'd always done right by her. She'd talk to him about it when he eventually got home.

***

With nothing else to do, she researched Jeremy Wright. She wanted to call Jaime and get his police detective's input on the voice she'd heard, but she recalled how he had stressed research, not going off half-cocked. Last night, she'd gone off completely unprepared and had landed in trouble. Today she'd do things the right way and learn enough about Jeremy Wright to make other people doubt him also.

An hour later, she hadn't learned much new. Despite being younger than Jessica, he didn't have much of a social media presence. In an online newsletter from The Way, they'd announced him as the incoming high school spokesperson for the organization in far west Texas. That was it. She didn't find any information about how long he worked there.

She traveled further back in time, cross-referencing his name with Pecos, Texas, where he'd allegedly grown up. Strangely, there was no information on a Jeremy Wright in the small daily newspaper. She searched for The Way and Pecos. Jeremy's name didn't come up, however, she did find an article that listed a William Burnett as the liaison to The Way's youth group at Pecos High School. There had to be a connection. A little more digging showed that Mr. Burnett also taught physics and chemistry at Pecos's only high school. Bingo.

She'd just written down Burnett's information when someone knocked on the door. When she opened it, she found a contingent of women. Her mother and Alma stood in front. Paz and Lucía lagged slightly behind them, and Sarah and Luz brought up the rear. Luz held a giant white paper bag with the Charcoaler logo on it. El Paso's best burger and onion ring place.

"Hi. We thought you could use some dinner," her mom said.

"This looks like more than dinner." It looked like an intervention. And it wouldn't be Jessica's first. She'd hated her first talking to about how she lived her life. Back then, she drank too much and slept around. Her friends wanted her to straighten up and get in touch with her parents. She'd done both. Looked like that wasn't enough.

She backed into the room and started pulling chairs into a circle. These women would be impossible to beat, so she might as well make people comfortable.

Jessica noticed Luz pulling plates down from the cabinets. "Just make yourself at home," she said. She didn't keep the snark from her voice.

Jessica dropped into a chair and Lucía sat beside her. "I'm surprised they brought you. This looks like a beat down."

"Yeah, I hate when they get this way. You were just trying to help me. I asked if I could come."

"Well, you're in for a treat. Should you ever falter from the straight and narrow path you're on, they'll come for you too."

"You know, just because I believe in Jesus doesn't mean I'm straight and narrow." Lucía lobbed the words back at Jessica.

She took a good look at the young woman. She wore jeans and a simple V-neck T-shirt. Her wavy black hair spilled over one shoulder, and Jessica noticed a new plum-colored gloss on her plump lips. She looked more grown up than she had just a few days ago. Jessica hoped she had an easier path than most of the women in the room.

"You're right, I shouldn't have said that. I'm in kind of a mood. I wasn't expecting all of this." She flung her hand toward the kitchen.

Luz walked over and set a plate in her lap with a burger and onion rings on it. Jessica grabbed one of the crunchy, salty rings and popped it in her mouth. "Thank you," she called out, her tone flat. "Best dinner ever."

Luz returned with a plate for Lucía. She looked at Jessica. "Well, you better eat up, because you're going to need your strength."

Jessica gave her a smirk and popped another onion ring in her mouth. Maybe if she kept her mouth full, she wouldn't have to talk at all.

Eventually, the women filled the spaces around her. Jessica ate slowly and deliberately, keeping her mouth busy, and thereby keeping her from engaging.

Sarah spoke first. "So, how are you doing?"

Jessica looked at the faces surrounding her. "I'm not sure. You tell me."

Luz started. "Well, we're gathered here today because your mom is really worried about you. She's terrified that you'll follow in your father's footsteps and get into serious trouble with the law."

Tension landed on Jessica's shoulders and billowed about the room. She remembered an old-fashioned barometer her father had hung on the wall to measure air pressure. She wished she had one now, just to see how it would react. "Yeah. She told me that this morning. I thought we'd talked it out."

Jessica caught the hard stare Luz gave Sarah. That statement had come as a surprise.

"That may be." Alma jumped into the conversation. "But I'm also worried. The man you went to the ranch with had a rap sheet a mile long."

"I didn't know that before you told me," Jessica answered truthfully. "But I did know he had a drug problem once, that's how he came across Brother Bill and Nora. Were any of his legal issues recent?"

"Not in the past few years, but it looks really bad when you're hanging out with people like that."

Criminals. People like her dad. Alma didn't have to say it for everyone in the room to get the reference. But she wasn't like her dad. Allegedly, her dad had tried to protect people in the office. Jessica had never been sure that was true, but if it was, then he had risked his career and family to protect crooks. Jessica held her head high. At least she was trying to protect the innocent.

"You said I would likely just get a fine." Jessica directed her comment at Alma.

"That's correct, but your friend may get much more. If the judge thinks you two are particularly close, he might take it out on you too."

"Can I just say the one thing I think everyone here is ignoring?" Burger-fueled frustration lunged from her chest. "I went out there for a reason. A woman is missing. When I was there, I heard another woman in a padlocked barracks. Let me repeat that. The door was padlocked from the outside. There's something wrong out there, and someone needs to look into it."

"That someone does not have to be you." Her mom's demanding tone just made Jessica angrier.

"I called the sheriff's office this morning," Alma said. "They said they went out there and the buildings were empty."

"That's not true." Jessica couldn't have imagined it. "For some reason I'll never understand, this man has deep connections with important people in this community. How did that happen when he's only lived here a couple of months?"

"And you think the sheriffs deputies would lie?" Alma asked, although she didn't sound sure about it.

"It's possible," Jessica said.

"Oh, Jessica." Her mom shook her head, disappointment etched into her features.

"One of my colleagues warned me that it's not just the sheriff who has taken an interest in Jeremy Wright, and an ex-mayor has as well." Alma's comment surprised Jessica. Alma did have some doubts.

"Is it Dick Saunders? I know him. Maybe I should talk to him." Every eye in the room turned to Clarice.

"I thought we were here to convince Jessica to back off." Luz's tone threaded a line between incredulous and frustrated.

"I really don't think anyone should do anything right now, Clarice." Alma's firm tone quieted the room. "I've talked to Jaime Castro. He said he counseled Jessica to research this guy. If this guy has a sorted past, that can help us get beyond anyone who might want to protect him. But he specifically said he did not want Jessica going off and causing problems. Which is exactly what you did." Her glare caught Jessica dead on.

"You're right. But Stan was super concerned about Nora, and it seemed like I could help. We just wanted to see if she was there and needed anything. We weren't trying to do anything bad."

"And what about Grace?" Lucía asked. "Jessica might have found her also."

Alma turned to her niece. "Grace is not a part of this conversation. Her parents get to decide what happens to her."

"But what if she's at the ranch? What if she doesn't want to be there? What if he hurts her?" Panic and pleading filled the words.

"If your mom decides to send you to calculus camp in Alaska, you have to go whether you want to or not," Alma said. "At least until you're eighteen. The same goes for Grace. And you have to trust her parents to protect her."

Lucía harrumphed and crossed her arms. Jessica wouldn't have gone back to sixteen for anything. Way too many emotions there.

"Jessica, I'd like you to leave this case alone." Alma's steely voice reminded Jessica that without her she didn't have a career. "If there's something wrong, leave it to the police or the sheriff. It's the best thing you can do for your future."

"Agreed," Luz chimed in. Sarah nodded at the words.

"Honey, I just don't want you getting in trouble. I barely endured your dad's conviction. I wouldn't survive you going to jail."

Jessica sighed. "This isn't about you. It is, perhaps, about women who actually need help." Jessica saw the hurt cross her mother's face and didn't care. Yes, her mom had been ensconced with her dad for over a decade with little other human interaction, but at least her mom had been safe. Jessica doubted Nora or anyone else at that ranch had safety.

The room quieted with Jessica's jab. Now it was her turn to cross her arms. She would not apologize for anything she'd done. At least she'd tried to do the right thing.

"Can you promise me you won't go back out to the Wright's property?" Alma asked.

Alma was right, that clearly hadn't worked. Twice. But maybe she would uncover something in this guy's background that would bring Jaime and the El Paso Police Department into the mix.

"I promise." She sounded like an indignant child, but the words had already left her mouth.

"Thank you. Now, I need to get home." Alma rose from her seat. The others filed out as well.

Paz grabbed her shoulder on the way out. "You are one tough lady. I'm glad you're on our side."

Lucía reached up and hugged Jessica fiercely. "Thanks for trying," she whispered in her ear. "I love you."

Jessica squeezed her back. She'd do anything for that kid.

Chapter 19

Jessica spent the next morning on the couch, laptop in hand, researching local attorneys. Alma had given her thirty days, and she needed to take advantage of each one. She had never looked at the options before. One of the bigger, more traditional firms in town, Cohen Garcia handled almost any type of law. Their clients included businesses and individuals, but their biggest clients commingled those two. They often ended up doing work for individuals at business client companies.

Her Google research returned firms like Alma's, followed by the sue-happy attorneys looking for car accident victims, people wanting to sue their employers, and similar. New-aged ambulance chasers. But below these companies, several pages into her search, she started to find attorneys who practiced family and immigration law, specialties that appealed to her, even though family law encompassed divorces.

She added the work she'd done for Alma's firm to her résumé, then sent it to a few firms. One had three attorneys who shared the same last name, another had two male attorneys, and the final one only listed one name, a woman's. She liked the small size of the firms and their narrow focus. She hoped one of them needed paralegal work as badly as she needed a job.

Angus had come home after midnight and had barely grunted at her when she asked how he was as he crawled into bed. She assumed his anger hadn't abated, something unusual for him. They'd have to talk about it. She just needed some time with him, hopefully this morning.

The second Angus stirred, Tela left the spot where she'd been curled on top of Jessica's feet and trotted into the bedroom to help him wake up. He came out groggy and looking for coffee.

"Hey," she said, wanting to ask him about his night, really wanting to ask about their relationship, but not quite having the courage.

"I'm going to take Tela out for a quick run," he said, filling his coffee cup and returning to the bedroom.

Now that they had a backyard, they didn't have to take Tela for walks anymore. The dog loved the yard and raced the fence with the Australian Sheppard next door. It seemed like Angus wanted excuses not to be around her. That made her blood boil. They needed to work through their issues, not avoid them.

She'd done what she thought was right in the moment, even if it had turned out wrong. She'd gotten in plenty of trouble, been chastised for it, and still couldn't make things right with him. Just what the hell was she supposed to do to make things better? And why did she have to feel so damn guilty about trying to do the right thing?

"Hey. How are we going to get past this?" She hurled the question at Angus as he walked toward the front door, Tela in tow.

He stopped, looked at her, and ran a hand through his unruly hair. "I don't know. I'm really mad at you. I didn't think you'd ever lie to me. It's going to take me a while to figure out what to do with that."

He was too polite to slam the door on his way out, and she barely stopped herself from getting up and slamming it for him. He could be mad all he wanted, but the bad stuff had already happened. She wanted to move on from there.

For the hundredth time, she asked why only she and Lucía cared about what happened at that ranch. She'd heard nothing back from the school district. Every time she visited the ranch and seemed about to uncover something, the sheriffs office stepped in and shut it all down. Alma and Jaime were right. She didn't know enough about Jeremy Wright. She had two main questions. Had he been in trouble in the past? And why did he seem to have an in with important people in El Paso?

She turned her laptop back on. Pecos only had one high school and fewer than thirteen thousand people. Someone had to remember him. Plus, it was just two hundred miles away. No one seemed to want her around here. Perhaps she should take a little time to go do some of that research Jaime had mentioned.

So many emotions swirled in her, she couldn't sit still. She had hurt people she'd loved. She'd put her career in jeopardy. And yes, she'd lied to Angus. He'd taken it really hard. It wounded her that she'd hurt him. She'd done it too many times before. And she'd promised she'd stop. She'd tried to become the person he deserved, the one who didn't drink and fuck her way through life, the one who chose family over vice instead.

Committing to him, marrying him, had changed her. Hell, they'd been the best months of her life. She'd always wanted the security of her own home, and with him, she could afford it. But now that she lived in her dream home, she realized that security did not come from property, at least not in whole. It came from the bond they'd formed. They'd admitted they were each other's people, had stood up in front of friends and family and promised that. For her, the bond had become something physical, a chord that bound them.

Entwined with him, she'd found safety and security. For the first time in forever, she could release her loneliness and fear. She'd thought the relief in that alone would make her whole. And it almost had.

Maybe she'd tried to change too much at once. If it had just been Angus and the job had come later, or vice versa, maybe then she wouldn't have split herself in two, the Jessica who tried to behave and the woman with a dark side who pushed things too far. But her life hadn't worked out that way. She'd thought she could bury the old Jessica and live in the new one. But that life plagued her with dissatisfaction.

That dissatisfaction now melded with the anger and disappointment of others. It made her want to escape this new life. Some part of her wished to return to her former self when she wouldn't have cared about hurting others. But she did care.

Caring wasn't enough. It didn't lessen the danger the women at the ranch might face. She had to *do* something. That overrode all other emotions.

She went into the bedroom and pulled her old backpack from the top shelf of the closet. She'd take a little break, let things here calm down, and perhaps uncover information Jaime could use to open an investigation into the Wrights. Perhaps then, they would find out what happened to Nora and uncover whatever was going on inside the locked barracks. If something terrible had happened, it might also save Grace from Jeremy's clutches, despite her parents' desires.

Jessica threw clothing into the pack, just a couple of days' worth. She didn't have a firm plan, but the open road would soothe the feeling of wanting to crawl out of her skin and leave behind all the disappointment she'd wreaked. Also, some plumb line of justice wouldn't let her give up on the women at the ranch. She would learn a little more, then leave it to others to deal with what she'd found.

She heard the front door open, then the jingling of Tela's collar as she shook herself post walk. She threw her toiletries into her backpack while listening for Angus. If he didn't want to deal with her right now, she'd make sure he didn't have to. She hated the feeling of acting like a hurt child, but she didn't want to spend days tiptoeing around him, and besides, she didn't have a job to go to. Researching from the road seemed like an excellent use of her time.

He didn't come into the bedroom. She could leave through the back door. It would be a quick escape, but she wouldn't be that much of a child. Instead, she turned toward the kitchen.

"Hey, you don't have to worry about staying out late with friends. I'm going to be gone for a couple of days." She gazed at his back, broad shoulders under a thin T-shirt. He wore basketball shorts, and she had to stop herself from snuggling up behind him and running her fingers just inside his waistband until she reached the firm muscles of his lower belly. His hot skin over hard muscles got her every time.

He swung around, a jar of peanut butter and a spoon in his hand. Man one minute, boy the next. Only his face didn't carry its usual smile.

"Where are you going?" His voice wasn't accusing. Not exactly.

Her plan suddenly didn't seem like such a great idea. "I thought I'd take a little road trip. You know, since I don't have work right now. I did send out a few résumés this morning."

He raised one eyebrow. "I asked where you were going."

"I'm going to Pecos. And maybe to Big Spring."

"Is this about that case you're working on?" He set the peanut butter down and leaned against the counter, arms crossed. Frown lines creased his brow.

"Jaime said the police might be able to do something if I did some research." She hoped he'd said that, or something close to it. He probably just wanted her to stop going to the ranch. She felt a tightwire under her toes as the ground quickly slipped away.

"Why can't you just leave this alone? How many people do you have to hurt before you'll stop?"

"I can't leave it alone because I believe there are women on that ranch who are in trouble." Her own anger sparked back at him.

"But no one asked you to do anything. Nobody wants you involved."

"I'm not someone who can just stand by in a situation like this."

"No matter who you hurt?"

She wasn't doing this to hurt anyone. "What if something really bad is happening?"

"What if it's not? What if you're just tormenting these people?"

She took a ragged breath, stung by his comment. He'd supported her in the past, not challenged her. "Way to believe in me." She shoved her way past him and toward the door.

He didn't stop her, didn't ask her to stay. He stood in the doorway as she backed her truck down the drive, just staring at her. A piece of her heart broke. It made her angry, made her want to hit something or drive over it. Underneath the facade of anger, sadness took hold. Count on her to destroy the best thing in her life.

Chapter 20

Jessica sped down the highway with the music turned high. AC/DC, Guns N' Roses, Judas Priest. Anything to crowd the regret from her mind. All the songs reminded her of Angus. Of course, she hated music like country and pop, so she continued torturing herself with Angus's favorites. For two hundred miles.

By the time she reached Pecos, she longed for a shot of tequila and a cool dark bar. Or at least the old Jessica wanted that. The new one wouldn't give up on her new life quite so easily. Instead, she drove to the high school.

The entire town reeked of desolation, including the school. Flat as a board and an unvarying shade of desert tan, the land around Pecos didn't leave much to the imagination. The low-slung high school with its campus full of desert-colored, one-story buildings echoed its plain surroundings. Only the football stadium provided any visual relief. The sparkling white structure had far more height than any other in the neighborhood.

Jessica scrolled through her phone and found the Christian fellowship club at the school. The website listed its liaison, the name she'd seen before, Mr. Burnett, science teacher.

She'd solved the who, now she just needed to figure out how to get to him. Lying might get her the farthest. Telling the truth certainly hadn't won her any prizes lately.

She concocted a story. She'd use her real name in case they wanted to see her ID, but she'd say her husband might have to relocate to Pecos. Her son was good at science and loved physics, and she wanted to make sure he'd excel at the school. Would anyone buy that story? It couldn't hurt to try. If she got kicked out, she'd just stop by Burnett's house. She found it amazingly easy to locate people in a town like this. Thank you, Google.

She walked into the administrative office. The elderly white lady at the front desk looked like someone's grandma who got her hair set at the beauty parlor once a week. Jessica introduced herself and said she'd come to speak with Mr. Burnett.

The woman's gray eyes looked into Jessica's, and her face held no hint of a smile. "Concerning what?" she asked.

"I'm trying to find some information on a former student, Jeremy Wright." Her lies quickly fled. She might as well be honest. This woman looked like she'd sat at that desk for the last century.

"Hmm." The woman did a slow blink, and when her eyes opened again, something cold shone through them. "Is he back in town?" she asked, her voice icy.

"No, he and his wife just moved to El Paso."

"Well, that's good." The woman paused for a moment. "Where is his wife from?"

"Big Spring. Why?" This woman had a lot of questions. Jessica hoped answering them would get her closer to Mr. Burnett.

The woman harrumphed and shook her head. "I thought it might be the one from Fort Stockton." The woman looked down and shuffled some papers at her desk. She pulled out a business card and wrote something on the front and back. "Room 331, like it says on that card. School's out in ten minutes. You can wait here until then." The woman motioned to three metal chairs along one wall.

Jessica slipped the card into her wallet. The lax security surprised her. With all the school shootings in recent years, she'd expected all sorts of barriers.

She texted Angus. "I love you."

She didn't expect and didn't get a response, but she'd figure out a way to fix their relationship.

The bell clanging scared her with a terror she hadn't felt since high school. Why did those bells have to be so loud? Even when they brought the release of the school day, they did it in the most shocking way possible.

She thanked the lady at the desk and headed into the hallway, her first mistake. The scrum of teens heading out the main entrance almost bowled her over. They smelled like sweat and anxiety. Man, she'd never go back to those days.

The hallway cleared quickly, and she found the classroom. A skinny kid with spiky hair spoke to the teacher. Mr. Burnett was probably only five-eight to Jessica's five-ten. His curly auburn hair bobbed as he nodded at the student. She waited outside until they'd finished talking.

The student nodded at her as he left. Jessica entered the classroom, which had desks in the front and a few rows of lab tables in back. She'd never done well in science, and even now, the smell of formaldehyde made her skin itch.

"Mr. Burnett?" she asked.

"How can I help you?" He gave her a big smile along with the words.

"I'm Jessica Watts. I'd like to ask you a few questions about a former student here."

"Oh?" He looked curious and a little suspicious.

"He's the liaison to a Christian high school group in El Paso. Do you know Jeremy Wright?"

Burnett's guard dropped, and a smile crossed his face. "Oh, I remember Jeremy. We used to travel together with The Way. How's he doing?"

"He and his wife recently moved to El Paso." Jessica wondered how much information to give the man. He did seem willing to talk.

"He's married? I'm surprised I hadn't heard that, although I haven't heard from him in a while."

"Is there someplace we can go? I'd be happy to buy you a cup of coffee." She needed to learn more from this man, but the awkwardness of standing in the classroom had her fidgeting like a teenager.

"I've got to clean up the lab and then was going to catch up on grading. Why don't we just talk here?" He gestured to a student desk in the front row.

She sulked over to the desk and dropped into it. The surliness of her high school days crept into her skin from the wood and metal. Burnett perched on his teacher's desk at the front of the room and looked down at her.

"Well, this feels disturbingly familiar," she muttered.

"Excuse me?"

"Nothing. Sorry. So, when did Jeremy go to high school here?"

"Well, he probably graduated about ten years ago."

"Was he a good student?"

"I should probably ask why you're so interested in him." He leaned back, as if he'd realized this wasn't a social call. She needed to find a way to disarm him.

She wondered what tack to take and decided to go with a little honesty. "He recently started running the youth group at El Paso High School. My, well, she's like my niece, is involved in that group and she seems especially taken with Mr. Wright. My family would tell you I'm always sticking my nose into places it doesn't belong, but I'm concerned about her interest in him and wanted to talk to someone who knows him. I figured Pecos was small enough that I'd find that person."

"You drove all the way out here for that?"

"Yeah, I know it seems a little rash, but you can't be too careful these days. My niece is a very sweet girl, and she just seems so taken with Jeremy."

The teacher chuckled. "Well, some things never change. The girls always did like Jeremy. He's a good-looking guy, and being a man of God, he didn't threaten them. So many young men in high school want to take advantage of women their age. It's really a hard thing for a young woman."

Jessica hoped her mouth hadn't hit the ground. Men thought they could explain anything. To anyone. Unbelievable. She forced her thoughts back to Jeremy. "Did he ever date any of the girls in these programs?"

Mr. Burnett moved his hand to his chin as if deep in thought. "No, he never did. I guess that's why it surprised me he got married. That must be some woman."

She was something, all right, but he didn't need to know that. "Isn't it unusual for a teenager not to date? Especially when they're surrounded by women who like them?" She had a hard time believing in the righteous Jeremy this guy remembered.

"I respect that you're here to protect your niece, but I can promise you, you don't have to worry about Jeremy. That boy had a hard life. His mother, well, let's just say he didn't have a good home life. I think that's why Jeremy didn't want to date. At least not in high school and the years we traveled together for The Way."

Man, this guy dropped leads everywhere. "I'm so glad to hear how much you trust him, and I didn't realize you two traveled together."

"Oh, yes. For several years. I tried to look out for Jeremy in high school. You know, on account of his family life. Once he got involved in our club here, he became the perfect representative. He got others to join, organized events, you name it, Jeremy was there to help. I used to buy his meals when we traveled and even bought him some clothes, so he'd look presentable."

She had to keep this guy talking. "That's incredibly generous of you. How did you get involved in The Way?"

"I had a contact at the organization, my roommate from college. At that point, The Way wanted to expand into schools throughout Texas. They actually paid us to travel to different high schools in far west Texas and start these programs. I couldn't have had a better partner, the kids adored Jeremy. They don't always trust teachers, but having someone their age speak about the program attracted them like flies to honey."

Jessica cringed at the comment. "So, you and Jeremy always attended the meetings together?"

"Usually. Sometimes I'd meet with the administration once things got going. Jeremy made friends with the kids. He always identified the ones who were struggling, probably because of his own home life. He'd give them extra attention."

Yeah, I'll bet. Jessica didn't speak the words, but she could almost see how these meetings unfolded. Surely Jeremy's concern covered more than religion, although this guy would never buy that. "Then what happened?" she asked.

"Once he graduated, The Way hired him full-time to start youth programs. He developed strong relationships with religious leaders throughout West Texas. It's really amazing how he built himself up after such a rough beginning."

"Wow. That really is amazing." She might as well lay it on thick, after all, this guy seemed to think Jeremy was the second coming. But Lucía had wept over what this guy had done. He couldn't be innocent. "I'm really glad I came here today. I can't tell you what a relief it is to speak with you. And I'm so sorry to hear about Jeremy's early life. Is he still in contact with his mom? Believe me, I know how fraught those relationships can be."

Burnett shook his head, seemingly overcome by obligatory sadness. "His mom disappeared his freshman year. No one ever found out what happened to her. She worked as a waitress down at the truck stop. Some people said she ran off with a trucker. Others suggested she might have died, although no one ever found a body. She had a bit of a drug problem."

"Oh my god." A stab of compassion hit Jessica. Perhaps she'd gotten the story wrong.

"That left poor Jeremy living with his stepdad. I don't think they got along too well. That's why I took Jeremy under my wing. When he first showed up at our group, he was painfully thin and always wore the same ratty clothes. You could tell he needed a father figure. I'm just glad I was there to help. Once The Way started paying him, his life took a turn for the better."

"You seem like a real saint." Jessica needed to leave. Something about this guy made her queasy. He seemed genuinely nice and caring, but he'd shared too much and had played too big a role in Jeremy's past.

She pulled herself out of the desk and made herself walk forward to shake Mr. Burnett's hand. "Thank you for speaking with me today. I really appreciate it."

***

Jessica checked into a no-name hotel painted a garish orange and turquoise. Fortunately, clean rooms, a relatively comfortable bed, and an extremely cheap rate made up for the unfortunate exterior.

She hadn't eaten all day and found a BBQ place with a high rating on Yelp. She couldn't decide between the pulled pork sandwich or the meat and sides, and she damn near ordered both. She settled on two meats—sliced brisket and sausage—and two sides, chile cheese hominy and green beans. The delicious food had her half-convinced to stay a few days.

She returned to the hotel, turned the A/C on high, and opened her laptop. She hadn't done much research on The Way. She figured they preached that new form of conservative, hate-filled religion popular on extremist media sites. Growing up, being a Texan made her proud, but the state had recently taken a hard turn toward extremism, at least in the rural areas.

When she looked into The Way, it surprised her to learn they donated to all kinds of charitable causes throughout Texas, including religious organizations outside of their own churches. They seemed to have a partner in every Texas town, be it a Baptist, Presbyterian, or other religious sect.

Jessica hated how The Way had infiltrated itself throughout the state. Even though its largest church sat just outside of Dallas, the organization's headquarters resided in Lubbock, a relatively small city in West Texas. A man named Tim Jeffries had founded the organization back in the 1980s and funded it still. Like most extremely rich Texans, his money had originated in the oil and gas industry.

The more she read, the more uncomfortable she became. This guy's money backed some of Texas's most restrictive laws and a slew of obnoxious politicians. He'd funded legislation that allowed the Texas Rangers to deliver immigrants to cages, that paid people to tell on neighbors they thought might have ended pregnancies, and all sorts of vile laws—along with the politicians to enact them.

Jessica had never been overly religious. She had friends in El Paso who belonged to one of the Catholic or Episcopal churches or the synagogue. She hadn't run across many super-right-wing Christians. Tim Jeffries had built an industry that fed extremism.

She jerked with surprise when her phone rang. Angus.

"Hey. I miss you." The words tumbled out before she stopped them.

"I miss you too." His heavy sigh rang through the phone. "I wish you hadn't run away."

She wanted him by her side, wanted to wrap her arms around him, but she wouldn't take all the blame. "You ran away first."

The miles stretched between them. She longed for him, craved the many good months they had before she'd taken a hatchet to his trust.

"I did," he said. "I was so angry. Things had been going well. But then there was the tension with your mother. And you seemed to keep getting into deeper trouble with this Jeremy guy and getting others in trouble too. I'm so worried we're going to fuck this up."

"You mean you're worried I'm going to fuck this up." That was as plain as a scorching desert day. She worried about it constantly.

"We're both responsible for this relationship."

"I don't ever want to lose you. But I am me. I know you think I should drop this, but as long as I'm truly worried about those women and girls, I can't leave it alone. But I'm not going to chase this forever. I met a guy today who thinks Jeremy is the second coming."

"And?"

"And I want to follow the trail a little further. If there's something out there that Jaime can follow up on, then I'll find it and pass it on to him. This isn't a life goal for me, but I want to do right by Lucía and the others involved."

"I think passing this one off to the police is a great idea. How long will you be gone?"

She wished she had a firm answer. She'd originally planned to continue to Big Spring, but she'd rather be home. Answers about The Way and the work Jeremy did there had risen to the top of her list.

"I may go to Lubbock tomorrow, but I'll try calling first. If I can get the information I need over the phone, I'll come home tomorrow." She sounded like she had a solid plan, but she'd winged it the whole way. She wondered if Angus knew that. If he cared.

"It'd be great if you were home tomorrow. I miss you."

"I miss you too. And I am not going to screw this up." She prayed she'd told him the truth.

Chapter 21

Jessica drove to the truck stop near the highway, hoping to learn about Jeremy's mother. The truck stops from her youth featured diners with sassy waitresses and delicious pies. A recent remodel left those visions far behind. This one still featured the requisite convenience store with an amazing variety of goods for sale, but instead of a diner, McDonalds and Subway divided the counter space like a mall food court.

Most of the people working there were her age or younger, and Jessica figured Jeremy's mom had to be at least in her forties. The only person old enough to have worked there ten years earlier was a gray-haired lady at the Subway cash register. Jessica got in a line ten people deep and ordered a sandwich. Still full from her late lunch, she ordered a six-inch veggie.

She took a chance at checkout and asked the woman if she was around when Ms. Wright worked at the truck stop.

"You mean Candy? That was a long time ago," the woman said.

Paydirt. "I know her son Jeremy."

"Oh, that poor boy. How's he doing?" The woman talked while she bagged Jessica's sandwich.

"I think he still struggles some. Did they ever find out what happened to his mom?"

"No. But she was a sad case. We worked together for years. I always warned her to stay away from the temptations of the truckers, but she seemed to like that excitement in her life."

"Temptations?" Jessica asked. She stood to the side of the register, and the woman continued to process people, ringing them up and wrapping their sandwiches.

"They'll offer a woman just about anything—fun, drugs, money. I thought Candy had gotten all that out of her system after she married Eli, but I think she probably went off with some trucker in the end." She glanced at Jessica, then turned to the next customer.

"Eli, that's Jeremy's stepdad, right? Is he still around?"

"Naw. There wasn't anything left for him here after Candy and Jeremy left. He was a good man. A little strict maybe, at least according to Candy. But he stayed here until Jeremy finished high school."

"Thanks for the information. It helps me understand him a little better." Not that it did, really. Most people had issues with their parents. Jeremy's sounded a little worse than most. But then again, so did Jessica's.

"You tell him hi for me next time you see him. My name's Maybel. He'll remember me. He used to spend a good deal of time here when he was little, and this place was a real truck stop." Maybel sounded almost wistful.

Jessica couldn't imagine working in a truck stop, whether in the old days or new. She didn't have the personality to be nice to total strangers, hour after hour. Of course, if she didn't figure out how to salvage her career, she might easily end up in a place like this.

***

The next morning, Jessica called The Way at 8:00 a.m. sharp. When she said she needed to talk to someone about a former employee, the receptionist transferred her to human resources. The woman who answered the phone refused to give Jessica any information except the dates Jeremy Wright worked for The Way. He'd stopped working there three years ago, but the woman wouldn't tell her if he'd resigned or been fired. She also wouldn't let Jessica speak to a former supervisor and wouldn't even mention the name of anyone Jeremy might have worked for.

"Listen," Jessica said. "We believe we have an issue with some inappropriate behavior with a young woman, and we need to know if he had a history of this type of behavior."

Jessica hoped the question might help the woman open up, or at least prompt her to let Jessica speak with someone else.

"Ma'am. I'm sure you know we would never give out any personal information on one of our employees. If you have a legal issue beyond that, you can contact our attorneys." The woman's tone had gone from uninterested to ice cold.

Jessica paused, wondering if the attorneys would help or get her into additional trouble. She must have waited too long to respond, because the woman said, "Thank you for your call," and hung up.

She had no reason to remain in Pecos, and certainly wouldn't receive additional information if she showed up at The Way's headquarters. When she'd started the trip, she'd thought about continuing to Big Spring. Perhaps she would learn a little more about Jeremy, or the sudden death of the pastor there. But she had nothing more to glean from the pastor's wife. Since she wasn't working in an official capacity, she likely wouldn't get additional information from the authorities. She could try to find more information from the family of Jeremy's wife, but strange didn't equal suspicious.

She might as well head back to El Paso and see if Jaime had learned anything. She'd share whatever she'd gained from this trip, but nothing she'd learned would change people's thoughts about the man. Despite Jeremy's creepiness, what did she really have on him? His inappropriate behavior and the locks on the barracks. She had heard someone inside, hadn't she? She had.

***

The drive home gave Jessica plenty of time to think. Jeremy was a creep, but maybe she'd focused on the wrong area.

Clearly, some people loved the guy, from his high school teacher to perhaps the El Paso sheriff. Jessica had gotten hung up on looking for Nora, but she didn't know Nora. Perhaps the woman had left, despite what Stan thought.

She needed to deal with Lucía and the threat he posed to girls like her. A compass inside her swung back to true north. She'd lost her way. She shouldn't have sneaked onto the ranch. She needed to focus on his inappropriate behavior. A history of this, even one case, would make it easy to talk to the school district and get him removed from any contact with kids. That vice principal she'd met, Charles Jackson, he wouldn't tolerate that type of behavior. It would also give Jaime something concrete to investigate even if the ranch lay outside his jurisdiction.

Each mile she drove gave her a little more confidence. Focus on the easy things that would make a difference. No school wanted someone hanging around kids who had a whiff of sexual harassment in their background. Not in the post #metoo era.

She used the phone's speaker system to call Stan. She needed to let him know she wouldn't help him find Nora. The last time she'd gone after a missing woman, it had been a mistake. Jessica ended up helping the woman escape again to keep her out of danger. She'd give Nora the same benefit of the doubt.

"I've been waiting for you to call," Stan said as soon as he picked up.

Ugh. He must still want her help. "Stan, I've done a lot of thinking about this, and I can't help you find Nora. I just don't know her well enough. There are lots of reasons she might have chosen to leave the ranch."

He didn't respond immediately. He cleared his throat first, as if trying to get the words out past his emotions. "I'm sorry to hear that, but I understand. I appreciate that you took me to the ranch, even though you didn't know me that well. I didn't mean to get you in trouble."

"I'm sorry we didn't find her. I hope, wherever she is, she's doing all right." Jessica really didn't know what else to say. She had to leave this one alone.

"Me too." His voice quieted, and she barely heard it over the road noise. "I'm certain that something terrible happened to Nora. But that guy who bought the ranch has some powerful friends. I appreciate your attorney putting in a good word for me and getting me out on bail, but I won't go back to jail."

"What do you mean?" Alma had helped Stan. It wouldn't look good for her if he disappeared. Alma's act showed her kindness, but maybe she also had her own doubts about Jeremy, despite what she'd told Jessica. Perhaps she didn't let Jessica know because it might have encouraged her to get further involved.

"I said I'm not going back to jail," Stan said, louder this time. "You won't be able to reach me after we hang up."

"I doubt they'll put you in jail. We trespassed, but we didn't damage any property. Alma thinks at most I'll be fined, and probably not much."

"Maybe they won't give you a harsh sentence, I truly hope not. I'm sure they'll give me the maximum penalty."

"Because of your prior arrests?" She hadn't looked up the maximum sentence, but she did not want to go to jail. She needed to end this call and get on the phone with Alma.

"The guy who checked me out of the sheriff's office told me I'd really pissed off the wrong guy. He said he'd see me back here soon, permanently this time. I've done some things in my life I truly regret, but looking for Nora wasn't one of them. Thanks again for trying to help, but I have to warn you to stay away from this one."

"That's what I plan on doing. I'll get this guy, but not this way."

"Well, be careful. You're probably best off dropping the whole thing."

Even the guy who'd convinced her to get further involved wanted her to step away. This Jeremy Wright guy had some influence. She'd tread more carefully in the future.

"If this ever blows over or if that guy gets caught and put away for something, would you do me a favor?"

"Sure. If it won't get me in trouble."

"Please don't do it if it will. But if there's no danger, there's an old cabin between the twin hills on the property. It's hard to get to. You need to hike in or have a good four-wheel drive. Just follow the road past the barn and you'll eventually get there. That's the one place we didn't look for Nora."

"Okay. So that's it. You're skipping out on your hearing?"

"It's better not to ask questions like that. And it's far better for you if you don't know the answer."

***

Jessica pulled into El Paso, determined to get her life back on track. Angus had left for work, but Tela greeted her as if she'd been gone for weeks, not just over twenty-four hours. Jessica let the dog crawl into her lap. Tela leaned heavily against her. Jessica wrapped her arms around the dog, certain she'd sensed the tension between her and Angus.

"Don't you worry. I'm not going to let anything happen to our family." She pressed her cheek against the dog's short fur and held on, hoping the ground would solidify beneath her feet.

She decided not to call Jaime, at least not yet. Instead of spending additional time on Jeremy Wright, she needed to figure out how to contribute to the household expenses.

"Mama's gotta work," she said as she gently pushed the dog off her. Tela bounded up, scampered to the back door, and whined. Jessica let her out, then sat at the table with her laptop. She'd heard back from two of the law firms. The first said they didn't have any open positions. The second, the single woman, asked her to call to set up an interview.

She hadn't expected her ploy to work, and relief thrummed through her. She pulled out her cell phone and typed in the numbers. She crossed her fingers, then tried to exhale any tension through a long breath.

"Linda Reed."

"Ms. Reed? This is Jessica Watts. I sent you my résumé, and you said to give you a call."

"Ah, yes. Jessica, thanks for calling. So, you want to be an attorney?"

"Yes ma'am. I just finished my second year of law school, have my paralegal certificate, and have more than a year's experience at Cohen Garcia."

"Can you come in for an interview this week?"

"Yes. I'm available tomorrow." Might as well get this thing done. This lady sounded no nonsense. Jessica needed a little of that in her life.

"Perfect. Come in at nine. I'm at 800 St. Vrain Street near the courthouse."

"Great. I'll see you tomorrow. Thank you, and I look forward to meeting you."

"See you then." The woman hung up the phone, dismissing Jessica.

Jessica wondered if she was as abrupt with clients as with potential employees. She'd also answered her own phone, which seemed highly unusual for a law practice. Oh, well. She'd learn more tomorrow. A current of electricity ran through her. Alma had done so much to help her, but getting an interview on her own brought back a little of the pride she'd lost since the autonomy of her real estate days. Then, she'd had to hustle for every deal. She'd faced tough times and lucrative years, but she'd always made her own luck. Maybe she needed a little more of that.

She called Tela in from the backyard and put a leash on her. The day had turned around, and she wanted to keep it on a forward trajectory. Tela's excitement translated into her trotting excitedly around Jessica's feet and almost tripping her. The dog had no end of energy.

"Sit," she said in frustration. One look from those eyes, one blue and one bright green, made Jessica sorry she'd snapped at the animal. "You're a good girl. Let's go get some ribs."

They walked a few blocks down the street, to the State Line, a restaurant that literally sat on the Texas, New Mexico border. It also had the best barbeque in town. Funny how once you'd eaten barbeque, you craved it again almost immediately.

At the restaurant, she ordered one rib along with all the sides. The ribs were gigantic, twice as big as you'd get anywhere else, and with the perfect spicy, tangy sauce. They sat on a bench in a tiled courtyard near the restaurant. She ate the rib first, then gave the bone, with plenty of meat scraps on it, to the dog whining beside her.

Jessica savored the potato salad, her favorite, and the coleslaw with a sauce that hit one hundred percent flavor and zero percent sweet. Full, she decided to take the sides of beans home for later. When she tried to take the bone from Tela, the dog growled from deep within her chest. "Fine, but it's going to be an awkward walk home."

Tela brought Jessica back to herself. This dog had seen the best and the worst of her owner and loved her anyway. Maybe Jessica could find a way to balance the dark and the danger with the straight and narrow instead of swinging between the two. She had to try.

***

Jessica looked forward to a late evening with Angus. He probably wouldn't be home until after eight, but she planned on picking up dinner for them and continuing the conversation they'd had on the phone last night. She loved him, and they would work this out.

She did not expect her mother to show up at six. She hoped she didn't look as annoyed as she felt when she opened the door after her mother's knock.

"Hi, Honey. Sorry to drop by without calling, but I just returned from meeting with Dick Saunders. You remember him. He's married to the gallery owner showing my work."

"And the ex-mayor. I remember him." She looked at her mom for a moment, wishing this was an email or phone call she could ignore until a more convenient time. But she stepped back and invited her into the house.

"Would you like something to drink?" Jessica asked once her mom had plunked herself down at the table.

"A glass of wine would be nice."

"We've just got beer and water. And tequila." Jessica smiled inside at the unsuitable options.

"I'll have a glass of water. Thank you."

Jessica grabbed herself a beer and filled a water glass from the tap. She hoped Clarice had an update on finding a house, but she didn't want to ask in case she'd decided moving in with her and Angus was her best option.

Her mom started speaking before Jessica had a chance to sit down. "As I said, I met with Dick Saunders, and I asked him if he knew Jeremy Wright."

"What?" No, no, no. She did not want her mom involved in any part of this. "We told you not to. Remember? The night you staged the intervention?"

"Well, I remembered you talking about how all the big wigs liked this guy, so I thought I'd see if he knew him. And it turns out he does. He said he and Robin have known him for years and have done what they could to help his career. They're thrilled he's moved out this way. Honey, he sounds like a fine, upstanding young man. Maybe you've got the wrong idea about him."

The ice cold prelude to panic formed in her gut and spread through her body, pooling in her joints. "Did you tell them I've been looking into the Wrights?" *Please say no.* Jessica tried to silently force the words into her mother's brain.

"I said you were concerned about him and wanted more information. After all, that's why I went to talk to him." Her mom's blue eyes looked innocent and so fucking gullible. Jessica got up and stomped to the back door to whistle for Tela. Her hands shook with rage as she opened the door.

Finally, she turned to her mother. "How could you do that? Didn't you realize you might get Alma and me into worse trouble by talking to a guy like that? That man still pulls a lot of strings around here. I've got to go stand in front of a judge, and guess who knows all the judges? Alma's already in trouble at her firm because of me, and the partners are some of his best friends. What were you thinking?" She'd meant to keep her voice calm, but the anger flew out.

Her mom looked like she'd been slapped, all bright red cheeks and round eyes. In fact, Jessica had never wanted to slap someone so much in her life.

"You know I was just trying to help." Her mother stood. "I know something about politics and how things work in this town. At least I used to. And you certainly seem like you're in over your head."

"God damn it, Mom. I know something about politics in this town too. I've been living and working here for a long time. I've met that guy a dozen times at chamber of commerce events. He'll shake anyone's hand, but he only notices people who can help him in some way. And believe me, he never wanted help from Joe Watts's kid. Not when my dad was the disgraced district attorney." Jessica hoped her mom felt even a tiny bit of the sting of embarrassment she'd carried all these years.

"Well, the Saunderses are very respected in El Paso, and they think Jeremy Wright is a fine young man. You're the one getting into trouble about this, and I just wanted to give you some perspective. Have you even considered you're wrong about him?"

"Do you think Lucía is lying? You do realize that's where this started."

"I thought Lucía liked him." Her mom sat back down. Jessica wished she'd leave and never come back. Like she had before.

"Mom. He touched Lucía's boob. He was supposed to be the liaison for a Christian youth group, and he abused that position." Every muscle in Jessica's body tensed with all the things that had gone wrong. Lucía. Nora. Alma. Stan. Jail. A lot of the blame fell on her shoulders for handling things poorly, but underneath that, something was rotten.

"It was probably just an accident." Her mom's feeble voice took a moment to reach Jessica's consciousness.

When it did, her anger turned cold. "You choose to believe a rich white man over the girl who's been devastated by this?"

Her mom stood at the table, her cheeks glowing red. Tears made her blue eyes glassy, but they didn't fall. Who was this woman?

"Out." Jessica raised an arm and pointed toward the front door. She noticed Tela cowering by her food dish. The dog hated arguments between the people she loved.

"Let's talk about this." Her mother had grabbed the table as if Jessica would have to pry her from it.

All those years caring for her dad in a place with few friends and no family must have taken its toll on this woman, but that didn't excuse her. Jessica had vowed to stand up for the people without power. She wanted to be a force of good in the world. Her mother evidently played by different rules.

"Out," she repeated without dropping her arm.

"You are so damn mean." Her mom released the table, then left, sobbing as she made her way through the door.

Jessica watched her mom leave, but all the tension she'd brought with her remained in the room. Jessica sank to the floor, and Tela crawled into her lap. Dogs should rule the world.

After a while, she got up, an old familiar beat thrumming through her system. What she wouldn't give for a dark bar, all the tequila she could drink, and someone to go home with. She showered instead.

She ran the water hot, then cold, trying to turn that dangerous anxiety down a notch. But the burden of the last few days, maybe weeks, wouldn't subside. It demanded to work its way out of her system in all the old, bad habit ways.

She put on jeans and a low-cut blouse, blew out her hair, and lined her eyes in kohl. She fed the dog, then pulled out her phone.

Meet me at the King after work. Pretend you don't know me.

She pressed send.

Chapter 22

"Well, look who the weather dragged in."

"Hey, Scottie." Jessica plopped up on the faux red leather stool, careful to keep her arms off the sticky bar. The dim light, the aroma of stale beer, men, and danger, and the colorful parade of bottles in front of her unwound the live wires keeping her muscles taut.

"I haven't seen you in a long while." He smiled, and the lines around his eyes crinkled a little deeper than she remembered. God she'd missed this place.

"I missed your hospitality. Can I get a Pacifico and a shot of tequila? Also, some quarters for the jukebox." She slapped a dollar bill on the table.

"Coming right up."

He placed four quarters on the bar, and she ambled over to the glowing music machine. She queued up "Wild Thing," then a couple of AC/DC hits. She turned around and surveyed the shadowy bar. She swore the same group of men had been playing pool at the same table every time she'd been here. And she'd been here a lot back in the day. A group that looked like frat boys had taken over one corner of the bar. Once, they'd have interested her, now they just looked young.

A man with a gray, shellacked helmet of hair sat at the bar with a bottle-blond wearing too much makeup. Probably the local university's football coach. They all had the same look.

Scott put her drinks on the bar, and she strode across the room, slamming back the tequila first. She coughed. The well tequila didn't match the quality of what she drank at home, but it would definitely get the job done.

"Another, please." The words came out hoarse, as if the alcohol had actually burned her throat. She took a long swig of cooling beer and popped back into her seat, waiting for the waves of booze to course through her body. She wanted to forget the bullshit, release all the heavy responsibility of the Jessica she should be and return to the knife-edge of danger from her past. She caught the scent of the desert at night as she and Stan tramped through it, saw the incomprehension of what she'd done wrong in her mother's eyes. She closed her own.

When she heard the shot glass hit the bar, she opened her eyes and sat up at attention, like Tela waiting for a treat. The liquor slid down her throat, burning straight through to her heart. It burned through her worries about Lucía, Jeremy, Alma, her marriage. It released them all and turned her into an unknown woman at a bar, not someone with responsibilities.

She took a long sip of beer and stifled a burp while Scott cashed out the coach and his girlfriend. When he sauntered back her way, she pointed at the shot glass.

"You driving?" he asked.

"Not if I can help it."

"The pickings aren't so great tonight, although those guys all have IDs that say they're twenty-one." He gestured toward the corner.

"I'll have another beer too," she said when he set down her latest tequila shot. "I have faith that the perfect guy is going to walk through that door."

"Well, if not, I'm happy to help out," he said. "Although you've told me you don't do seconds."

She looked at him appreciatively. He hadn't been bad in bed, especially at certain things. But that had been years ago. "Not tonight. But thanks."

She leaned back and held the shot glass up to the light, The amber elixir looked innocent, but when she brought it to her nose, she smelled its secrets. Man had used tequila for centuries for everything from the courage to go into battle to a lubricant for love. And it still worked every time. Her body warmed thinking about the adventure ahead, and a lazy fullness took over.

The bar door opened. A man walked in. Six feet, two inches of lean muscle in faded Levi's and a Bad Honey T-shirt. He sat at the bar across from her, and she raised her shot glass to him then poured the liquid down her throat. He ordered a beer from Scott.

She'd found her target. She adjusted her already low-cut shirt to expose even more cleavage. Scott dropped off the guy's beer, then brought a fresh beer and another shot to Jessica. He stared straight at her breasts. "These are from the guy across the bar. I think I should warn him about you," he said.

"Don't bother. He looks like he can handle it." She looked at him and the guy tipped his beer in salute.

Jessica took her drinks around the square bar and sat on the stool beside the man.

"Hey, babe," he said.

She straightened and narrowed her eyes at him. "Hi. I'm Jessica. It's nice to meet you. Thank you for the drink." She kept her face still and serious.

He cleared his throat, then offered her his hand. "I'm Angus. Nice to meet you."

"So, Angus. Tell me something about yourself." She spun his chair toward her and trapped his knees between her legs. A thrill of power, and, yes, freedom, grew from her boldness. Wet heat rushed through her.

"Well, I heard a beautiful woman comes in here every now and then and picks a man to have her way with. I'm hoping to get lucky." Angus said it with a straight face, but Jessica heard Scott chuckle. She turned toward him, but his back was to them.

Jessica sipped her tequila and appraised the man in front of her. How far would he go? There were so very many things she wanted from him. She placed a hand on his knee, ran it up soft denim so slowly it lit her on fire. From what she could see, he enjoyed it as well.

"Drink." He pointed at the half a shot of tequila remaining.

She followed his command and drained her glass, staring into his brown eyes the entire time.

"Finish your beer," she said, relishing the command. She sipped her own brew like a high priestess ruling her very own depraved corner of the world.

He drank the entire beer in one long sip like a college parlor trick. "What now?"

"What do we owe you?" she asked Scott.

She left cash on the bar. In the parking lot, she pushed him against his car, then pressed herself into him. The searing heat of his lips sent a tremor through her. She couldn't get close enough. She lifted her arms and wrapped them around his neck, pulling him into her. Her breasts scraped against his chest in exquisite pleasure. She dropped a hand to his jeans and unbuttoned them.

"Here? In the parking lot?" he asked, sounding bewildered.

Jessica looked around the lot. It happened to have a dark corner. "Go park there. Now." She pulled open the car door and practically shoved him in. Craving the thrill of danger from her past, she marched after the car feeling strong and reckless. She played a devil's game, and tonight she would win.

Angus jumped out of the car, his pants still half undone. "Let's go home."

Jessica walked up to the front passenger door and opened it. She maneuvered the seat back as far as it would go and reclined it all the way. Then she looked at him. She could almost feel the hard muscles under soft skin. She knew the moan he'd make when she wrapped her fingers into the hair on the nape of his neck and pulled.

In the past, she'd used men to pound the emptiness out of her. Now she wanted to be filled with the joy and passion and love that spilled from him. She teetered on the edge of desire and madness. "Get in the car. Spend five minutes making out with me and then let me know if you want to go home."

His eyes half closed. Sultry, with a fire underneath. He came to her, lifted her onto him, and then sank into the car.

They didn't talk. They did kiss and nip and grope, all in a space preposterously small. Somehow that made it hotter.

After, she lay half-clothed and spent atop him, small flashes of electricity still tingling in her fingers and toes. Her woozy head spun when she lifted it off his chest. "I think you're going to have to drive me home."

"I'll drive you anywhere you want. That was amazing."

She smiled at his comment, pressed her lips into his. Just kissing him started a stirring deep in her belly. Again.

She pulled herself off him and climbed into the driver's seat. "I've got to find my pants." She reached between his legs and found them on the passenger seat floor. She leaned over further, her bare breasts pressing against his denim-clad knee. He ran a warm hand down her shoulder, her back, around a bare ass cheek. She moaned, knowing the strength of his guitar playing fingers. The same fingers that played her so well.

Part of her wanted to climb right back on him and have another go. But her brain felt sloshy from the booze. They should go home. She laid a hand on his bare chest. "Thank you. You saved me tonight. All of my demons showed up, and you satisfied every one."

"Christ, Jessica. I've been stiff from the moment you sent me that text. I could barely work. I'm happy to slay your demons anytime you want."

"Do we need to talk about everything that happened this week?"

He chuckled. "Nah, we're good."

Chapter 23

When the alarm blared, it sliced through Jessica's head. Someone had stuffed cotton balls into her mouth, but her body felt plump with satisfaction, and the demons had fled her psyche, leaving her refreshed.

She slapped the top of the old-fashioned digital alarm, hopefully hitting the right button, and pulled herself from bed, trying to not wake Angus. It might not have been a good idea to drink so much the night before her big interview, but hungover and sane had to be preferable to yesterday's mood.

She stayed under the hot shower too long, loving the way the water pounded on her shoulders, then spun off in rivulets down her back and legs. Last night had opened a portal to the dark animal in her soul who'd loved her former life.

Instead of trying to hide that piece of herself, she'd claimed it. And she'd shown it to Angus and shared it with him. Given his response when they returned home, a new ravishing where he held her wrists behind her back and took complete control, he might have his own dark side. She ached with desire at the thought.

She turned the water to cold and let it douse the flame. This wasn't a morning for lust and sexcapades. She needed to go nail an interview and bring in some money.

***

Jessica pulled up in front of a home the color of pound cake with crisp white trim. She must be hungry. Located on a block of houses built roughly a hundred years ago and now mostly converted to offices, this one had a peaked roof, a narrow, covered porch, and a "Law Office" sign hanging in the front yard.

She opened the gate and wandered up the path, trying to decide whether to knock on the closed door like a house or just open it like she'd do with a business. She hesitated a moment, then pushed the door open.

The room seemed far dimmer than it should have, given the bright sun outside and colorful tile floors. Banks of files lined one wall, and a beautiful old desk with an inlaid top greeted her. Only no one was there.

"Hello," she called into the empty space. She could see into the next room. It had likely once been the home's dining room and had made the minor transformation into a boardroom. A hallway on the right side of the house paralleled the dining room, but she couldn't see where it led. She eyed two comfortable looking leather armchairs across from the desk but didn't want to sit. "Is anyone here?"

"Grab a chair in the boardroom. I'll be right out."

Jessica recognized Linda Reed's gravelly voice from the phone call. She obeyed and entered the boardroom, where she met another dilemma. Should she sit at the head of the table, or would that look obnoxious? She chose the first chair on the side.

Banging and slamming came from the back of the house cum office, and after a few minutes, a thin blond woman strode in. She carried a tray with two brown ceramic mugs of coffee, a bowl with different kinds of real and fake sugar, and a stack of napkins. She set the tray down carefully, then sat across from Jessica.

"Help yourself to some coffee. I'm Linda Reed." The woman reached in and grabbed a mug for herself.

"Thank you." Jessica took the second mug, all the while studying Ms. Reed. She had wavy blond hair that fell past her shoulders and wore a tailored navy suit. She had the hands of an older woman and the highly arched eyebrows of a drag queen. Linda clearly knew a plastic surgeon or two.

"So, tell me about the kind of work you've been doing at Cohen Garcia."

"I've drafted a few real estate and business contracts. Lots of divorces. I work primarily for Alma Rey." The work didn't sound too impressive to Jessica's ears.

"God, I hated big law firm work. I'd rather not eat than handle another divorce." Linda rolled her eyes.

A little of the interview tension lifted from Jessica's shoulders. "You've worked for a big firm?"

"Yes, years ago. It's a lot more lucrative than the work I do now, but I like to feel like I'm making a difference. And I sleep with a clear conscious."

"I like the way that sounds." Jessica relaxed into her chair. Linda Reed was an interesting woman. Jessica couldn't tell her age. Definitely well over fifty, despite the carnation-pink lipstick and heavy concealer that didn't hide the dark circles under her eyes. She'd paired her suit with a starched white shirt and gold cufflinks that looked expensive, yet she worked in a converted house.

"Good," Linda said. "Let me tell you about the job. I need someone who can work as a paralegal, receptionist, court researcher, basically someone willing to handle any task. I'm the only attorney here and my last assistant decided not to return to work after having a baby. She'll still come help in a pinch, but she's got other priorities now. Also, I only pay about half what the big firms pay. On the other hand, you won't have to work divorces. We do a lot of immigration work, take some criminal cases, and I'm known for helping women in need. That doesn't always pay well, thus the low salary. We do have a healthcare plan, and you're welcome to study here when we're not busy. I expect you to do well in school and pass the bar. This town needs more women attorneys."

The salary cut would be tough, but she already liked this woman and wanted to learn more about the kind of law she practiced. She and Angus would find a way to make it work. Jessica lifted her mug and took a sip of coffee to buy herself time to think.

She almost spewed the vile liquid across the table. Lukewarm, it tasted like three-day-old coffee that someone had cut with motor oil. She managed to swallow, barely. She blinked away the tears of disgust that formed in her eyes. Certain Linda had noticed her reaction, Jessica cut to the chase. "Can we get better coffee?"

Linda laughed. "I've been really strung out looking for help. If you can start Monday, I'll put you in charge of supplies. Sorry. I don't pay attention to stuff like that."

Who was this woman with a strong fashion sense and zero taste buds? Jessica looked around the homey building set in a run-down neighborhood. It felt like a place she could love. Just a block and a half from the county courthouse, near the police headquarters, and surrounded by bail bondsmen, she'd probably get a far better legal education here than in a downtown high-rise. Excitement and adventure crackled in the air around her and emanated from the woman across the table.

Jessica reached an arm toward Linda and shook her hand. "I'll take it."

Linda gave her a tour of the small office. Behind the boardroom sat a tiny kitchen with a door to a backyard of dirt and weeds. Two offices converted from the original bedrooms lined the hallway, along with the lone bathroom. Dark wood or tiled floor contrasted with ivory walls. A few bright paintings hung in the hallway.

Other than Linda's office, which looked like the aftermath of a hurricane, the space had a soothing vibe. Jessica would work in the front room, greeting clients and doing the thousand other things Linda seemed to expect of her. Linda asked her to make herself at home, then came back several minutes later with a contract.

The salary ended up being three quarters of what she made at Alma's. She'd make it work.

She half wanted to hug Linda when she left, but something told her not to. Instead, she shook her hand and said she'd be back Monday. With coffee.

***

Jessica stopped for beans at the coffee shop where she used to work on the way home, determined to convert Linda to decent coffee. She'd have done anything to get the taste of Linda's awful brew out of her mouth. When she walked in, she noticed Lucía sitting at a table, her laptop open.

"Hey, can I get you something to drink?" Jessica asked.

"Hi, Jessi. Sorry about the other night."

"Oh, you mean the intervention? It wasn't my first one. I'm sorry you had to witness that. What are you up to?"

Lucía closed her computer. "Sit." A defiant look came over her face. "I'm investigating Jeremy Wright."

"Oh, no. Please tell me you're not doing that. You need to stay far away from that guy." Damn, this was the case that would never end.

"I have to. I think my friend is in trouble. You're the one that said we just needed to find dirt on him so that we could get Jaime involved. So, I'm trying to find it."

Damn headstrong child. They didn't need two people getting into trouble for this. But if she wouldn't be dissuaded, how did she expect Lucía to be?

"What's your strategy?" Jessica slid into the seat beside her.

"Well, he told me he had been a youth liaison for The Way. So, I called them and said I was interested in working for them in the future. They sent me a job description. His job would have been to travel around one of the Texas regions, meet with high school kids, and help them grow their chapters. Look, you can see the different sectors on this map." Lucía opened the laptop and turned the computer screen toward Jessica.

"I'm sure he worked in the West Texas sector because he never mentioned Houston, Dallas, or San Antonio."

"You are brilliant," Jessica said.

"Not really. Now I'm searching towns against his name, but there are a million small towns in Texas. Happy, Van Horn, Kermit. I haven't gotten very far."

"Fort Stockton." Oh, shit. Jessica pulled her wallet from her pocket. She remembered the receptionist's strange words at Pecos High School. She'd wanted to know where Jeremy's wife was from. Jessica opened her wallet and pulled the business card from between the ones and tens. The receptionist had scrawled *Room 331* under the principal's name and title. She flipped the card over. On the bottom, the woman had written *Fort Stockton Pioneer* 2017.

"Oh, my god. I think I've got it." She'd worried for a second about sharing the information with Lucía, but she deserved to know. And given her talent for research, she'd find it soon anyway. "Check Fort Stockton, 2017. I think they've got a paper called the *Pioneer*."

It took fifteen minutes, and inconceivably for a tiny rural newspaper, getting past a paywall, to find the miniscule article hidden in the May issue. *Jeremy Wright arrested on suspicion of criminal harassment.* An eighteen-year-old had accused him of sexual assault.

"Wow. I was right." Lucía looked at Jessica, her eyes big.

"You were totally right. I'm proud of you."

"What's next? I mean, I have to get to school. I had a late block this morning, but . . ." her voice trailed off.

"You can't miss school. Not when you've got a brain that big to train. Do you need a ride?" The high school was at least a couple of miles away.

"No. I dropped my mom off at work this morning and she let me have the car."

"I'll call the Fort Stockton Police Department and find the records on this. Worst case scenario, I'll put in an open records request. We finally have something concrete on this guy."

"Fine." Lucía stood, but she didn't leave. She stared at Jessica, wanting something else from her.

"What?" Jessica finally asked.

"You were right from the beginning about him. I was wrong. Grace was wrong. We've got to help her."

"If we find out the truth about Jeremy, the police will get him."

"That's going to take too long." She turned to leave.

"It's the best way. Do not do anything until we have more information." Jessica talked to Lucía's back as she left.

Jessica continued the search for information, but the Fort Stockton police records proved to be more like the razor-wire topped metal border fence than a scalable brick wall. They seemed to have dropped the case and expunged all the data. She finally called Jaime to see if he had any police force wizardry that would get them answers about Jeremy's past. She left him a message when he didn't answer.

As a last resort, she called Stan, even though she expected him to be deep in Mexico by now. He answered on the first ring.

"I told you not to call me at this number." He whisper-spat the words, his anxiety clearly turned up to eleven.

"You told me you were leaving town. Are you still here?" Calling him had likely been a mistake, but curiosity pulled her into the conversation.

"I can't share that information, but I'm making progress."

"What the hell does that mean?" she asked.

"There's still no sign of Nora, but three more girls have moved through the ranch. The same guys in the same pickup trucks brought new girls. A different vehicle, one of those two story Mercedes things, took the first two girls away."

Jessica didn't know exactly what to ask, but a steel trap clamped shut in her belly. Girls being transported through the ranch—she hadn't heard of human trafficking in this area, but what else made sense?

"Stan, are you sure about this? And did you happen to get a license plate?" This meant he was back out there, might be there now. The sheriff's deputies had already arrested him for trespassing. If they caught him, he'd surely do time, if he was lucky and law enforcement got to him first.

She'd thought of Jeremy Wright as a certain type of evil, the kind of person who preyed on the weak. Trafficking would be a deeper circle of hell—one where he delivered the weak to be preyed on by others. A chill ran through her.

"I'm too far away for that. Maybe if I had binoculars." He paused for a moment, then his voice broke. "I still haven't found Nora. I just know they've done something terrible to her."

"Hey. You need to be careful. I think this is a whole different level of danger than we expected." They'd been caught so easily the first time.

"I know this land pretty well. Remember, I told you there were hiding places out here. And it's a lot easier without you making all that noise."

That stung, but she had been the one who got them caught. "Is there any way I can help? I think we're closing in on him at this end. He was arrested for criminal harassment in Fort Stockton. We're trying to get the details."

"Harassment sounds about right. Although there are lots of reasons people get arrested. Listen, if I need anything, I'll let you know. Bye."

The call ended. She sat back in her chair, completely ill at ease. Today had ratcheted up the tension in the Jeremy Wright case, but she had no path forward.

Jaime called her back. He'd received her message but hadn't had any luck with the Fort Stockton police. The records had been formally expunged. They no longer existed.

Jaime said he'd run a Texas-wide search on Jeremy and get back to her. She needed to let the professionals handle this one. Well, the professionals and an agitated ex-druggie stranded in the desert. If only she could help.

Chapter 24

The orange sun burned on the western horizon as Jessica left the coffee shop and headed home. The day had given her too much and too little information at the same time. She opened her car window to air out the sunbaked interior and caught the smell of woodsmoke, odd for a warm afternoon.

She drove down into the valley, slightly off kilter. The potential for a new job excited her, but the unfinished business of Jeremy Wright, Nora, Grace, and the mystery girls troubled her. Hopefully, Jaime would find enough information to finish what she'd left undone.

When she pulled into the driveway, she spied a blue card stuck between the door and frame. She hurried over and saw her name scrawled across the paper in her mother's handwriting. The memory of kicking her mom out of her house flitted through her mind, but the accompanying anger had passed. She should have called and apologized.

She brought the paper to her nose before opening it and caught the faint scent of jasmine. It smelled like childhood. She had to try harder to negotiate this new relationship with her mother, but her mother had to respect certain boundaries as well.

Jessica flipped the envelope over and opened it with a finger. A drawing of the historic Plaza Theatre in downtown El Paso decorated the card. She opened it and read.

Jessica,

I love you, but I'm going back to Fort Davis for a bit. I still plan on moving to El Paso, but I need to figure some things out first. I hope someday we can have a better relationship. You are the only important thing in my life.

Love, Mom

A fist gripped Jessica's heart. Why did she suck at this relationship stuff? Finding a missing woman in the desert would be far easier than not hurting her mother, or Angus, or the other people she loved. Although she hadn't found Nora either.

Feelings spun around her in disarray. The unfinished business in the desert. The fragmented relationship with her mother. She wanted to run away from these ghosts or revert to plastering them over with sex and booze. But even more, she wanted to find solutions so they'd quit haunting her.

She opened the door to a bouncing dog full of uncomplicated love. Maybe she should become a crazy dog lady. It seemed a simple, fulfilling life. But that was a cartoon or a meme. She had a real life to live. She texted "I love you" to her mom. And then to Angus.

An urge to do something with her hands overtook her. She wanted to make chili or dig a hole in the backyard like Tela. The wind kicked up and banged a shutter. Things left undone kept her unsettled. Angus texted back three hearts. Everything was good. She had a good life. This unaimed energy would pass.

She started cleaning the house, not her favorite job, but something to do. First, she swept the floor with vigor and placed the dishes in the drying rack back on their shelves. She found a bottle of cleaner deep under the bathroom sink and sprayed every surface in the small room. Then she scrubbed, burning through fumes, through energy, through worry.

The phone rang. Alma. Jessica longed to tell her about the intriguing woman she'd met who offered her a job working a side of the law she'd yet to see. Less buttoned up, more her speed. But that also meant telling Alma she wouldn't be returning, even if asked. And Alma had given her so much more than a job. She'd given her a chance at a better life. Was wanting to leave a betrayal? Or perhaps not listening, getting arrested, and endangering Alma's job were the betrayals. She answered, but Alma had already hung up.

Jessica called her back. "Hey, how's it going?"

"I just saw Lucía when she came to pick up Paz. She said you two had found something on Jeremy Wright. I don't think she should be involved in this."

"Honestly, I just happened upon her in the coffee shop. She was already researching him." Christ. Had she yet again done something to upset everyone?

"And then?" Alma didn't sound happy.

"We researched him together and found something. The cops in Fort Stockton arrested him, but we couldn't figure out anything else, so she left for school, and I kept researching. I turned the information over to Jaime Castro like we should. Everything seemed fine." But the entire afternoon had pressed in on her with its odd energy. She looked out the window. The horizon still glowed where the sun had set, but a deep, inky blue covered most of the sky.

Alma sighed. "Thanks for letting me know, and I hope you did find something on that guy that will stick. I'm sorry if I sounded accusing. I worry about Lucía and Paz. I'm glad my kids aren't teenagers yet."

"Hey, I have a question for you. Do you know Linda Reed?" She hoped Alma would approve of Linda and would see this as a way out of a difficult situation for both of them.

"The attorney? Of course." Alma didn't volunteer any additional information. Jessica pictured the files piled on Alma's desk, especially now that she was down a paralegal.

"I met with her earlier today. She offered me a job." Jessica held her breath, waiting for a response.

Alma's silence spoke volumes. Another sigh. "You're leaving us."

"Well, I am on double secret probation, and you told me it didn't look good." Suddenly, some of Jessica's burden lightened. This was the right thing.

"Did you tell her about your recent arrest?" Alma's question slapped the burden back down, ten times greater.

"I didn't think about it." She hadn't. She should have.

"Well, you should have. She might not want to work with someone in legal jeopardy. Honestly, Jessica, you've got to grow up and take responsibility for your actions."

Jessica deserved the hit. "You're right. I'll call her back."

One more huge sigh from Alma. "Listen, I understand that everything you did, you did to help. But Linda is a good person, and she deserves to know what's going on with you. I do think you'd learn a ton from her. And you're right, it would be hard to keep you on here. I'll miss you though. You do good work."

"Thank you." The compliment surprised her, a shaft of light in a dark conversation.

The second they ended the call, Jessica tried Linda. No one picked up at the firm, so she left a message. She'd have to get her cell phone number.

Jessica fed the dog and thought about cracking a beer. But Angus wouldn't be home for hours, and booze wouldn't be the best way to deal with her unsettled emotions. She drank a glass of water instead.

***

Thirty minutes later, her phone rang. She hoped for Linda or Angus. It might be her mother. Hopefully, she'd call when she got to Fort Davis so Jessica would know she'd made the trip all right.

She didn't recognize the number. "Hello?"

"Is this Jessica Watts?" a woman whispered.

"Yes. Who is this?"

"It's Emmy Wright. You've got to come out here."

A tight knot formed in the pit of Jessica's stomach. She swallowed. "Where? To the ranch? Why?" What the hell?

"Jeremy got a call that there's going to be a raid on the ranch tomorrow."

"Good." Jessica couldn't have thought of a better solution to this whole fiasco. She wondered if the information she'd provided Jaime had helped.

"Not good. He's going to hole up in some cabin in the hills here. And he's got Grace and two other girls. And Lucía. That stupid girl came back out here."

Nausea swept through her body. Not this. "What are you talking about, and why are you whispering?"

"Shhh. I'm not going to be able to talk long. A sheriff's vehicle showed up a couple of hours ago. After he left, Jeremy made us pack things into the truck. Then Lucía showed up."

"Why is Lucía there? What have you done with her?" Jessica couldn't keep the panic from her voice, but somehow, she managed not to scream into the phone.

"Jeremy handcuffed her. I don't know what he's planning, but you have to come save us."

"No way. Let me get the cops out there. They'll be able to help."

"No!" If he sees lights and sirens, he'll kill us all. He's killed before. Poor Pastor Harris. He was such a good man." Emmy sobbed. "Please, you have to help."

"If he's got a gun, then I'm no match for him. I have to get help. You should have called the police, not me."

"I can't call the sheriff's department, Jeremy's benefactors have too many connections with them. You gave me your card. You're the only person I know in this purgatory."

"I promise. I can get help. I'll call right now."

"Don't hang up. If you want Lucía to live, you'll do exactly what I tell you. I have a plan, and it's the only way." The woman sounded desperate.

"What's your plan?" Jessica asked, trying to buy time.

"I can distract him. I know how. Then you can get the girls out."

Worst. Plan. Ever. But Jessica needed as much information as possible. "Will you be in the house?"

"First, promise me you'll come alone. He'll shoot them if the police come."

"Sure," Jessica lied. "Where will I meet you?"

"There's a house or shed or something in the hills behind the barn. Just follow the road. Please come quick."

The call dropped. Dread sunk through her like a lead weight, but she had to move, fast. Rushing, she put on black jeans and the same black hoodie she'd used the night they'd arrested her. She grabbed her flashlights and headed to the truck.

Jessica let her phone tell her the fastest route to the ranch and did her best to keep the truck's speed just below where she thought she'd get pulled over. Somehow, the truck kept sliding above that speed, and she had a hard time slowing back down. Time was everything right now.

Chapter 25

She debated whether to call Jaime or Paz first. If she called Paz, she might go out there and make the situation worse. But if she didn't tell her and something happened, she'd never be forgiven.

She asked her phone to text Paz. "Is Lucía there? I wanted to follow up on our conversation."

It took less than a minute for Paz to respond. "She's studying late at a friend's"

She directed her phone to send Paz the thumbs up emoji, then asked it to text Lucía. "Are you studying with a friend? Please answer. Emergency."

Nothing.

Maybe Emmy had lied. Maybe Lucía was studying and had turned her phone off. Not likely. Maybe she'd snuck off with the flaming hot Cheeto boy. Her gut told her Lucía was in trouble. Jessica pressed on the accelerator.

She called Jaime. He didn't pick up. Damn. She wanted to leave a detailed message about Emmy's call, including that they might have Lucía and that she'd been told to go to the ranch alone or Jeremy would kill his hostages. But what if Emmy was right? Finally, she just said, "Call me back. It's an emergency."

She didn't call Angus. She didn't know what to say. She'd caused this, turned up the temperature on Jeremy Wright, bumbled around without accomplishing anything. She needed to get to Lucía more than she'd ever needed anything. And she wanted Jaime to return her call.

She didn't want to imagine what Lucía faced tonight. She remembered her own dark night in Juarez. Just when her life had been about to turn around, thugs had shown up to kidnap and kill her. She'd managed to escape. But she'd been twenty-eight, not sixteen. And she'd been fueled by anger and regret. She definitely had not been trying to help a friend. Her foot pressed heavily on the accelerator.

She tried Jaime again when she left the road. Still no answer. She didn't trust the sheriff's department and debated calling the El Paso Police dispatch number, but the ranch was far outside of their jurisdiction. Protocol would force them to send the call to the sheriff's office.

When she reached the Dominion sign, she tried Jaime again. No signal. She calculated the time it would take to drive back to where her phone would work. Five minutes. Ten. Fifteen. If Jaime didn't answer, she could try someone else with the police, or maybe Alma knew someone.

Emmy said he'd shoot the girls if the police came. Some furious animal deep inside her yelled at her to go get Lucía. To stop wasting time.

She hit the gas, and the truck skidded on dirt as she turned into the drive. She pushed the truck harder, and it rattled over the gravel and drifted in the curves. Finally, she arrived at the eerily dark house. One of the barrack doors hung open.

She headed alongside the barn, then past the motorhomes. She'd looked up the trail to the cabin after Stan told her about it. From the satellite view, it couldn't be called a road, just faint tire marks through sand, rock, and sage. She hit the accelerator again.

She thought about turning her headlights out. They'd surely be able to see her coming. But she had miles to go, and her fear of driving into a gully kept the lights on, for now.

The road quickly became worse. Her truck swung into holes, then climbed back out. Corners of soft sand threatened to entrap her. Mounds of dirt topped by creosote blocked her view as the trail weaved between them. She wanted to go faster, to catch up with them before anything bad happened, but she'd easily break an axle if she drove faster.

She spun around a particularly high dune and almost crashed into Paz's Camry. Emmy hadn't lied. Dread threatened to immobilize her, but Lucía needed her.

Jessica stopped the truck and hopped out. She listened. Nothing, just the sound of wind rustling the sage and sparse grasses. Sand had swallowed the front left tire of the Camry. A mound of freshly turned grit at the back of the tire showed Jessica that the car's driver didn't know the desert.

She'd probably driven a couple of miles from the ranch and had a couple more to go. The Camry's passengers must have gotten into Jeremy's truck. She hadn't seen it at the ranch, and wide tire tracks continued past the Camry. She listened in the night gone silent. Surely, she'd hear them if they were close.

Jessica returned to her truck. She rolled the window down and this time kept the headlights off. She drove more slowly, using whatever light came from the slim moon and glowing stars to illuminate her way. Barely touching the accelerator, she let the truck roll through the solemn night.

Time seemed to move in inches instead of hours. The truck shuddered over a large rock she hadn't seen but kept going. She crossed a wash that would turn into a raging flood during a rainstorm. The road turned up the next wash, and the driving became more difficult. The tracks turned from mostly sand to fist-sized polished stones. Tiny cliffs marked the height of the last flood.

The road turned off the wash and climbed toward one of the hills. A set of fresh tire tracks lit her way. The truck's engine strained up the hill. She had to be getting close.

The road swung around a boulder twice her height. Behind it the tracks continued, but a flat area just the right size for her truck sat between the boulder and a scrubby tree. She pulled in and turned the vehicle off. The noisy truck would alert them to her arrival. She'd walk from here.

Jessica opened the glove box. The blue flashlight hadn't saved her from trouble last time. Tonight, her eyes would have to adjust to the darkness. She reached for the taser.

She continued down the path, feeling eyes on her. Did Stan know she'd arrived? Perhaps a mountain lion watched her. Worst case, Jeremy had seen her coming, but since she hadn't seen the cabin yet, hopefully, he couldn't see her. Hopefully.

She paced along the fresh tire tracks, winding deeper into the chasm between the two hills. They crowded her, she'd have preferred the open desert where the moonlight stretched along the ground instead of a canyon that sucked in all the light. She chose not to use the flashlight. She wouldn't become a target, and she refused to give Jeremy a reason to hurt anyone.

She imagined the scene ahead. A dilapidated wooden cabin. Two adults and four children. One or more of the kids with their hands tied. There would likely be a gun. Hopefully, Emmy would side with her, as she'd said. But she'd likely sided with Jeremy in the past.

What kind of woman would stand by and let other women get hurt? It pained her to consider even someone as strange as Emmy a party to that level of depravity. Women could be such damaged goods. She was. But there needed to be a social contract to help each other. After all, didn't men cause most of the trouble? They had in her life, although her mom had helped.

She couldn't think about her own troubles. Not tonight. She paused, hearing rustling in the brush, but whatever it was became silent when she stopped. She had to be close.

She came to a fork in the road, one she didn't remember seeing on the satellite image. The fresh tire tracks led up a rise to the right. She followed, hiking up a steep twenty yards. Atop the rise, she could almost feel the ground shallowing to a small bowl.

She thought she caught the glint of a vehicle in the faint moonlight. For a moment, silence surrounded her, save for her labored breathing. As her eyes adjusted to looking into the distance instead of at the track at her feet, she noticed a dark patch on the far side of the vehicle. That must be the cabin, but it was completely black. Surely, they had lights—flashlights, lanterns, something.

About halfway to the cabin, a low wall ran along a portion of the road. Strange. Staying in the fresh tire tracks, she headed that way.

Anyone in the cabin might see her, especially since they had their lights out and the moon and stars may have lit her form despite her black clothing. But she had no choice except to move forward. Every step brought her closer to Lucía.

She reached the wall and realized it formed a square. Within the wall lay an ancient cemetery. Perfect. She prayed they wouldn't need it tonight.

She left the trail at the edge of the graveyard and cut through the brush. The obvious choice of the road left her too exposed. She closed in on the cabin, doing her best to remain silent. She tried to clear her mind of snakes and tarantulas, which only made her think about them more. A soft patch of sand grabbed her foot and brought her to one knee. She rose, and step by difficult step, she closed in on the cabin.

Finally, she stopped behind a creosote topped mini hill. Now what? Her thoughts admonished her for coming out here without the police and pushed her onward toward a confrontation with Jeremy.

She stopped the rambling thoughts and focused on the truth. She hadn't gone back for the police because she feared they wouldn't do anything. They hadn't so far, and the ranch lay beyond their jurisdiction. She'd made the decision to come out here the second Emmy had called and told her about Lucía.

Jeremy had packed up and left, taking his human cargo with him. For some reason she'd never understand, people and agencies she should depend on for safety protected the bad guy.

Jaime had done his best, but even he had trouble making progress on this case. It was like the sheriff, the mayor, and others couldn't believe one of their own would do something wrong. That's why they'd arrested her and Stan. That's why the ex-mayor fed her mom a load of bullshit. That's why she couldn't rely on them tonight. Tonight, she would rely on herself.

So now she needed a plan. She had to draw him out and incapacitate him. Once she'd accomplished that, she'd escape with Lucía. The heft of the flashlight gave her a sense of security. She could do this.

Jessica crept as close as possible to the truck. The sand softened near the vehicle and cabin. It allowed her to move silently. When she took off with her half-assed plan, she'd worried she'd freeze from fear. Instead, the calm of the desert night steadied her. She belonged in this land of sand and rock. Out here, she was the hunter, not the prey.

She sidled up to the rectangular building. Its wood planks had gone silver with age and moonlight. The front of the cabin had a closed door and no windows. She settled along one side of the building. It had a window once, but someone had boarded over it long ago.

With each step she'd taken across the desert, her fear had diminished. Rage replaced it like a long-lost friend. When thugs had kidnapped her, driven her to Juarez, threatened to kill her, this same fury had washed through her. Why did women have to deal with injustice over and over? The constant threat men held over them infuriated her. That she couldn't trust the sheriffs flamed her rage. Men like Jeremy grasped at power, and the more they seized, the more they used it against others.

She welcomed back the anger coursing through her veins. It made her stronger and meaner. It made her a threat as dark and evil as the night.

She'd found three rocks slightly smaller than palm sized as she cased the building and had slipped them into the front pockets of her jeans. Now she removed them. She gripped the stun gun flashlight in her right, dominant hand. That meant throwing with her left. She figured it'd work out, given the size and proximity of the truck.

Jessica lifted the first stone and tossed it overhand into the middle of the truck's windshield. The sharp smack of stone hitting tempered glass rang through the quiet night and the rock skidded off the far side of the vehicle.

Murmuring started inside the cabin followed by shushing. Jessica let the second stone fly. This one soared wide and clanged on the roof of the truck before skittering away.

"Who's out there? I know you're out there. I've got a gun." Heavy footfalls on a wooden floor, then the door creaked open. A dim shaft of light spilled into the night. Jessica slitted her eyes to preserve her night vision. She let her anger completely take over, and it slowed her heartbeat and breath. This would be over soon. She would win.

She heard him step into the sand and hoped he'd move toward her. That's why she'd chosen the windshield. He'd walk toward her, past her hiding place on the side of the building, to investigate the damage.

Just like she'd envisioned, he walked toward the truck, into her line of sight. He had a rifle. She wished for time to assess this new information, but time no longer existed. It had disappeared the second she laid eyes on the devil in front of her. Only action mattered now. Would he step forward again, turn toward her, return to the cabin?

He swung the gun wildly back and forth as she melded into the cabin wall, dark as night. At least she told herself that. Then he stepped toward the truck and leaned forward to examine the windshield.

She ran two steps toward him, the taser part of the flashlight already turned on. He swung toward her, but she managed to slip past the rifle's snout. She jammed the flashlight into his side. A loud crackle pierced the night, followed immediately by Jeremy's guttural yell.

She slammed him into the side of the truck, her body making contact with the arm that held the rifle. He dropped it, then fell to his knees.

She owned him now. Still trapping his arm against the truck with her body, she pressed the stun gun into his neck, and he whimpered and jerked. It took all her strength to keep him pinned to the truck. She imagined the reverberations of electricity traveling from his body to hers and back out the hand that held the stun gun to his neck.

Finally, he went limp and dropped to the sand. She reached for the rifle and flung it out of reach. The sharp smell of ozone burned through her nostrils, fueling her adrenaline. She wanted to kill him. Quickly, she lifted the flashlight and brought it down hard on his temple. He stopped moving. Perhaps she had killed him, although probably not. She wished she had a zip tie like the one the sheriff's deputy had used to handcuff her. She still felt the burn from when it cut into her wrists.

Hate for this man flooded her. She wanted to cut off the hand that had touched Lucía. She wanted to bring the flashlight down on his skull again and again. *Stop*. Jessica inhaled. She had to pull herself together, get beyond the warped joy of conquering this devil.

She took two deep breaths. Lucía. The thought brought her back to herself.

She turned off the flashlight's stun function, stepped away from Jeremy, and grabbed the rifle. Heavy and awkward, she managed to get the gun under one arm while still holding the flashlight in the other.

She moved to the door of the cabin and stood beside it to give herself a little protection in case there was another gun. Then she shone the light inside.

Chapter 26

A huddle of bodies formed a mass in a back corner of the small room. "Lucía?" Jessica croaked, struggling to get the word past the fear of what she'd find.

"I'm here." Her small voice came through the pile which slowly disassembled into individuals.

Thank god. Jessica shone the light around the spare cabin. Emmy slumped in one corner, hands behind her back. Her head lolled to one side, eyes closed. Her mouth hung open. What had Jeremy done? Hopefully he'd just incapacitated the woman, not killed her.

Jessica leaned the gun against the door. She'd have these girls out of the cabin and headed back toward the ranch in a few seconds.

She ran toward Lucía. Kneeling, she pulled her up to a sitting position, but the girl yelped in pain.

"Ow. My arms."

Here were the zip ties she'd needed, wrapped around Lucía's bleeding wrists. But she was okay.

A gunshot blasted through the night.

Jessica spun around, shining the flashlight through the single room building. Emmy was gone, as was the rifle. Terror clutched her.

"Get down," she told the girls. Four sets of terrified eyes stared at her. She turned back to the door, wishing she could hide them all, and doing her best to place her body in front of theirs. She shone the flashlight at the door, hoping the light provided some small measure of protection. Perhaps it would blind the person on entry.

A blond woman carrying a rifle appeared in the doorway. Emmy. She held the gun comfortably in her arms, cradling it like she knew its curves.

"Stop shining that light at me," Emmy said.

"Put the gun down." Somehow Jessica's voice remained calm, authoritative even. But she despised the position she'd put these girls in. Perhaps Emmy and her husband were equally evil.

Silence stretched between them. "I heard a shot," Jessica said.

Emmy laughed, an ugly, eerie noise. "Yes. Someone finally got what he deserved."

Jessica could no longer rely on tricks and tools. As long as Emmy held the gun, she'd have to keep her talking. "Did you kill him?"

"Yes. I felt the power of God for one of the first times in my life when I pulled the trigger. Tonight, the angels sing."

Jessica slow-blinked, while the girls whimpered behind her. The woman sounded insane. Maybe insane enough to keep killing. "Did he hurt you?" she asked.

Emmy raised the gun, pointed it at Jessica. "Isn't that what men do?"

"Some of them. Not all of them." Jessica tried to sound soothing.

"All of them!" Emmy screamed. "All of them!" The gun swung wildly.

Jessica raised her hands, as if in surrender, but kept the flashlight trained on Emmy. "It's okay. He's gone now."

"It will never be okay. Not as long as there are women and girls to feed the beast. You know what these men do."

"Did he come to your high school?" Jessica asked. It was a longshot, but the second she asked, the light in Emmy's eyes changed.

No longer wild, she seemed trapped in a memory. "He spoke there, long ago. All the girls liked him. Those slutty girls in their little cheerleading outfits with shirts that bared their navels. They'd shove their breasts in his face, rest their hands on him. I knew what they wanted. But he didn't want them."

She paused, and Jessica feared they'd lose the momentum of the story. She had to keep Emmy talking or get her to break down crying and hand over the gun. Or Jessica would figure out a way to disarm her. "He wanted you, didn't he?"

Emmy straightened, but the gun still pointed at Jessica. "He said he could tell I'd been touched by God. He knew I was a good girl and that I wanted to learn to serve the Lord. For the first time in my damned life, he made me feel unique. And beautiful." Emmy paused. "Then he showed me the bad girl hiding inside me. He made me want what I'd always hated." Her face and voice morphed into something ugly.

So, Jeremy had a formula. He knew how to pick out the girls who most needed attention. Those soft-hearted women who endured lectures about promiscuity but had love in their souls and sex in their bodies. Easy targets. "I'm so sorry."

"Sorry?" Emmy looked confused.

"I'm sorry you had to go through that."

"There's no need to be sorry. We're all the devil's work. Me. You. Those girls." She lowered the gun just enough that Jessica worried she might shoot someone just to make a point.

Jessica waved her empty hand near her head, just a little, hoping Emmy would raise the gun to that position. "You're not the devil. He took advantage of you."

"It is a woman's work to serve man," Emmy said. "In every way they need to be served. I thought I could control him when he came back. I knew The Way had fired him. The things he did to me, he did to others, and they found out." She looked and sounded like a robot, a Stepford wife.

Then, someone sobbed behind Jessica. The room, which had narrowed to Emmy and Jessica, became wide again. Jessica tried to quietly shush the girl.

Emmy lit up like a lightening flash. "Do you think you're better than me? We are all the devil's work." She stepped forward, gun raised.

"Emmy, don't," Jessica snapped. The woman's face shot toward Jessica. "What happened in Big Spring? Were you able to control him?"

"Ha! What a stupid woman I was. He saw right through me. He told me he knew how much I hated him. He said he wanted me to love him.

He bought me gifts, but I paid for them in so many ways. Pastor Harris paid too. Jeremy stole from him."

"Did he kill Pastor Harris?"

An evil smile lit Emmy's lips. "Did you know I was a nursing student before Jeremy came back to Big Spring? My daddy had heart problems too. I found a permanent solution to Daddy's problem. Then, when Pastor Harris found out about the money, Jeremy needed my help."

"So, you—helped—him?" Had this woman really admitted she killed two men? She had to get these girls away from Emmy. Her eyes scanned the cabin and found nothing but a few backpacks in a corner too far away to reach.

Emmy's face transformed again. "I set it up perfectly. Jeremy should have taken over the church once Pastor Harris was out of the way. I told him that, but he panicked when he found out what I'd done. He said he needed to move so he could hide me. Liar. He moved here to feed his vices. We should have stayed in Big Spring instead of coming to this filthy place." She swung the rifle as she said the last words.

"What happened to Nora?" Jessica had to ask and prayed it wouldn't set Emmy off. Clearly, she'd had some kind of psychotic break.

"She got in the way. Jeremy didn't mean to kill her, he just got scared when she started yelling at him. He hit her with the shovel, then buried her with it. It doesn't matter. She was just another whore."

"No." Jessica whispered. "She was a good person." Grief crawled through Jessica. She hated Emmy, seemingly so unaffected by murder.

"There are no good ones." Emmy looked Jessica straight in the eye. "We are all whores. We all must pay." She lifted the gun to her shoulder.

Terror flooded Jessica. She wouldn't let four girls die in an isolated desert cabin. She took a deep breath and rose. Standing as tall as possible, she raised her arms wide. "Take me," she spat. "I'm actually a whore. I've fucked more guys than you've probably even met." She took a step forward as she spoke.

Emmy seemed taken aback and actually looked awake instead of crazed. But she still held the rifle at shooting height.

"You're not a whore," Jessica continued. "He hurt you. I'm the whore. I did it for pleasure. I took comfort in strangers." Her booming voice filled the room, and she took another step forward. "I lusted after men, found them in bars, searched out the ones who would please me." Holy shit, if she survived this, she'd have a lot of explaining to do to Lucía.

"We are all evil!" Emmy lowered her head to the gun sight.

Suddenly a body flew out of the darkness toward Emmy. It was Lucía, head down and hands still clasped behind her back. Lucía roared as she ran, then screamed. "You can't shoot her!"

Jessica jumped toward Emmy. One hand touched the cold steel of the deadly instrument, the other shoved Emmy away from it. A blast from the gun shook everything around them, seemed to ignite the very air with fury.

"Lucía!" Jessica didn't know if the scream had passed through her lungs or remained in her head. Emmy fell backward. Lucía slumped to the ground. Jessica's momentum drove her forward, into and on top of Emmy, pushing the gun away the whole time.

Time slowed. Emmy's head bounced on the wooden floor. Jessica fought to control the gun clutched in Emmy's hand. She moved so that she lay on the woman's arm, keeping her from maneuvering the rifle. Emmy lay limp beneath her, and Jessica pried her fingers from the weapon. She moved Emmy's head, opened her eyes. The woman seemed truly unconscious this time.

Jessica got up and staggered to the cabin door, checking to make sure Jeremy was indeed dead before flinging the weapon into the sand. She wished she hadn't looked. Most of his upper torso and head were gone, and blood splattered across the pickup.

The second she let go of the gun, she spun around and ran to Lucía who sobbed on the dirty wooden floor. Somehow, she was alive. Jessica patted her down. She hadn't been shot. Kneeling down, she embraced Lucía in a giant hug. "Everything is fine. It's okay now. You're safe."

She'd lied. After this, Lucía likely wouldn't feel safe for years. Jessica had rarely felt safe since thugs had kidnapped her from her own home.

This kind of trauma changed a person. Jessica looked toward the corner of the cabin where the other girls still huddled.

"Is everyone okay? Was anyone shot?" Jessica asked. She hadn't seen any blood on Emmy, and Lucía seemed whole. As Jessica looked at the three girls still huddled together, she recognized Grace, her light brown hair falling out of its conservative bun and her face wet with tears.

"Are you all right? Can you check the others?" Jessica asked. The other two girls leaned into each other, their faces turned toward the floor. Grace pointed toward a hole in the ceiling and the splintered wood above it. Thank god.

"They don't speak English," Lucía whispered.

Jessica looked down at her. "I'm so glad you're all right. You really scared me."

"I couldn't let her shoot you."

"You shouldn't have risked your life, but thank you." She'd give her life a hundred times for this girl with the bright future.

"But if she'd killed you, then she would have come for us."

"You're probably right." Jessica squeezed Lucía fiercely. This ridiculous brave girl. "Sorry about all the slutty stuff. I was trying to distract her."

"It's cool. I knew you had a reputation."

Jessica laughed at the total nonchalance of Lucía's statement. She did have a reputation, and tonight wouldn't help it.

Jessica carefully grabbed her flashlight, which had fallen to the ground in her tussle with Emmy. She double checked that the stun device remained off. Then, she extricated herself from Lucía to check out the backpacks in the corner. She rummaged through both, finding water, snack bars, zip ties, and a multiuse knife. She cut through the girls' zip ties and gave them each a bottle of water.

Next, she leaned Emmy against the wall and zip tied her hands behind her. The woman still had a pulse but was out cold.

Finally, she spoke with the other two girls. Grace was right, they only spoke Spanish. Jessica learned they were cousins who had traveled north from Guatemala with ten other people. Two turned back at the

US border, while the remaining eight paid coyotes to help them cross. Jessica hated coyotes, the human devils who agreed to cross people into the States for a fee. Far from honorable, they often set people up to be captured, or worse, took their money and then left them to die in the desert.

When Jessica asked what had happened to the people they traveled with, the girls began to cry. They'd crossed the river, then walked for miles, following the coyote's directions. When they reached the pickup location, men waited for them in trucks.

The older of the two spoke about how her father whooped with joy, happy to have completed their journey. Then one of the men shot him. They shot everyone else. Then they put the two girls in one of the trucks and brought them to the ranch. The girls waited for someone to kill them too. At least then they could be with their families again.

Jessica dropped her head into her hands. What an incredibly cruel world. Immigrants headed north in hopes of finding a safe place to live and raise their families. They weren't here to steal jobs or hurt Americans. They just wanted to survive. And instead, they'd been slaughtered. Except for these two who might have faced a future even worse than death. Who knew what lay ahead of them, even now?

Jessica vowed to help them however she could. She would also find the rot on her side of the border that had allowed, maybe even encouraged, this to happen. Her spine straightened with resolve. And purpose.

Emmy stirred. Jessica got up, opened a bottle of water, and sprayed it into her face. She sputtered, tried to lurch forward, but her bound wrists stopped her. She blinked the water out of her eyes.

"What were you going to do with the girls?" Jessica couldn't control the rage in her voice.

"I have no idea." Emmy's face was closed, her words sharp.

"I don't believe you. You had other girls go through the ranch. You said you were the devil. What hell did you have planned for them?"

"I. Don't. Know. They come in. I'm supposed to teach them to do household chores. I clean them up, teach them manners, make them look nice. We were supposed to get someone to teach them rudimentary English, but that hadn't happened yet. Jeremy didn't share all of his plans with me, but I think we can both figure out what grown men want with young women." She seemed indignant.

"Where do they go when they leave the ranch?" The lack of answers frustrated Jessica.

"The same guys who drop them off pick them back up again. It's a group that works to stop illegals coming in from Mexico. People like them don't deserve to be here." She nodded toward the girls, a sneer in her voice.

Quick as a rattlesnake, Jessica slapped Emmy. "You bitch. They are just as deserving of a life as you and me. Maybe more so."

"Don't. It's not worth it." Lucía's voice reached Jessica, snapping her out of her anger. She was right. They'd each been broken in different ways. Emmy through what she'd endured with Jeremy. The traumatized girls who'd seen their family shot before them. Grace and Lucía who'd found themselves in the belly of a world that would haunt them. And Jessica had always found her own way to break. Tonight, she'd likely broken her marriage, her career, and her relationships with the people she held dearest.

She turned away from Emmy. Except for Lucía, the others still cowered in the corner. She couldn't do much to help them here. They needed to hike to her truck, and then she'd get help.

She looked at the Guatemalan cousins. They'd likely be held in a deportation center. With no family here to help them, who knows how long they'd stay in a subpar facility with no one to advocate for them? They had already faced so much.

She hobbled over to the cabin's wall and sank down, leaning against it. Suddenly bone tired, she didn't know if she had the energy to keep going. Was this truly the same day as her interview? That seemed like a century ago. And last night with Angus hadn't exactly been restful. Her mind traveled across everything that might have exhausted her but didn't settle until she remembered the fight with Jeremy and her thirst for violence.

He'd transformed her into everything she'd ever hated. She'd wanted to hurt him, to kill him even. That level of darkness took up new space in her body and robbed her of a part of herself. Jessica had always thought of herself as a badass, but she'd just played a role. She'd worn black denim, cussed, mainlined tequila.

Tonight, she met evil with her own darkness, and it flowed deeper than she'd ever imagined. Deep enough to kill. In the past, she'd hidden that dark, depraved part of herself. Tonight, she embraced it, and she'd do it again and again if it protected people like Lucía and the Guatemalan girls. That meant she'd have to drag her tired ass off the floor and help them now.

She thought about the men in pickup trucks. They needed to be stopped. Somehow, they'd tied themselves into the coyote network, Jeremy, and maybe even the sheriff. That knot of snakes would be tough to unravel, but it had to happen. She'd talk to Jaime about that one. Her flashlight/stun gun couldn't take on men stocked with guns and cruelty.

She turned to Emmy. "Why'd you set me up?"

Emmy's ugly smile transformed her face. "We each had something to give the other. I wanted an end to living in a barren land with nothing but a stream of young women passing through for my husband to taunt me with. You wanted to be a hero. Anyone could see that. You'd stop at nothing, no level of stupidity, to save someone. Someday you'll figure out that no one is ever saved."

Jessica looked around the cabin, fearing some kind of booby trap, then realized Emmy meant God. The same God that Jeremy had turned into a weapon of evil. The God that lit Lucía's life. Dark and light. Blessing and curse. Perhaps everyone shared the struggle.

Chapter 27

Jessica pushed herself up from the floor. "Girls, we've got a long walk ahead of us. Let's go." She'd addressed Lucía and Grace who sat together near the backpacks, then she turned to the other two and repeated herself in Spanish.

They all looked like they'd trudged through hell, and they'd have to parade past a dead body before the hike even began. Jessica heard shuffling and saw Emmy trying to rise to her feet.

"No. You're not going anywhere." She crossed to the woman, zip tie in hand, to bind her ankles. Emmy would certainly wander off into the desert and find a way to die. Snakes, mountain lions, stupidity. The desert gave a person a hundred choices about death. Jessica wouldn't be responsible for that.

"You can't leave me here like this." She kicked a foot at Jessica.

"Lucía, come help me." Jessica shot a look at the young woman who returned a frightened glance. "It's for her own good. I don't want her to leave the cabin and find a way to get killed out there."

"But I want to die. I have to die. You can't send me back to that world of men." For the first time, Emmy looked afraid.

Jessica pushed her legs down and pressed her shin into Emmy's just below her knees. "I have a feeling you'll be surrounded by women." Although the abuse wouldn't end in a female penitentiary. Lucía grabbed the zip tie and tightened it around Emmy's ankles.

"What happened to you?" Lucía asked.

"You're one of the whores. You already know." Scorn pierced Emmy's voice.

Lucía sat back, shock on her face. Then Jessica watched as defiance took over.

"I am not a whore."

"Didn't you go with him in his car?" Emmy nodded toward the door. Jessica pictured her decapitated, bloody husband. Emmy had killed him. Jessica would have, but only if he was a threat.

"No." Lucía said with conviction, and the solitary word turned a girl into a woman. Lucía crossed her arms.

"Well, you would have. I did. When I was fifteen. He got me pregnant. Maybe. It might have been my daddy's. All their talk about God and salvation, yet they ripped my baby from my womb." Emmy didn't cry. She'd returned to the unemotional, robot-like woman from earlier. Jessica knew what toll that kind of emotional displacement took on a person.

Lucía did cry, as did Grace. Fortunately, the two Guatemalan girls hadn't understood Emmy. They'd been through enough.

"Well, I certainly can't walk you through the desert with four innocent girls." The words sounded harsh, if true. "You just murdered your husband. As soon as I've got cell service, I'll call the authorities and have someone pick you up."

"No!" Fear returned to Emmy's voice. "They love him. They act like he's the second coming. Who knows what they'll do to me when they find I've taken their golden son away?"

Jessica looked at the woman, now visibly distraught and so caught in her own nightmare that she couldn't see the truth.

"They didn't like him because they thought he was the second coming. They liked him because he was useful to them. Whatever those guys in pickups are doing, it's illegal. You and Jeremy provided cover for that activity. This is not about God."

Emmy looked at her with desperate eyes. Blue irises pulled her in as if she were falling down a well, then, just as she was about to sink into a pit of terror, the light cut out. Emmy's face relaxed, her shoulders sank against the wall, dull eyes staring blankly ahead.

"We're leaving now," Jessica said. No response. Nothing. Just a vacant stare without even the twitch of a muscle. Emmy's derangement scared her more than men with rifles.

"Girls, let's go. Vámanos."

They walked into the night. The cousins had on filthy sneakers with duct tape around the toes. Grace wore sandals. Not great options for trekking through the desert. "This is going to be a long and difficult walk. It will help if you don't complain. The night will be over soon." She didn't bother repeating her words in Spanish. Those girls knew about walking through this arid land.

She grabbed the rifle and tried to keep her body between the girls and Jeremy as they left. Of course it didn't work. She heard the gasps. "Just keep going around the back of the truck," she said.

They found the faint tire tracks and began their journey. Twenty yards from the cabin, Jessica heaved the rifle into the desert. She didn't trust Emmy not to find a way out of her predicament. She'd never find the rifle out here and wouldn't be able to shoot herself or whoever came to rescue her.

Grace tripped and fell to her knees, sobbing. Lucía rushed to her, but Jessica gently pushed her away and knelt in front of Grace. "Sweetie, this has been a terrible night. But you have to be strong now. We must get out of here." The girl just cried harder.

She stood back up and pulled her special flashlight out of her back pocket. After turning the light on, she handed it to Grace. "Please don't touch any other buttons, this thing is very dangerous. I'll explain later." She hoped giving the girl a job would help her stay focused.

Jessica hadn't wanted anyone else to carry the flashlight and accidentally deploy the stun gun. But she also needed to be at the back of the group, between the girls and the horror behind them.

Lucía pulled Grace out of the sand and led her to the front of the group as her tears subsided. As they walked, Jessica kept glancing toward the Eastern horizon, searching for that faint white glow that signaled daybreak. She had a feeling morning wouldn't arrive for hours. She'd stowed her phone in the truck. Reception didn't exist out here. She'd also worried some sound or light from it would give her away.

She'd have to make phone calls as soon as possible. Jaime needed to know first. She sure as hell wasn't going to call the sheriff. She wished she could figure out how to protect the quiet cousins who walked in front of her. Perhaps she'd call Alma or Linda. Jessica hadn't even started working for the woman, but she seemed wise and didn't have an entire law firm to drag her down.

Angus was last on her list, and he wouldn't be happy about that. She'd thought once she'd said yes and stopped screwing around, literally, that things would be easy. But she'd forgotten how truly difficult she could be, and as perfect as he seemed in comparison, he had his own set of needs.

A memory of the glint in his eyes when he'd spied her across the bar made her smile. He'd looked like a puppy who'd stolen a steak off the countertop, a little unsure about what would happen next, but defiant enough not to give up his prize. It wouldn't always be easy, but working through their relationship issues might sometimes be fun.

She wrapped her arms around herself because of the chill. Deserts became cold at night. The temperature often dropped more than forty degrees from the daytime high. But the sun always came up again. She glanced east. No faint glow signaled morning.

By the time they reached her truck, it seemed that hours had passed. Her phone told her it was just past midnight.

The truck only had one row of seats, and some of the girls would have to ride in the back. Of course, Jessica wanted Lucía with her. But Lucía might want Grace in front also, and Jessica didn't want the cousins in the back alone.

Lucía solved the problem first. "We'll all ride back here." She climbed into the bed of the truck and beckoned the others.

"Hang on tight. The road sucks," Jessica said. Lucía translated for the cousins. Then Jessica began the slow drive back to civilization.

She didn't try to call from the ranch, not with visions of men with guns pulling up in their pickups. She might never trust the sheriff again.

Instead, she drove to the outskirts of El Paso. As soon as she passed the city limits sign, she pulled into an empty parking lot next to a paintball park and stopped the truck.

Driving further, she risked a police officer or sheriff's deputy pulling her over for having the girls loose in the truck bed. She also didn't know where to take the girls. Showing up at Jaime's house wouldn't be good for him and taking them home would likely get her, and maybe Angus, in some kind of trouble.

Jaime picked up on the third ring, his voice gruff with sleep. "Jessica. Finally. I must have fallen asleep. I've tried to reach you for hours. What the hell is going on?"

"I need your help, and I've got a long story for you." The tale sounded surreal as she rehashed it. Emmy's call. Her warning Lucía would die unless Jessica came alone. Luring Jeremy outside and disarming him. Stupidly leaving the gun unattended to check on the girls. The crack of the rifle. Emmy returning with the gun. Pointing it at them. The words became harder to get out. The horror of staring down that crazed woman, realizing how she'd been played and how the girls might have paid with their lives. Would she ever learn?

Jaime, fully awake now, started asking questions. Where was she? Was everyone all right?

"Stop," she finally said, recovering her voice. "There's more. Everyone is fine except Jeremy Wright. He's dead. I saw him after I heard the gunshot. Emmy is tied up in the cabin. Physically, she's fine. Mentally, there's something terribly wrong. I threw the gun into the desert in case she got loose. I didn't want her to find it."

"I need to come get you."

"Jaime, there's so much more, and I think the sheriff is involved." She proceeded to tell him about the girls and their horrific story. "I have them with me, and they've already been through so much. How can we protect them?"

Silenced met her on the other end of the phone. Jessica's heart swelled for those girls, pushing tears out of her eyes.

"You know we have to turn them in to immigration." The softness in his voice made her imagine him breaking the way she had. "It's not fair, and I'm sorry."

One sob escaped, and then she pulled herself together. She would find a way to help, even if she couldn't make things better tonight. She gave Jaime her location and told him the girls would probably be hungry.

She wiped her face on a sleeve and got out of the truck. The four girls huddled together in the back, sleeping. As she looked at them, the younger of the cousins opened her eyes and looked back. It was as if she stared into Jessica's soul, asking if they'd be all right, but not expecting a positive answer.

Jessica tugged on Lucía's sleeve. "What?" Lucía said, slapping at her arm.

"Wake up. I want you all to get into the cab, It's warmer in there." She repeated the words in Spanish. The girls eventually climbed onto the bench seat and Jessica closed the doors, leaving herself outside in the chilly air.

She looked down at her phone, at the missed messages from Paz, Alma, and Angus. She texted Angus and Alma, let them know she was okay, and said Jaime was on his way to meet her. She told Angus she'd call as soon as possible. Then she called Paz.

When Paz picked up the phone, her desperation slapped Jessica across the face. "Is Lucía with you? She never came home."

"She's fine."

Before Jessica got a word out, Paz started in on her. "I've been calling you for hours. Why the hell didn't you call back? I've been terrified, but afraid to call the sheriff's department. Let me talk to her."

"There wasn't any service. I'm sorry." Jessica held the phone away from her ear and knocked on the car window. She heard Paz screaming through the phone—or perhaps her voice had carried over the mountains and halfway across the desert.

Lucía took the phone, and Jessica happily gave up the responsibility of explaining the night to another person. She still had amends to make, but the battle had ended.

***

Within ten minutes the lights of a police vehicle became visible, but no sirens interrupted the quiet night. Soon an El Paso Police Department car pulled into the parking lot. A young female officer emerged.

"Hi. I'm Officer Martinez. Sergeant Castro said the girls might be hungry." She turned around and pulled a large bag from the car, the Taco Cabana logo emblazoned on the side.

"Thanks. I'm Jessica Watts." Jessica reached for the bag.

"There's a bunch of different tacos in there. I also brought you a large coffee."

"Oh my god, you are an angel." Jessica turned to the truck, vowing to stop talking about God and angels so casually. From Lucía's devotion to Jeremy using God as a shield for despicable behavior to Emmy's skewed view of religion, she could no longer easily borrow the words.

She distributed the tacos to the girls and retrieved her phone from Lucía.

"Mom's going to be okay." Despite Lucía's declaration, Jessica figured she had a lot of trust to earn back. The phone rang. Angus.

"Hey. I love you," he said.

"I love you too. I think everything here is going to be okay. Jeremy's dead. His wife killed him. They had Lucía and three other girls. They're with me now. The cops just arrived, and I need to go."

"Where are you?" He sounded desperate with worry. And he didn't even know the whole story yet.

"I'm at that old paintball place on the way to Hueco Tanks. There's probably going to be a lot of police stuff this morning. I'm not sure when I'll be home."

"Okay. Take care of yourself." He ended the call, taking a part of her with him and leaving her hollow. She wanted to fix things with him. Her compulsion to help others, to make a difference, drove so much of her life. There hadn't been a choice about going after Lucía, just like she'd once had to find Doraliz Velasco. That deep-seated need to save others probably sprang from the clawing longing for her parents for so many years, despite hating them and refusing to see them. But want, not need, drove her feelings toward Angus. He was the only thing she purely, selfishly wanted.

She turned her attention to the police officer and explained all the horrible things that had happened. More officers arrived, including Jaime, who must have made it across El Paso in record time. Jessica told her story again and again.

Alma drove up and Paz flew out of the car. She grabbed Lucía in a fierce embrace, then started sobbing. Jessica had never seen Paz cry before. After a few minutes, Paz pulled herself together and approached Jessica.

The energy billowing off Paz backed Jessica up a step. She glanced nervously at Paz's hands, afraid of a coming slap, or punch. Although maybe she deserved that. Jessica found it hard to think straight. Now that the danger had passed, exhaustion took over.

Lucía must have sensed her mom's energy because she ran up to her and pulled on her arm. "Mom, Jessica saved us. You can't be mad at her."

Paz visibly trembled, then she grabbed Jessica in a hug. She could barely breathe through the overpowering squeeze, but she hugged Paz back as hard as possible.

Just then, a truck came skidding into the parking lot, spraying dirt and gravel everywhere. The second the truck stopped, Grace's father leaped from it, already yelling. Jessica saw Grace slump down in the cab as if wanting to hide from her dad.

Several police officers approached the man, and Jessica could see why. He was a walking threat. His wife quietly slipped out of the other side of the truck. Grace ran to her mother and embraced her. The dad never even noticed as he loudly accused Jaime and another police officer of interfering with his family and wasting taxpayer dollars.

Another car drove into the lot. Angus parked right in front of Jessica.

She wrapped him in a hug before he fully extricated himself from the vehicle. "You're here!" She hadn't expected him, but having him here made her finally believe this ordeal would end, and she'd survive it.

"I'm here for you." He whispered the words into her ear, and they beelined straight into her soul. "Always."

She closed her eyes and snuggled into his warmth in the still chilly morning. "I was afraid you'd be mad," she whispered back.

He pulled her back and looked into her eyes. "You do make me mad. Sometimes you completely exasperate me. Most of the time you amaze me. But I am always here for you, even if I act like a dick sometimes and forget that. You're my person."

That broke her. All the tension of the last few weeks came out in one overwrought sob, and she plunged into him. And he held her tight.

Chapter 28

Eventually, immigration showed up along with a woman from the Office of Refugee Resettlement. Jaime brought Jessica over to meet her.

"I'm Gabriela Ochoa. The middle-aged woman had kind eyes.

Jessica retold the story of the night, with a special emphasis on the trauma the cousins had told her about. "What will you do with them?" she asked when she'd finished.

"They witnessed a crime. More than one actually, and we'll need to talk to them," Jaime said.

"I promise, we'll make sure they're taken care of. They'll be held in a shelter while we evaluate them and try to find their relatives. If there aren't any, then foster care might be an option." Gabriela reached for Jessica's shoulder as she spoke, a gesture of sympathy.

She focused on Jaime. "We can keep them in the area, but we'll need you to fill out some paperwork."

"Of course. Whatever it takes."

Reluctantly, Jessica led her to the girls. She didn't have a better option, yet. But she'd find one.

The cousins sat in Jessica's truck cab watching everything that happened with wide eyes. Jessica opened the door and leaned in, speaking to them in Spanish. "I'm so sorry about what happened to you. There is a lady here who will take you to a place to stay. I want to keep in touch with you and help you." It took everything she had not hug them to her and cry. But that wouldn't help them.

One of the girls gave the slightest nod, and Jessica introduced them to Gabriela, who spoke to them for a few minutes and then took the girls away. Jaime promised Jessica he'd keep an eye on them.

The sheriff's deputies arrived, causing a chill to run down Jessica's spine. Jaime assured her the El Paso Police would stay on the case.

Lucía left with Paz. Grace's dad hadn't calmed down, and the officers had eventually forced him into the back of a police car. When Officer Martinez took Grace and her mother aside to speak with them, Mr. Randolph started kicking at the glass in the back of the police car. After a few minutes, an officer drove him away. Grace and her mother cried as he left, and Jessica had to turn away. Grace needed support right now, but her father had made the night about him.

Jessica knew she wouldn't be lucky enough to go home. Sure enough, Jaime approached her. "A team of police and sheriff's deputies are going to the site. We'd like you to come with us."

"Can I ride with you?"

"Of course."

She said goodbye to Angus and left her truck in the parking lot. The ride back to the ranch took forever. She pointed out the rutted path to the cabin. Eventually, they passed the Camry. The sheriff's deputies examined it and said they'd pull it out on the way back. Jessica wondered how long it would be until Paz got her car back.

A white glow grew on the horizon, eventually tinging the sky lavender and pink. Finally, the trail of four vehicles made it to the cabin. Jessica prayed Emmy would still be inside, and she'd be okay. The thought of walking past Jeremy again almost made her ill. The flies, and who knows what else, would have already found him.

"Would you mind staying in the car?" Jaime asked.

"I would love that. Thank you." Her shoulders unhitched in relief.

She watched the officers tramp through the sand past the pickup truck. Several stopped near Jeremy's location. Others continued into the cabin. One of the men carried a large paramedic's case. The minutes ticked by, and Jessica's body grew heavy with fatigue. She leaned her head back on the rest and let sleep come for her.

***

"Hey, Sleeping Beauty. I need to ask you a few questions." Jaime gently shook her shoulder.

Jessica came to, wondering if her head had been run over by a Mack truck. She rubbed itchy eyes and tried to swallow past her dry throat.

"Water?" she croaked.

Jaime left and returned a minute later with a cold bottle of water. She drank half of it immediately.

"I can't believe I slept so hard. Did you find Emmy? Is she okay?"

"She's on her way to El Paso. She's not speaking. Being exposed to stuff like this—he gestured toward the cabin and the desert beyond—it will do a number on your body. And your mind. Take it easy for the next few days."

She nodded and took another slug from the bottle. "Is Jeremy still out there?"

"Yeah. It will be a while before the coroner comes. So, tell me again how he died?"

"Emmy took the gun, and then we heard the rifle blast."

"And how did she get the gun?"

"I set it down near the cabin door when I saw the girls. They were all huddled together, and I had to make sure they were okay. I couldn't tell if they'd been hurt." The moment of panic returned full force.

"Where was Emmy when you set the gun down?"

"She was slumped against the wall. I thought she was asleep or passed out. I've told you this." Frustration laced her words. Why did she have to keep repeating the same thing?

"Jessica. You are going to have to tell this story over and over again. Right now, it's your word against Emmy's, and she's not talking. I know there are other witnesses, but I want to make sure your version of the story doesn't have holes."

"You think I killed him? I didn't." She thought back to the thunk of the flashlight hitting his head. "Well, I don't think I did. I stunned him, and then I hit him really hard in the head. As far as I know, he wasn't dead."

"Great." Jaime's voice didn't portray great. "Of course, the coroner won't be able to identify your blunt force trauma because the guy no longer has a head."

"And my prints are all over the gun."

"So are Emmy's. How did you hold the gun when you carried it into the house and later into the desert?"

"I picked it up by the wood part. It was heavier than I thought, so I also grabbed the nozzle."

"So, probably the grip and the barrel. Your complete lack of knowledge about firearms may work in your favor. You said you threw the gun into the desert. Do you think you can find it?"

"Yes. I'm sure I can." She got out of his SUV. He signaled to two sheriff's deputies who met them at the car.

"Jessica, I'd like you to meet Deputy Foster and Deputy Ramirez."

"Hey." Jessica nodded at them but didn't offer her hand. "We've got to walk down the trail a bit to get to the place where I got rid of the gun." She pointed to the trail.

"Lead the way," Jaime said.

The sun, now high in the sky, had changed the landscape by throwing shadows into a land once completely dark. She walked roughly the same distance she thought she had earlier. She passed a yucca she'd last seen in the moonlight. She'd tossed the gun just past the spikey desert plant.

"It should be out there about ten feet or so." The deputies followed where she'd pointed.

"Here," one of them yelled. She watched as they photographed the ground. One of them donned disposable gloves and picked up the rifle.

"The safety's not on," the deputy said.

"You threw a loaded rifle without the safety?" The tone of Jaime's voice was accusing. "You could have killed someone."

"It was night, and I don't even know what or where the safety is." She'd hidden the gun to keep them safe, not to risk their lives. "I didn't want Emmy to find it if she got away."

"You are one lucky woman. And I'm signing you up for a gun safety class." His stern voice meant he'd follow through.

"I don't plan on being around guns. I don't particularly like them." She'd never believed in having guns at home. Too many times, they ended up killing those they should have protected.

"And yet, you keep running into them. Trust me, you need to learn how to use one."

She didn't respond. The group walked back to the cabin.

"Guys, I'm going to take Ms. Watts back to her vehicle," Jaime said.

One of the deputies glared at her. "We need to take her in for questioning."

"Ms. Watts has been answering questions for hours now. I'm sure she'd like to get some sleep and a shower. We can bring her back in for a joint statement to both of our departments later today. I'll vouch for her whereabouts."

The deputy didn't look happy but deferred to Jaime. A sheen of sweat crossed Jessica's shoulders under the deputy's gaze. Perhaps the walk through the desert or the growing heat of the sun was responsible. Perhaps the ordeal was far from over.

On the drive back, she asked Jaime how much trouble she was in.

"As long as the prints on the gun come back consistent with your story, and the other witnesses corroborate it, you should be okay."

"But you left the gun with them. I don't trust them. The sheriffs are involved with this somehow." Panic and anger threatened to erupt. She'd already been through so damn much.

"Jess, it's going to be okay. There were four girls in the cabin. If they all tell the same story, things will be fine, even if Emmy says you killed him."

"Fuck."

"Right now, she's not talking. In fact, she's hardly moving. It's like she's not all there." Jaime gave her a quick glance before returning his eyes to the road.

"She's disturbed," Jessica said. "I'm pretty sure she's been abused for a long time. She does this thing where she's present, and then she checks out and acts like a robot or something."

"She needs a good lawyer."

Jaime's comment made Jessica think about Linda. She needed to talk to her and come clean about all of this. Hopefully, she'd still have a job after that. She'd started to think of the little converted home as a refuge. A place where she'd finally fit in.

"Hey, do you know Linda Reed?" she asked Jaime.

He almost flinched at the name. "I know her very well. She was my training officer when I joined the force."

"She was a cop?" Jessica couldn't picture the older woman in her fancy suit wearing police blues.

"It was a long time ago, but she was one of the best. An incredible investigator. How did you run across her?"

"She offered me a job."

"Huh. That's kind of a surprise." Even from the side, Jessica saw his brow furrow.

"Why? What's up?" Everything she'd heard about the woman so far had been good. Why did he seem reluctant?

"It's nothing. I thought you worked for Alma."

"I'm on probation because of the incident at Jeremy Wright's ranch. Man, I wish I'd never gotten involved in any of this."

"You know what, Jessica? You did good out there. You saved those girls."

Validation. And from her cop-hero, no less. She'd done good. Maybe it didn't matter so much whether you were good as long as you did good. She could be hard to deal with, drank and cursed too much, but she used her ornery darkness to help others instead of turning away from that part of herself. Maybe that was enough.

Chapter 29

Later that day, Jessica attended her interview at police headquarters, where the deputies were decidedly less friendly than the police officers. After that, Jessica walked the two blocks to The Tap. When she'd called Linda and said they needed to talk, Linda had suggested Jessica's favorite downtown bar. Astounding. With only about fifteen feet of storefront, The Tap had a neon sign worthy of Las Vegas.

Inside, a bar top stretched the depth of the establishment, barely leaving room for passers-by. A few high top tables and a jukebox were shoved against the wall. Wood paneling darkened the already small space, and one-hundred years of grime could probably be pulled from seams and corners. Nonetheless, they had ice cold beer, a vast array of hard liquor, and the best nachos in town.

Jessica's interview had ended earlier than she'd expected, and she'd texted Linda to let her know she'd arrived. She ordered a Shiner after Linda texted back that she'd be there in ten minutes.

Jessica stretched her neck from side to side, then took a sip of the icy beer. The chilled liquid ran down her throat, loosening muscles along the way. She'd managed to get a couple hours of sleep before her interview but needed far more to make up for last night. And the night before that.

At least after she spoke with Linda her course would be set. She hoped the attorney still wanted to hire her. Certainly, after last night, Alma's firm wouldn't give her another chance. They wouldn't want their highbrow name associated with her low doings, regardless of right or wrong. Still, even if she had to work at Starbucks, she'd find a way forward.

Last night had reminded her of what her life could be. She didn't think of herself as a hero, even though Lucía had texted her that three times today. She'd just done what she had to do to protect people in need. And while she hoped she never had to deal with such a frightening situation again, it felt great to do something that mattered.

The sheriff's deputies clearly weren't as impressed and had acted like she'd put people in danger instead of saving them. But they had their own behavior to answer for. Jessica was certain they'd helped protect the Wrights and perhaps the men with guns and trucks. And she didn't even know who they were. Yet.

Unfortunately, before she left the courthouse, Jaime let her know they'd found Nora's body. Jessica didn't call Stan. It wouldn't help, and she hoped he'd escaped.

She took another sip of her beer. When would the strings of her life come together and braid into something that would support the future she craved? She had parts of it. Angus. A home. As tedious as law school could be, it would serve her well. But the loose ends seemed permanently out of reach. How would she find some sort of balance with her mother? Could she find a job that she both liked and found meaningful? How would she satisfy her desire for justice? She didn't want to be a vigilante, but she was driven to help those who needed it. To right the wrongs.

"You're deep in thought." Linda slid onto the barstool beside her and signaled the bartender, a curvaceous Latina woman about Jessica's age with truly spectacular lavender sparkle eyeshadow. Her chola T-shirt and full sleeve tattoos completed a look that would keep any patron from messing with her.

"The regular?" the bartender asked.

Linda nodded. "Irina, meet my new friend Jessica."

Jessica smiled and nodded at the woman.

"I've seen her here before," Irina said as she set a longneck and a shot of tequila in front of Linda.

Jessica stared at Linda's drinks. Her past and her future slammed together like a shot glass hitting a table. Who was this woman who'd copied Jessica's perfect pairing?

"What's the matter?" Linda asked. "Don't like tequila?"

Jessica chuckled. "I definitely like tequila. It's been one of my most reliable friends."

"I'll drink to that." Linda raised the glass toward Jessica, then emptied half of it. "So, what did you want to talk about?"

Jessica took a deep breath, wishing she had her own shot of fortune. But she should do this without the drink. "You never asked me why I was leaving Cohen Garcia."

Linda's eyes scanned Jessica. "Unless you're sleeping with eighty-four-year-old Saul Cohen, I don't care. Actually, I don't really care even then."

"Yeah, I can promise you that'll never happen." Jessica smiled, happy to still have a job, although wanting to confess everything to her new boss. "I'm on probation there. I found out that an adult male inappropriately touched a teenager I know, and I confronted him on his property. He was a Cohen Garcia client. The sheriffs arrested me for trespassing the second time they found me on his property."

Linda drank the rest of her tequila, seemingly lost in thought. "If the guy really did it, it seems like he should be the one in trouble."

"Well, he's dead now, so we don't have to worry about that."

Linda's eyebrows slid up her forehead. Jessica had surprised her. "Did you kill him?"

"No. His wife did."

Linda snorted. "That sounds about right. Irina, bring over a couple of tequilas."

"So, you're telling me you're trouble." Linda fixed her eyes on Jessica.

"Yeah. I've been known to find it a time or two. The thing is, I want to make things better where I can. Last night, I received a call from the man's wife saying he had the young woman I mentioned earlier. She said I needed to go out there, alone. So, I went."

Jessica settled into the story. Irina set down the tequilas, but Jessica didn't touch hers. "I found them in an abandoned cabin in the middle of nowhere, the man, his wife, and four young women hostages. I neutralized the man first, with a stun gun and the butt of my flashlight."

Despite the number of times she'd told the story, the words spewing out of her mouth shocked Jessica. No wonder her friends and family worried about her. Everything sounded so nonchalant, but it hadn't been. She'd been terrified, but mostly she'd been enraged at Jeremy, for what he'd done and what he might do to Lucía.

She kept talking. "He had a rifle, but I disarmed him. Unfortunately, I didn't realize the wife was a threat, and while I checked on the girls, she took the rifle and shot her husband. Then, she returned to the cabin and threatened us."

"Holy shit." Linda was glued to the story. Who wouldn't be amazed at such a preposterous but true tale?

"The wife was unstable, but we eventually disarmed her and tied her up." Jessica stopped. She didn't know why she sounded like an automaton when every action of that night had overflowed with emotion. It reminded her of Emmy's strange voice. She would not be like that.

"It was terrible. I was afraid she was going to kill us. The four girls, two of them were cousins and refugees from Guatemala. They're currently being held in detention, and I'm really worried about them."

"Well, maybe we can do something about that. I do specialize in immigration law. If they witnessed a violent crime, they're eligible for a U visa, although those take about eight years to process."

"Eight years!" The cousins would be adults by then. "How can it take so long?"

"Welcome to the world of immigration. Do they have any family in the US? That might be a faster way forward."

The horrible story of the girls' family had faded to the back of her mind in the busy day, but now it roared back. She couldn't help the tear that escaped her eye. She hoped Linda didn't mind emotion.

"A coyote led the girls and their family across the border. He led them into a trap. Men in pickup trucks with guns waited. Only the two girls survived the massacre." The horror of that act, of those violent men still on the loose, crushed her.

Linda finished her tequila, then took a swig of beer. "I've heard of things like that." Her voice, rough and low, barely made it to Jessica's ears.

"I want to do something important with my life. I love this city and the people in it. I want to help them, protect them, make things better." Jessica gripped her cold beer as if it might save her from her own ambition.

"Welcome to paradise. We'll see what we can do about the girls. Get ready to work hard starting Monday. This is a tough job. A tough life. But given the story you just told me, I think you've got what it takes." She knocked her beer against Jessica's.

Funny how the rest of her life would start in a dingy bar with a beer and a tequila. These familiar liquids had often flowed through her veins like water in the desert after a rainfall. Fitting, actually, to have a part of the past to go with the future, akin to melding the dark and the light.

Irina looked at the two women and shook her head. Jessica smiled at her, imagining her thoughts. They might not look alike, one of them small, blond, and in her sixties, the other black-haired and tall, but Jessica recognized a kindred spirit. This was going to be one interesting job.

She downed her tequila. "Thanks. I look forward to working with you."

***

"You smell like tequila and beer." Angus looked at her, one eyebrow cocked, but a smile played at his lips.

"Yeah. I had a drink with my new boss. Imagine my surprise when she ordered a tequila and a longneck." She sounded innocent. She was innocent, despite the strange coincidence.

"Sounds like trouble."

Jessica treaded carefully across potentially hurt feelings. "She wants to find a way to help the two girls from Guatemala."

"That sounds good." His voice didn't match his words.

Jessica pulled him toward the couch and forced him to sit beside her. She turned to face him and threw her legs across his thighs, pinning him in place. He had to understand. He knew her. Perhaps better than anyone.

"You know who I am," she said. "I need to try to help them."

He took her hand in his, squeezed it, linked their fingers together. "Do you think this need to save others is about your parents leaving you?"

She thought about the question. He deserved the right answer. "Maybe. But it's more than that. It's part of my DNA. Remember in college how I helped you and the band get gigs in Juarez? That was the first time I learned I could get stuff done. Then, when I searched for Doraliz and everything that happened after that, well, I realized that I could do this. I should spend my life helping people.

She took his hand, willing him to understand. "The night you picked me up downtown after those thugs kidnapped me—that night changed my life. So many people need help here on our border. Rich, poor, Mexican, American, I don't care who they are or where they're from. I don't want to sell industrial buildings. God knows, I don't want to work on another divorce. I want to do meaningful work. Like you."

The air between them stilled as the echo of her words faded away.

"Teaching kids about music isn't dangerous." His voice was soft when he finally spoke. "I want to know what the future holds."

"What do you mean?"

"If you're out there risking your life all the time, where does that leave me? Us?"

The question didn't fit. It itched and constrained, and she couldn't get the buttons undone. "My goal isn't to risk my life. Never. I don't like being in danger. I want to become an attorney, win cases, help people that way. I can't explain how I've ended up in a couple of weird situations."

He stroked her cheek and looked at her with intense black eyes. "Danger courts you."

The phrase sounded odd coming from Angus, as if some deeper truth used him as its spokesperson. She had courted danger many times. It fed the darkest part of her. Perhaps it wanted something in return.

"If that's the only way to justice, I am not afraid. But I don't think it is." She paused a moment and let the words build within her before releasing them. "I want a meaningful life. I want a life as tall as the mountains and as vast as the desert. As passionate as our love. I'll take going into battle on a dark desert night to save someone I love over a thousand safe divorce cases every time."

Every empty spot in her filled with fervor. Her darkness, the very part of her she'd tried to push down and hide, had given her the courage to go into the desert, to take on a criminal with a gun, to win. She could bring her whole self to everything she did. Her dark side had repaired her relationship with Angus. It helped her survive.

"Not every day at the office is going to be an adventure, even with your new boss. Sometimes life is boring." Angus ran his fingers along her cheek, tucking a strand of hair behind her ear.

"You're right." He was in many ways. "Occasionally, it might take hooking up with a stranger in a bar." She smiled as she pulled him in for a kiss.

"I make a really good stranger," he said. Their lips met.

He definitely did. She felt the darkness unspool within her and meld with the forward-thinking, responsible Jessica she'd tried to become. Her whole life stretched in front of her, and she'd embrace it with every part of herself.

THE END

Thank you for reading *El Diablo* by Kathryn Dodson.
Please submit a reader review.
Join Kathryn Dodson for updates, events, book info, and more at
www.KathrynDodson.com.

Other novels by Kathryn Dodson
Tequila Midnight
Hired to find a tycoon's daughter, Jessica Watts, a hard-drinking woman needs more than tequila to survive the night.
The Podcast Chronicles
She traded suits for mom duty, but she'll risk everything to save the Colorado mountain paradise she loves.
Portrait of Deception
A photographer on the brink of fame. A dictator with a fatal agenda. A terrifying trap she may not escape.
Five Tries to Get It Right
When her lifelong friend hits rock bottom, a widow tries to reawaken their zest for life on a voyage retracing their wild youth,

About the Author

Kathryn Dodson

Kathryn Dodson grew up writing and riding horses in far West Texas. She graduated from SMU in creative writing and went on to get an MBA from Thunderbird and a PhD from Clemson.

She has worked on both sides of the US/Mexico border and has held jobs with governments, chambers of commerce, and other businesses. Now she spends her days writing about interesting women in fascinating places.

Join Kathryn for updates and extras and receive the *Tequila Midnight* prequel, *La Paloma*, at https://www.kathryndodson.com/

NOVELS

Tequila Midnight

The Podcast Chronicles

Portrait of Deception

Five Tries to Get It Right

El Diablo

Acknowledgements

Thank you for reading *El Diablo*, you make my novels possible.

El Diablo was a devil a book to write because I'd never written a sequel before. Fortunately, the writing community is generous, and I had a lot of help. Nancy Yeager and Marta Lane read very early copies of the novel and really helped me find the balance between linking to the first book and ensuring this novel could stand completely on its own. My critique partners Claudia Armann and Sydney Clark provided sage advice about how to make the novel better. I also had more beta readers than usual on this novel, and I owe Marsea Nelson, Jessica Ames, Theresa Munroe, Jocelyn Lindsay, Lisa Ulrich Hoffman, and Renita Bradley a huge thank you for their input.

Growing up in El Paso, I couldn't wait to leave. I think most kids feel this way about where they grow up. Clearly, the city left its mark on me and continues to haunt my dreams and my novels. I was lucky to spend my formative years in such an interesting part of the country. I forgave my parents for dragging me there kicking and screaming in sixth grade, and now I finally appreciate the move.

Thank you Jack for always inspiring me. Finally, I'd like to thank Tom for supporting my writing in so many ways. You may not read my novels, but you make them happen.

Printed in the USA
CPSIA information can be obtained
at www.ICGtesting.com
CBHW020312090824
12908CB00028B/399